Robert William Eastwick, Herbert Compton

A Master Mariner

Being the Life and Adventures of Captain Robert William Eastwick

Robert William Eastwick, Herbert Compton

A Master Mariner
Being the Life and Adventures of Captain Robert William Eastwick

ISBN/EAN: 9783337077167

Printed in Europe, USA, Canada, Australia, Japan

Cover: Foto ©Raphael Reischuk / pixelio.de

More available books at **www.hansebooks.com**

A MASTER MARINER.
BEING THE LIFE AND
ADVENTURES OF CAP-
TAIN ROBERT WILLIAM
EASTWICK

EDITED BY HERBERT COMPTON

ILLUSTRATED

LON·DON : T. FISHER UNWIN
PATERNOSTER SQUARE. MDCCCXCI

$\mathfrak{To}$

S. E. R.

THIS RECORD OF

HER FATHER'S LIFE

IS

AFFECTIONATELY

INSCRIBED.

INTRODUCTION.

PON the death, in 1889, of the last surviving son of Captain Robert William Eastwick — the Master Mariner whose life and adventures are recorded in the following pages —a box of old family papers passed into my hands, and on going through them with a view to their preservation or destruction, I came across an autobiographical manuscript that at once arrested my attention. It was the story of my grandfather's life, dictated by himself about the year 1836. With a few additions from other authentic sources, and especially from some valuable papers placed at my disposal by a member of the family, the narrative is given in Chapters II. to XVI. of this book.

The autobiography was written in a queer little shagreen-covered album, and was in the form of an epistle addressed to the narrator's eldest daughter: "*As I fancy it will be gratifying to you, my dearest child,*" it begins, "*I sit down to dictate a brief and hasty sketch of my life, which, however, from the multiplicity of events attending it, must be*

abridged to so inconsiderable a portion as to reduce it to a mere summary of the Hardships, Trials and Losses sustained by your father."

From this it will be gathered that the original design of the narrative was of a purely private nature, a fact amply corroborated by the many domestic allusions abounding in its pages, but which are naturally omitted in this transcript. I mention this in order to dispel any idea that the manuscript might have been intended for publication, and contained the incidental embellishments indigenous to efforts having that aim in view. This was certainly not the case, for a very considerable portion of the original matter has necessarily been excised as containing family or business details of no interest to any one but the person they were addressed to, and which could only have been touched on in a strictly private communication.

No one seems to have known of the existence of this authentic record of Captain Eastwick's life, and although many of his adventures had crystallized into family legends, it was always a matter of regret that no memoir of his career was available. From the position in which the MS. was discovered, cheek by jowl with a budget of old accounts, and legal documents and releases, and in a receptacle that contained no papers bearing a later date than 1847, it is probable it had not been disturbed for a long number of years.

It was a labour of love to verify the leading

incidents related in the body of the work by an examination of the public journals printed at the period of their occurrence, extracts from which are given in sundry footnotes. The remarkable accuracy of the narrative—written, it must be remembered, long after the date of the events recorded, and by one who had been blind for three years at the time of inditing—bears testimony to a wonderfully retentive memory, and forces the conviction that those lesser episodes that cannot be so circumstantiated, are nevertheless equally exact. In this connection it may here be noticed that of the many ships Captain Eastwick refers to, both those he commanded himself and those he met or sailed in company with, he scarcely ever omits giving the names of the vessels and of the captains who commanded them.

Although this history carries the reader back to the days of the Lord George Gordon riots and the return of the *Resolution* and *Discovery* with the news of Captain Cook's murder, there are yet several people, born in the latter half of this century, who can remember to have heard the narration of those remote events from this Master Mariner who actually witnessed them in his own youth. Prior to 1866 Captain Eastwick was a well-known personage in parts of Brompton. To within a few weeks of his death he was wont to take his daily walk in that neighbourhood, where the "old blind Captain," with his gold-headed malacca cane, and his handsome patriarchal face, lifted to that angle peculiar to all blind men, was a familiar figure. Leaning on the arm of his attendant, or accompanied by some of his many grandchildren, he might constantly be seen pacing the streets in the vicinity of Thurloe Square. His loss of sight was in some measure compensated by a marvellous sense, that had almost become an instinct, of locality. Often, much to the alarm of his family, without saying a word to any one, he would slip out of the house alone, and make his way to some neighbouring friend's residence, never failing to find his destination, with unerring correctness, by counting his footsteps. If, perchance, he went out with one who was a stranger to the locality, he undertook to direct the way, and no matter how interesting the flow of conversation, never failed at the right moment to break off, in parentheses, with " *Now turn to the right*," or " *to the left*," as the case might be, and when the journey came to an end to say, with a decisive halt, " *This is the house*." He constantly went into the city to transact business, taking one of his children with him, and directing them from place to place until his visits were completed, and without once having to inquire the way from a passer-by. In many East India banking and mercantile houses he was a well-known client, for he always made a point of transacting business himself, following to the very last, with a sagacious prescience, the various phases and changing conditions of current commercial affairs.

His memory was so trained that it could not only retain every figure and incident relating to numberless investments, but without hesitation deal with each separate transaction, referring to the book in which it was registered, and even the page on which it was entered. He was executor to many friends and members of the family, and was consulted by all his acquaintances for advice, and it was a source of pride to him to be able to say that he had ever proved himself a just and faithful steward of interests confided to his care.

He is still spoken of by those who knew him as one belonging to these later days, even though he links them with the stirring epochs of a past century. And although twenty-five years have passed since he died, his memory is green in many hearts. Perhaps it is because he enchanted so many childhoods with his tales of daring and adventure ; or because the picture of the fine old man, with his snowy locks, his patriarchal features, his kindly smile, and his patient grace, as he sat sunning himself through his long blind hours, in the little western room, with its vine-trellised windows, wherein he passed his later days, is engraven deep in grateful hearts who owe him much; or because he was one of those rare men whose striking individuality fascinates and is never forgotten. Be it as it may, the following history of his life, written by himself and now rescued from the dust of oblivion, will be read by many who knew him, and loved him, and revered him; because he was an Englishman, manly and modest, and made of that stern stuff which has given this country her fearless sailors and her stout adventurers; and because he left behind him to his children, and his children's children, and their children after them, the heritage of a name that was stainless and honourable, a character that was unselfish and sincere, and a career of adventure and achievement that fills them with a not unjustifiable pride.

H. C.

LIST OF ILLUSTRATIONS.

CHAPTER I.

My birth and parentage—My mother is left a widow—Reminiscences
of my childhood—My mother goes to reside at Lower Edmonton
—Mr. English, my godfather—I grow up impatient of discipline ;
and often play truant—The Grey Ghost—I recognize him in
chains on a gibbet—The curious effect it had on me—I visit
London with my godfather—Am afforded opportunities of seeing
the shipping in the docks—Make friends with the sailors, who
spin yarns to me—My mother and I study geography—Return to
England of Captain Cook's ships, the *Resolution* and *Discovery*—
I visit them, and their sight determines me to become a sailor—
The Lord George Gordon Riots break out—I steal away to London
to witness them—The condition of the city—" The soldiers ! "—
My leg is broken in the rush of the mob—I am rescued and taken
to a neighbouring house—My mother comes to me—I am sent to
school at Pilgrim's Hatch—Mr. Lalteral's academy—I walk in my
sleep—A cure for it—I refuse to return to the school, and am sent
to Merchant Taylors'—The Reverend Mr. Rose—His opinion of
me—School companions—The Guinea Coast Captain—The recital
of his marvellous adventures fires my imagination—I determine
to become a sailor—My mother's dislike of the idea—I persist in
my intention—She consents to my wish at last.

 WAS born in London on the 25th
day of June, 1772, at a house in
Goodman's Fields. My father was
a native of the county of Suffolk, in
which his family had resided for
many generations. In 1771 he came to London,
and having made the acquaintance of my mother,
married her, and settled down to live upon the

remnants of a considerable fortune which he had once enjoyed, but the most of which he had run through. In the following year I was born, and shortly after my birth my father was seized with a violent disorder which carried him off in a week, leaving my mother, who was little more than a girl, a widow.

I cannot, of course, remember my father, but the memory of my mother, the most tender, the most affectionate, the most indulgent that ever lived, is as dear and quick in my mind now as she herself was in life half a century ago. I can recollect playing by her side in the little garden of our home (wherein she was fond of sitting in the summer weather) when I was but a brat in petticoats, and can call to mind how, oftentimes, suddenly laying down her work, she would snatch me up and set me on her lap, and begin to tell me of my father who was dead and gone. There was a great and intense earnestness in her manner when she spoke of him, which I can remember even to this day, and she would praise him, and bid me be worthy of him who possessed many rare virtues and accomplishments. And as she thus spoke, her eyes often gradually filled with tears, which caused me to wonder, and then she would bend down and kiss me, in order to hide them; and I, seeing her thus distressed, would whimper and ask her why she cried. At which she always smiled, or made pretence to smile, and said it was nothing but her foolishness and fondness of him and me, and that she wept for joy to have a son so like his dead father, to constantly remind her of him. Then she would bid me run and play. But I have never forgotten the constant tears and sense of sorrow that clouded those early years of her widowhood, nor has the affliction of blindness, with which it has pleased the Almighty to visit me, been able to hide from my inner sight the vision of her sad and gentle face, and her slight girlish figure dressed in black.

My mother was left in straitened circumstances, but, being a sensible and thrifty person, managed her means so prudently that she was able to continue to live in that station of life to which she had been accustomed. She left London after my father's death, and rented a small cottage in the village of Lower Edmonton, six miles out from the city by the Kingsland Road and the Green Lane, and here my childhood was passed. Her stepfather, Mr. Isaac English, lived in Church Street, which was the reason of her fixing upon this place for her residence. He had no family by my grandmother, whom he had married late in life, but she, by a previous marriage, had borne three daughters, of whom my mother was the eldest, and Mr. English always regarded them as if they had been his own. He was likewise my godfather, and I, being the only son born of his stepdaughters, was brought up to believe I should be his heir. In this, however, I was disappointed when he came to die many years afterwards; for although he always treated me affectionately, and never at any time appeared to be offended with me, he left his property and fortune (amounting to some ten thousand pounds) to my mother's youngest sister, who was never married, and whose name was Miss Elizabeth Archer. This, perhaps, was not to be wondered at; for he lived to an uncommon old age, and she kept his house, and obtained great influence over him; which is often the case where the memory fails, and a man is apt to forget all except those who administer to his declining years.

Though small in stature, I was always a forward and lusty child, full of life and energy, and constantly getting into boyish scrapes from the time I could walk. My mother taught me my letters, and how to read and write and cipher, devoting much time and patience to me, who was, I fear, but a dullard and a dunce. Books and figures were pains and purgatory to me, and I was always more ready with an excuse for a holiday (which she, most indulgent, constantly granted me) than a lesson well learnt, or a copy neatly written. There was something in my disposition that rebelled against the quiet of home life. From my earliest days I desired independence, and sought such adventure as was open to me, loving to flout authority and play the truant whenever I could. I would often rise early in the morning before any one was up or stirring, and calling one or two companions who, though older than myself, were always content to be led into mischief by me, we would wander abroad the whole day long and explore all the country round about Edmonton, and especially such wild places as Finchley, which was then a wooded waste infested with foot-pads, or the hills about Highgate and Hornsey.   Many desperate characters haunted these parts with designs against travellers journeying to or from London.   I remember one whom I often saw, a well-dressed man mounted on a fine grey horse, and who frightened me by his dark and sombre visage.   Whenever he met me on the high-road he would ask me what coaches or chaises I had observed passing, and question me and cross-question me in a bullying way, and fix me with his piercing black eyes until I felt inclined to call out from fright.   He had a wonderful way of appearing suddenly, and without warning, by bounding into the middle of the road with a leap when he was least expected, and drawing his horse up on to its haunches, all done so quickly and quietly that he seemed like a phantom horseman, and we used amongst ourselves to call him the Grey Ghost. Then a long time passed without our seeing him, and I began to think he had left that part of the country, when one day I heard that a certain famous highwayman had been caught, and condemned to death and executed, and was hanging upon an old gibbet on the high-road, there to dangle away in chains.   I knew where this gibbet was situated, and made a journey in order to visit it.   When I got near, whom should I see but him I had missed of late. I went quite close to him, and peeped into his face, which was hanging down in an awkward manner and difficult to see, his neck being broken. Sure enough it was the Grey Ghost, only his face was all livid, and his eyes protruded, and his jaw was fallen, showing a set of grinning teeth and a piece of dry black tongue, giving him a horrible appearance. It was the first time I had looked upon Death, and a great quaking seized me. But presently I recovered a little, and even drew closer to him, and impelled by some hideous prompting I caught hold of one of his feet and gave him a jog; whereupon the body began to swing slowly to and fro in the air, and with the movement his head wagged with a curious sort of jerk, and his eyes appeared to open and shut so that he seemed alive again. And now I desired to run away, but found myself unable to do so, being fixed fast there under the evil glance of his eyes, as he winked at me, standing just beneath him, and grinned. After a little while I felt myself beginning to grin too, and then a fit of laughter seized me which I could not control, and I laughed and laughed back at him, yet without any meaning in my laughter, until I fell down from exhaustion. There I lay for some time until I was recovered sufficiently to rise and go home, but without ever casting another glance at the grim spectre. That evening I was taken ill and confined to my bed for a long time, afflicted with strange uncontrollable fits of loud laughter which frightened my poor mother greatly, and deluded the doctors, who could give no name to my disease. It was a long time before I recovered from the effects of the shock, but I never told any one what had been the cause of my illness.

When I was getting on for my eighth year and able to be useful, my godfather, Mr. English, would occasionally take me to London with him, seated behind him on his horse, to mind which was my duty when he dismounted at any place he had to visit. Sometimes he had business near the river, or about the docks, and would then bait his horse at a tavern, leaving me free to wander abroad, whilst he conducted his affairs. These were verily red-letter days in my life, for I was able to loiter about the wharves, and inspect the shipping, and gaze with awe and wonder upon the great vessels, and especially the East Indiamen collected together there. These filled me with a marvellous interest, and I was never tired of standing watching the unloading of their cargoes, and wondering what all the chests, and bales, and bags and packages contained, many of which were marked with most strange letters, not in any civilized writing. And then I would try and consider how many storms and tempests they had contended against, and how many leagues of ocean they had crossed, and where they had been a month ago, or three months ago, or six months ago. After a time I got bolder, and, if I was not hindered, would steal on board some ship, and peer into the great dark hold, much tempted to hide myself in it, and be carried away to sea, and find myself presently in some lovely tropical country far away, such as my mother had described to me. And sometimes I would make my way into the fo'castle, and if I had a sixpence in my pocket (which was none too often) would invite one of the sailors to refresh himself at my expense, provided he in return rendered me some account of his voyages, and of the strange countries, and cities and people in Cathay and India. In this way I learnt not a little concerning Indostan and the far East, and the riches and magnificence of those parts, and their marvellous natural products. But most of all was I diverted by the descriptions of the barbarians who lived in those distant places, and their cruel and inhuman habits, who were accustomed to kill their own lawfully begotten daughters at birth, so as to be saved the expense of providing for them in after-life, and whose widows, however young and beautiful, were obliged to burn themselves to death when their husbands died, a heartless custom that made me grateful to have been born in a civilized country where my mother was not only permitted to enjoy life, but treated with kindness by all. I was never tired of listening to descriptions of all these things, or about the wild and fierce beasts very commonly met with, or the serpents and poisonous insects that stung with such severity as to cause instant death, or the sharks and alligators that infested the shores and rivers, and immediately devoured any person who happened by accident to fall into the water. It was passing strange what terrible and constant dangers surrounded those who visited the East, and yet how many survived to return home safe and sound to relate their adventures. I did not know then the habit of exaggeration which is common to sailors, but believed implicitly everything that was told me. And dreadful though it all was, and enough to scare the boldest and bravest man, somehow I never felt frightened at anything I heard, but was on the contrary seized with a great curiosity to see all these strange and fearful things with my own eyes, so that I too might come back with adventures of my own to relate, and be listened to.

On my return to Edmonton from these visits to the river or the docks, I would repeat all that had been told me to my mother (saving that information relating to the burning of widows, which I cherished as a secret from her, thinking it might cause her pain) and she would borrow a large globe of the world, that belonged to a neighbour, and point out upon it the various places that had been mentioned, and even study Mercator's projections, and endeavour to discover by what course the ships I had been on board of must have sailed out, and come back. In this way we ploughed together (in imagination) many leagues of ocean, experienced trade winds and set currents, encountered typhoons, cyclones, hurricanes, storms, and squalls, both black and white, narrowly escaped shipwreck on sunken rocks or isolated desert islands, weathered the Capes of Good Hope and Horn, and even came into contact with icebergs in Arctic latitudes. Observing me interested in these subjects, my mother encouraged me in every way, and I thus obtained a familiarity with the geography of the world such as no schoolmaster, setting the same as a task, could have drummed into my head.

On one occasion, never to be forgotten by me, my eyes witnessed a sight that stirred my ambition far beyond anything I had ever seen before. It was in the month of August, 1780, when those noble ships the *Resolution* and the *Discovery* returned from Captain James Cook's last voyage, and with flags flying half-mast high anchored off Sheerness, bringing the news of his foul massacre in the previous year by the savages of Owhyhee. Not a heart in broad England but mourned his untimely end. For whether as a British sailor, or as a navigator in dangerous and unknown seas, or as a discoverer of wild countries and wilder people, or as commander of a ship, he was an honour to the nation he represented and the profession he dignified. From that day forward I applied myself to the study of those books and descriptions of his previous voyages that had already been printed, and read them over and over again, until I knew them almost by heart. And I have always esteemed it a blessed thing that I was permitted to see with my own eyes the very ships he commanded, and to converse

with the gallant men who had called him captain.
It was this circumstance, more than any other,
that filled me with the fixed determination of
myself following a seafaring life.

I must not forget to mention an accident which
happened to me just before this time, and went nigh
to terminating my career. It was in the month
of June of the same year, when there arose a great
commotion about the No-Popery Riots, excited by
Lord George Gordon. The rioters were assembled
in the streets of London, and having broken open
Newgate prison, had released the felons and burnt
the building to the ground. When intelligence
of this reached Edmonton I was seized with a
mighty great longing to see what was going on,
it being reported that the whole city was in flames
and given over to plunder, and the streets littered
with articles of great value, pillaged and cast aside,
and which could be had for the picking up. This
created the greatest excitement in our village, and
all the folks were gathered together in Church
Street discussing the matter.

Such an opportunity for adventure was one I
could not resist, and I determined to make my
way to London on the following day. So rising at
daybreak, I slipped out of the house, and went to
that of a companion, who was always ready to join
me in any wild prank, and having awakened him
by throwing a handful of gravel at the window of
the room in which he slept, I called to him to
accompany me. This he joyfully consented to do,

and in the grey dawn of the morning we sallied forth for London.

The sun was well up when we arrived in the city, where a wonderful sight met our eyes. The whole place was in a state of siege, doors and windows bolted and every shutter closed. The shops had not been opened for two days, and even at this early hour a great mob held possession of the streets. Nearly all the city gaols had been forced open, and many of the released malefactors mingling with the multitude, urged it to greater excesses. We were soon drawn into the middle of the mob, and carried along to all manner of places, holding tight each other's hands in order not to lose one another. Now and then some one kinder hearted than the rest, taking pity on us, advised us to go home, saying that such scenes of disorder and commotion were no places for children; but we, enjoying the freedom, only laughed. It seemed to us the finest adventure we had ever been engaged in. There was no one to bid us do this, or do that. We were our own masters. And so we joined lustily in the shouting and cheered and huzza'd with our neighbours, not knowing in the least what it was all about, but thinking it very fine and grand, and doing exactly as those around us did.

Presently we found ourselves in the junction of two cross-roads, when suddenly some one raised the cry of " *The Soldiers !*"

Whereupon all the mad valour instantly died

out of the populace, and there came such a rush of headlong flight as lifted me completely off my legs. For some moments I was carried along, wedged in between the bodies of the people, who heeded not my cries, until I gradually slipped to the ground. Then came a sudden great pain in my right leg, and almost at the same time I lost consciousness.

When I recovered the streets were empty, saving for my companion (who, luckily seeing me fall, had returned to the spot) and two strange but very respectable men, who were bending over me. As I slowly regained my senses I heard the voice of my friend crying out, "Oh, he is killed, he is killed!" Whereupon I opened my eyes, at which he was vastly comforted. The two men lifted me up, and carried me into a house just opposite, in which it appeared they lived, and my companion immediately went off with the intention of acquainting my mother of what had happened. The good people who had succoured me sent for an apothecary who lived a few doors distant, and whom with the greatest difficulty they persuaded to come and attend me, he for a long time positively refusing to leave his house in such troublous times, being a God-fearing, peace-loving man, he said, and a good citizen to boot, who had no desire to cross his threshold on such a day. However, he came at last, and discovered that my leg was broken, and set it, but clumsily enough and causing me great pain. He then bandaged it up, and I was laid on a bed and told not to move—a thing I was not like to do with pain and exhaustion.

Late in the evening my mother arrived, having braved all the dangers of the road to reach me, which was no slight proof of her devotion. For the riot was now at its height, and all respectable citizens barred within their houses, and not so much as daring to peep through the windows, the most of which were broken.

I can recall my poor mother's scared face all pale and terrified (partly through fear on my account, but more by reason of the fatigue she had endured, and the rude buffetings she had met with on the way), as she entered the room in which I lay, and running to the side of my couch, threw herself upon her knees and covered me with kisses and embracings, trying all the time to upbraid me for my wickedness, yet unable to do so for joy and thankfulness at seeing me alive and safe.

I lay there for three weeks before I was permitted to be removed, but fortunately the bone was well joined, and I being young, it soon set. During this time I had to listen to many lectures concerning my wickedness and disobedience, especially from my godfather, Mr. English, who visited me from time to time, and talked of punishment to follow so soon as I was in a state to bear the same; all of which evoked from me the most solemn protestations of genuine and permanent amendment. But I had no sooner recovered, and was able to walk again, and found no further chastisement in store for me (my dear mother declaring I had already been sufficiently punished), than I forgot all my promises when I was sick, and returned again to my former bad ways, playing truant at every opportunity that presented itself, and deriving fresh audacity from the immunity I enjoyed.

At last my mother's patience was fairly exhausted, and, recognizing that I had grown altogether beyond her authority, she consented that I should go to a boarding-school, and set to work making inquiries as to which was the most suitable. And presently Mr. English heard of one, where the discipline was very excellent and suitable, he was assured, and here I was accordingly placed.

This Academy was situated at Pilgrim Hatch in the parish of Weald, near Brentwood in the county of Essex. It was conducted by a Mr. Lalterel, a person of French descent, and was a very large establishment, with a great many scholars, but very badly managed, and the boys sadly ill-used and ill-fed. The principal incident during my stay here that I can remember is that I used to walk in my sleep. One evening the schoolmistress met me on the stairs, late at night, and suspecting that I was endeavouring to run away, caught fast hold of me, and gave me a severe cuffing, which had such an effect upon me, that from that day forward I discontinued the practice, as no doubt any other sensible person would have done under similar circumstances. After that Mrs. Lalterel always bore

me a malicious spite, and showed it in many petty
ways, so that when I returned home after the
second term, I determined nothing on earth should
induce me to go back for a third. On my being
despatched after the holidays by Mr. English, I ran
away from the coach, bought a pair of fan-tailed
pigeons with my pocket money, and returned home,
where I got well punished. But I gained the day,
and was not sent back to Mr. Lalterel's Academy.

It was now decided, at my mother's request, to
place me at a school nearer Edmonton than Pilgrim
Hatch, and I was consequently sent to Merchant
Taylors', then considered a first-class public school.
Four clergymen attended the different classes, and
the Rev. Dr. Thomas Green was the head-master.
The usher under whom I studied was the Rev. Mr.
Rose, who made me feel the cane pretty often, and
said I was the most daring and mischievous boy in
his class. Doubtless he was right: my recollection of myself confirms his description.

At Merchant Taylors' I found an ample compensation for the pains and penalties of the school-
room in the companionship during play-hours of
two of my school-fellows, the sons of a sea captain
who owned and commanded a ship trading to
the Guinea Coast. These lads were primed with
accounts of their father's voyages and adventures,
which it was his custom to relate to them whenever he returned home. I was never tired of
listening to these tales, nor they of narrating
them. They were stirring and exciting beyond

measure. Such marvels as my companions discoursed surpassed even those that I had heard from the sailors at the docks, and so proud were they of their sire's achievements, that I soon came to envy them their parentage, who could talk of "our father that hunted and cut down lions on the Coast of Barbary—the skins whereof we have now at home"—or prate of how he had fought and captured such and such ships, mostly pirates, or at least privateers; or boast of a certain great battle with a black negro king on the Gold Coast, in which the captain had entirely vanquished the barbarian army, and loaded his ship with a free cargo of gold and ivory and ebony, sufficient to have made him the richest man in England, had not a storm arisen and wrecked his vessel on her homeward voyage, he barely escaping with his life, and all the rest of his crew miserably perishing.

Such stories as these fired my young imagination, until I came to believe that astounding conquests and successes were the natural concomitants of a seafaring life, and that one needed but to be a sailor to achieve certain and substantial wealth and renown.

I now began to plague and pester my mother to take me away from Merchant Taylors' School, and send me to sea. At first she smiled (not without a certain fond pleasure) at my ardour, and said it was so with all boys, and it gratified her to think I had a brave and adventurous spirit within me. But that I was young, and should become wiser as I grew older, and change my inclination, and not desire to follow a course of life so full of dangers and hardships, and to which she could never consent. "For," she would always end, stroking my hair off my forehead and looking me affectionately in the face, "I have but you, Robert, my son, and how can a widow let her only child go to sea?"

Then I would, by her sweet voice and manner, be irresistibly drawn towards her, and throw my arms around her neck and kiss her; but still maintain my point, and declare that those who sailed away to foreign countries always came back again, laden with riches and honour, and that I desired to do likewise, and buy her a mansion in which she might dwell happily, and ride in a coach till the day of her death. At which she would again smile, always very sweetly, and reply that she would rather walk barefooted for the rest of her life, with her son safe on land, than ride in the finest coach in the city of London, whilst he was tossing on the stormy seas.

But for all this the intention grew and increased in me to become a sailor. Nothing but sea voyages, and books of travel and adventure, interested me, and I could not bring my mind to consider any other course of life. I grew more and more urgent in my appeal to my mother, and gave her no rest night and day, vowing that I would be a sailor and nothing else, and threatening to run away from home and enter the King's navy if she did not accede to my request.

At length she began to realize how earnest I was, and how obstinate in my intention. For a long time she reasoned with me, often with tears in her eyes, attempting to turn me from my purpose—but all in vain. I was but a lad of twelve, yet masterful and pertinacious, whilst she, ever loving and indulgent, when it came to deciding, could say me nay in nothing. And thus it was that I won my desire, and it was at length settled that I should be a sailor.

Had I known how soon I was to lose her, who was so loving and so tender to me, it might have softened my hard and wilful heart, and inclined me to yield to her entreaties. Often have I regretted my obstinacy and determination. Had I but known—but there! the whole philosophy of life is discounted in those four short words!

CHAPTER II.

WHEN it was finally settled that I should go to sea, my godfather, Mr. English, who had some interest amongst people connected with shipping, exerted himself on my behalf, and presently obtained for me an introduction to the house of Messrs. Enderby and Sons, one of the best and most opulent firms in the city of London, who owned several vessels trading in the southern whale fishery. By them I was accepted as an apprentice; for it was the custom in those days to article a lad for a period of four years to the seafaring profession, however respectable he might be, and boys did not enter on the life in the merchant service as midshipmen, but as common apprentices, very dirty to look at, messing in the fo'castle with the sailors, and being expected to perform all the most menial duties on board.

It was in 1784, being just past my twelfth year, that I signed my articles, and was shortly afterwards sent on board one of their ships which was just ready for sea. She was called the *Friendship*, of four hundred tons, under the command of Captain Goldsmith, who in many respects, and especially from the natural kindness of his disposition, was suited to make a lad happy. But he held the idea that boys ought to be inured to the hardships of the profession from the commencement, and this induced him to overlook the tyrannical conduct of his chief mate, who was a savage (for I can designate him by no other term), of the name of Horton. To the brutality of an animal, this person added the vulgarity of a Custom's House officer, and he took a particular and malicious dislike to me from the first, because of my respectable birth and decent appearance, he himself being degraded and uncouth in manners and dress.

My mother had provided me with a very fine outfit of clothes. For days and weeks she had toiled, late and early, to prepare everything her devoted love considered necessary for my comfort, and the result was that I was by far the smartest dressed of all the sailors and apprentices. Moreover I took a certain pride in my person, having in this respect been very strictly brought up. It was this that turned Mr. Horton against me. To be neat and tidy was a reflection upon himself, I suppose, for I never saw him clean in my life. Whenever his eyes fell upon me he saluted me with a volley of oaths, calling me all manner of names to indicate his contempt for what he called my "proudbelliness," which he vowed to break. I soon learnt that to wear a clean shirt was a sure passport to being sent up aloft, with a grease-bag round my neck, to grease down one of the top-masts, and that each new article of apparel I put on at once set him discovering some filthy job to put me to. Captain Goldsmith never interfered in the chief mate's work, and there was nothing for me to do but to obey. Yet oftentimes, during the first month, when I was homesick and troubled, my boyish heart would almost burst with anguish when engaged in these duties, as I recalled the picture of my patient mother, plying her busy needle hour after hour by candlelight, and working away through the long evenings to provide me with the very articles of attire that had raised the tyrant's spite. It seemed to me then (as, indeed, it seems to me now) such a cruel compensation for all the love she had worked in with every stitch; and I would try and avoid soiling my dress, since every stain on it seemed to me undutiful. All this may appear foolish, but I was only a child then, and the purchasing and providing and fitting and packing of my first sea-chest, which contained all my worldly wealth and seemed to be so precious, had taken weeks in its completion, and formed the absorbing theme of our daily conversation at home for a month before I sailed.

The mate's conduct towards me soon made me repent my determination to become a sailor, but this being my own choice I could not relinquish it. It did not take me long to discover how different was the reality and practice of the life to the vague and fanciful dreams concerning it that I had cherished. To a boy brought up as I had been, the duties I was now forced to perform were of a most degrading description, and the fact of my being in the chief mate's black books gave every one a license to ill-use me, and I was subjected much more than my fellow-apprentices to the orders of all on board. During that first voyage I was nothing less than a slave, and at the beck and nod of the common seamen before the mast, even to the washing of their clothes and the cleaning of their pannikins and platters. Looking back now on these days, it is surprising to me that through it all I continued hopeful and persevering, and anxious to excel in a profession in which my commencement was so unpromising, so hard, and so truly humiliating.

There was only one person on board who was at all kind to me. This was an old man-o'-war's man, who had served in the King's navy for many years, and had sailed forty years before with Admiral Lord Anson in his famous voyages. After serving under Admiral Sir George Rodney in the great fight off Cape St. Vincent, he had left the service, but having settled on shore and married a shrew of a wife, he was glad to return to sea "for the sake of peace," as he explained it. I do not know what induced him to notice me, but being in the same watch we gradually struck up such a friendship as can exist between a lad of twelve and an old man of sixty-five, which was his age. I found him to be amiable and kind-hearted, though unwilling to show it, and disguising his true character beneath a gruff and taciturn exterior. He always spoke to me sharply, except when we chanced to be alone; but I got to understand this and did not mind it, always giving him a civil reply and a ready obedience. Sometimes in the trade winds, when the ship was sailing along under a cloud of canvas, and we, off watch, were lying lazily on the fo'castle head, mending our clothes, his manner would somewhat soften, which encouraged me to speak out and tell him my troubles, and how unjustly I was treated by the chief mate, and bullied and knocked about. To all of which he would listen very gravely, and then slowly and digestively reply: "There is no justice or injustice on board ship, my lad. There are only two things: Duty and Mutiny—mind that. All that you are ordered to do is duty. All that you refuse to do is mutiny. And the punishment for mutiny on a king's frigate is the yard-arm. In the merchant service you only get rope's-ended. Lads have to learn: discipline is good for them; and you will come some day to feel quite grateful to Mr. Horton for his trouble in teaching you your profession."

There was not much comfort in this, but a great deal of sound sense. I was learning to be a sailor, and though the task-master was cruel, I perceive now he made a man of me in less time than many others would have done.

My first voyage in the *Friendship* was an absence of sixteen months, and we returned home early in 1786 with a full cargo of spermaceti of great value. During the whole of this period we had been continually at sea, and I had gained a practical knowledge of many of a seaman's duties, and by the end of it there was scarce any operation on board in which I could not lend a hand if ordered; and I knew every rope on the vessel, and its use, by heart. On my return home I was so brown with exposure to the sun and weather, and so grown and filled out, that I was almost past recognition by those who had seen me start, an undersized boy. In spite of bullying and harsh treatment, of bad food and bad water, of night-

watches and short spells of sleep (to which a
young and growing lad takes long to get reconciled), of hard knocks and harder fare, I had
throve amazingly, and when I burst into the
cottage at Edmonton, and ran up to my mother's
side, she held me at arm's length for a moment
before she fully realized that it was her son come
back again.

Alas! she herself was much changed—as much
for the worse as I was for the better and stronger.
Her face was pale and thin, with a bright spot on
each cheek, and her complexion had become a
strange waxen delicate colour, whilst her eyes
seemed softer and larger than ever. I noted it
but lightly at the time, being young and careless,
thinking little and never cogitating upon anything
I saw. I heeded not the hectic flush that every
trifling exertion brought to her pale face, nor the
exhaustion that followed each physical effort,
however slight. But I know now that the seal
of death was set upon her at that very time, and
after I left her for my second voyage I never saw
her face in life again.

I passed a merry time ashore, being made much
of by all who had known me, and considered quite
a hero by my former young companions. When my
month's liberty was over, I bade good-bye to my
mother, and repaired to London to rejoin the
Friendship, the command of which had now been
given to Captain Melville.

This gentleman was as kind a man as Captain

Goldsmith in disposition, but with the additional feeling of protecting the boys against the ill-usage of the mates. All the apprentices were, in addition, allowed certain opportunities for acquiring a knowledge of the higher branches of navigation, and of these I quickly availed myself, and by my anxiety to learn attracted the attention of Captain Melville, who seemed pleased at it, and very kindly encouraged and helped me, which was greatly to my advantage.

During this voyage, I was ordered out one stormy night to the foreyard, to look out for land, which was expected to be sighted. This was a task often assigned to me, as my sight was particularly acute. Anxious to show my activity, I stood upon the yard-arm and leant carelessly against the topsail, when the sheet suddenly broke, and I fell upon the bowsprit, where I managed to hold on by a rope until taken on board by some of the crew. Having pitched on my knee, my agony was almost past endurance for about sixty hours; but I recovered in three weeks, and my escape was considered so miraculous that the incident was noted in the log-book.

On my return home after this voyage, I obtained leave at Greenwich, and immediately proceeded to Edmonton. Having reached the well-known cottage, I found, to my dismay, that it was empty and deserted. The weeds had grown in the garden plot in front, and this was the first thing to catch my eye, being so unusual, for the little flower-beds before the sitting-room windows had always been kept in neatest order, it having been my mother's particular delight and care to attend to them herself. I rang at the door, but no one answered. Then I made my way to Mr. English's house, and from him I learnt the news of my dear mother's death during the preceding winter.

I cannot describe the grief that overcame me. I was so unprepared for this intelligence that it burst upon me with an overwhelming shock. It seemed impossible that she to whom I had said good-bye so light-heartedly, believing I should see her again, was now lying beneath the little grassy mound in the old churchyard, and that we should never meet again on earth. Repairing to her grave, I knelt by the side of it, and sobbed my sorrow out in a tempest of unavailing tears and regrets.

I stayed but a short time with my godfather, Mr. English, although he offered me a home for so long as I wanted one. But it was so different to that to which I had been accustomed, and the place was now made so unendurably sad by the many memories that haunted it, that I felt it would be a relief to me to return to sea, and endeavour to forget my sorrows in the work and excitement of my profession. So I thanked Mr. English for his offer, but told him I proposed sailing again directly, having no heart for a jaunt ashore; at which he was somewhat surprised, but offered no objection. I therefore proceeded to town, and explaining my situation to Messrs. Enderby and Sons, they very kindly arranged for me to be taken on board another ship of theirs which was just sailing.

The name of this vessel I forget, but she was commanded by an American gentleman named Delano, who was a most clever, experienced man in whaling affairs, and an excellent seaman, but in his manners and disposition rude and overbearing. In my previous voyage with Captain Melville, I had considerably added to my stock of professional experience, and during this present one I completed my education as a sailor, and also worked out the full period of my apprenticeship; so that on my return in 1790, although under eighteen years of age, I was certified as eligible for the duties of first officer.

Very shortly after this I had the good fortune to obtain the situation of chief mate of a small trading brig called the *Salamander*, Captain Ellis, of which appointment I was mightily proud, for it was an almost unheard-of thing to step out of an apprenticeship into such a position. I owed this singular good-fortune to Captain Delano, and it was certainly a favour I could not have anticipated from his treatment of me when I was on board his ship, but it rewarded me for a prompt and willing obedience to orders, which I always endeavoured to show, no matter how harsh the manner in which they were conveyed.

I was placed in charge of the *Salamander* whilst

she lay loading in the Pool, just below London Bridge, and began my duties with a wonderful will, being very active in the fitting-out of the ship for sea, which seemed to please Captain Ellis very much. Matters went on smoothly till within four days of the date of our sailing, when, the *Salamander* being almost ready to start, I obtained leave to go ashore for the purpose of saying good-bye to a young lady to whom I was paying attention, and who afterwards became my wife.

Just about this time our Government was involved in a dispute with Spain. Four years before, under the protection of the East India Company, certain merchants and shipowners had opened out a trade in furs with the North-West Coast of America, for the purpose of supplying the Chinese market, and two ships had been despatched to Prince William's Sound, where the crews landed to winter, building houses and opening an extensive trade under the British flag. The Spanish Government, so soon as they heard of it, despatched two ships of war to this place, took possession of the English vessels, hauled down the British flag, and raised the standard of his Catholic Majesty, at the same time declaring that all lands comprised between Cape Horn and latitude 60° north belonged to Spain. There was great excitement in London at this insult, and satisfaction was at once demanded by our Government.

In consequence of this a fleet was ordered to be manned, under the command of Admiral Barrington, and to assemble off Spithead. These orders, being urgent, led to a very hot press taking place, from which not even officers of merchant ships were exempted if found on shore without an Admiralty protection. Captain Ellis procured me a protection ticket for three days, but meeting me on shore, he extended my leave from three to five days, as there was some delay in our sailing. On the fifth day he called for me at my lodgings, and we set out for the ship, both of us being dressed in private clothes, but with black neck-handkerchiefs. As we turned round the corner of a street near the river, we were accosted by two press-gangs, coming from different directions, the one under a press-master, and the other under a lieutenant of the *Inconstant* frigate. The latter coming upon us first, inquired who I was. My fear confused me, and I did not answer. Captain Ellis then said I was his chief officer, returning with him to his ship. My protection ticket was then demanded, and the date on it showed I was behind my time, so the lieutenant immediately claimed me, and carried me aboard the *Enterprise*, Captain Vanderbilt, the principal officer in London for pressed men, whose ship was lying in the river just off the Tower.

Being presently brought before this officer, I stated my case, and handed him my protection in confirmation of what I said. From the kind way he made his inquiries, and especially from his sharp rebuke to his first lieutenant for speaking without permission, I entertained hopes of being discharged, until he unfortunately referred to the time of my liberty, and discovered that I had overstayed it, which he had not observed at first. "I am sorry," he said, "that you have put it out of my power to accommodate you, for I perceive your protection ended yesterday."

"That, sir," I replied, "is true. But a protection was granted for the period of my leave, which was extended by my own captain, who will prove it."

"There is no need to do that," rejoined Captain Vanderbilt, "for your captain cannot extend the period of your protection, so that plea will not avail you."

"Then, sir, allow me to procure a substitute," I answered, "for I have just obtained my first appointment as chief mate, and if I am now pressed into the navy, I shall lose that which I have worked hard to obtain."

"What," cried Captain Vanderbilt, smiling, "you a chief officer! Why, you are but a lad. Still, if you have deserved such promotion, I take it there must be particular merit in you, and under the circumstances, seeing the great need there is of capable seamen to man this fleet, I should not be doing justice to his Majesty if I accepted a common sailor for an officer of your parts. In short, if you desire your discharge, you must provide me with two men."

This was beyond my power, for the price then

ruling was twenty guineas each, which was too much to pay when no actual war was declared, and when I might be free again in a few weeks. I therefore declined the proposal, and was passed for the *Inconstant* frigate, Captain Montgomery, fitting out at Woolwich.

The next day, in company with two hundred more pressed men, I was sent on a large brig tender proceeding to the *Inconstant.* At Greenwich we were obliged to anchor for the night, and the lieutenant in charge, having too few hands to guard so many men, proffered my liberation from the crowd below, if I would take a pair of pistols and a sword and stand guard over the hatchway during the night. It was so repugnant to my feelings to be cooped up with the drunken sailors and longshoremen who were crowded between decks in an atmosphere of reeking smell that nearly suffocated me, that I very gladly accepted the lieutenant's offer; and thus it happened that, although no one on the brig was more anxious for liberty than myself, it fell to my lot to prevent my fellows in misfortune from escaping. The next morning we dropped down to Woolwich, where I and eleven other enlisted landsmen were sent on board the *Inconstant*, and the brig continued her journey down the river to Gravesend, where several other men-of-war were stationed awaiting their complements.

The first lieutenant of the *Inconstant* mustered us on deck, and our names were put down, and then, having found out that I was an officer of a mer-

chant ship, he said he would like to satisfy himself
of my ability, and in order to test it, presently
ordered me to go into the maintop and see the
rigging set up, there being only a young midshipman in charge of the work, who did not know what
he was about. I obeyed him with alacrity, and
accomplished the task he set me in a manner
that pleased him so much, that on my return to
deck he said if I would pledge my word of honour
to return, it being Sunday, he would grant me
liberty to go ashore until eight bells.

I was not slow to avail myself of this chance,
and at once proceeded to Woolwich with another
respectable man, who had also been pressed, and
whose acquaintance I had made. His name was
Pearse, and he was carpenter of an Indiaman, and
had, like myself, been taken for overstaying his protection. He told me that he had many friends on
shore who belonged to the Dockyard, and invited
me to accompany him to the house of one of them,
which I did, and was most hospitably received, and
asked to join in a good dinner.

Just as the meal was finished there came a
knock at the door, and immediately afterwards a
constable burst into the room and demanded to
know if a man named Pearse was there.

"I am Mr. Pearse," said my companion, rising
from the table.

"Then you are my prisoner," cried the officer,
drawing a pistol from his pocket and presenting it
point-blank at my friend. "I apprehend you on
suspicion of robbery.

At this proceeding my young blood boiled up, for I could not suppose that such a quiet and decent person as Mr. Pearse could be a' thief, and I immediately demanded an explanation from the stranger, asking him on what proof or authority he acted.

" What ! " he bellowed, with a threatening gesture at me ; " and are you in league with him too ? Then I must take you as well ! "

This was too much for my indignation, and I immediately knocked the pistol out of his hand, and took him by the collar to turn him out of the house. But before I could do so Mr. Pearse interfered, and drawing me back, said :

" I beg you to desist. You do not know what danger you are incurring by laying your hands on an officer of the law."

" Officer of the law he may be," I replied hotly, " but he shall not accuse me of that which I am not guilty, nor act without showing his authority."

" Sir," rejoined Mr. Pearse, very earnestly, and with a mildness of manner that I could not understand, " I pray you moderate your feelings. Believe me entirely innocent, but should I resist I should be placing myself in the wrong at once. This constable is merely acting under the orders he has received from his superior authority, and only doing his duty. It is better for me to accompany him and have the matter cleared up. I beg of you therefore not to embroil yourself on my behalf, for were any harm to come to you on my account I should be much concerned. Therefore I will go with him of my own free will."

This seemed to me a tame submission; so I answered, "As you please, Mr. Pearse. If you are content to be treated like this and apprehended without a warrant, and do not require my assistance to resist, I cannot force it upon you."

The constable then took Mr. Pearse by the arm, and, holding his pistol presented at him all the time, led him out of the house towards a coach which was standing waiting at a little distance. On reaching the door he asked a well-dressed woman, who was sitting inside, "Is this the man who robbed you?"

" Oh, yes ; that is the rogue," was the immediate reply.

Then happened a most extraordinary thing, for the constable opened the coach door and pushed his prisoner inside, whilst he himself mounted the box, and the coachman immediately drove off at a rapid rate, leaving me staring at them and utterly bewildered. It seemed as though the constable was in league with the reputed thief to rob the lady a second time, only that she made no noise or outcry at the proceeding.

I determined to return to the frigate at once and report what had occurred ; but as I got down to the landing-place I met the first lieutenant coming ashore in his boat. Directly I told him what had taken place, he swore very roundly, and instantly despatched his boat's crew to overtake the coach if possible, and detain it. But they never came up with it, nor did Mr. Pearse rejoin the ship ; and I afterwards discovered that the whole affair was a stratagem between his wife and a friend. of his, and that its object was to secure his freedom.

I remained on board the *Inconstant* a week, continuing in my dress as a gentleman, and not being set to do any duty, and at the end of this time I was surprised at seeing a very great friend of mine come aboard.   His name was Beddick, and he immediately ran forward to where I was standing and greeted me in the most hearty manner, asking how it was that I was there without having previously informed him of my intention of coming to see him, for he believed that to be the object of my presence on board.   When I told him that I was a pressed man he expressed considerable sur-prise, observing that at times the press was very hot—a remark that was more commonplace than comforting.   It turned out that he was purser of the frigate, to which he had just been appointed, and an intimate friend of the captain.   Having heard my story he professed great concern at it, and said he would consult with Captain Mont-gomery what was best to be done.   Later on in the day he called me to his cabin and thus addressed me :

" I have been considering your present situation, and my advice to you is to give up the merchant service and enter the navy.   And I have obtained for you the promise of being entered at once as master's mate."

This was one step higher than a midshipman, and far beyond anything I could have expected under the circumstances. But the position was nevertheless a very subordinate one, and quite different to that which I had earned for myself in the merchant service, and I began to reflect over this before I replied. Mr. Beddick perceiving my reluctance, said :

"Why are you hesitating? Consider what an opening lies before you. There is quick promotion to be won, in these stirring times, and in such a frigate as the *Inconstant*, commanded by a captain notorious for his fighting proclivities. Believe me, you will here have many opportunities of promoting your own interests by zeal and merit ; whereas on such crafts as these "— he waved his ·hand disparagingly at some merchant ships at anchor hard by— " who and what are you? The king's uniform carries a distinction with it, which you can never hope to arrive at in the merchant service."

The result was that I determined to act upon Mr. Beddick's advice, which it was the more easy for me to decide on as the *Salamander* had dropped down the river and sailed three days previously. I therefore thanked him, and said I would avail myself of his kindness, and the next day I was entered on the ship's books of the *Inconstant* as a master's mate, and acted in that capacity.

Had I continued in the navy, I might have had the honour of serving under Admiral Lord Howe, or Admiral Lord St. Vincent, or Admiral Lord

Nelson, and shared in some of the glorious victories that added a lustre to the next fifteen years, when the battles of Cape St. Vincent, Camperdown, The Nile, Copenhagen, and Trafalgar were fought. Perhaps I might have risen to the command of a frigate myself, or (what is more likely) become food for the sharks! But as it happened, the Spaniards yielded satisfaction for the insult they had offered us, and there was no war declared. As soon as this was made known, I obtained a month's leave, and went to London, and during that time the *Inconstant* was paid off, and I never afterwards rejoined the king's navy.

CHAPTER III.

DURING my detention and subsequent service in the navy, I had of course lost my appointment as chief mate of the *Salamander*, and on leaving the *Inconstant* I found myself without any occupation. I have mentioned that at the time I was pressed I was returning from paying a visit to a young lady of whom I was enamoured; and now that I was master of my own time I had so many opportunities and so much leisure for courtship, that I soon found myself engaged to be married, and early in 1791, when I was only in my nineteenth year, I made the object of my affections my wife.

She was the daughter of independent parents living at Kingsland, and niece to a very rich gentleman, a Mr. Axe, who was sole owner of one, and part owner of two East Indiamen. Our marriage met with his approval, and he took an interest in me, and presently proposed that I should enter the Honourable Company's service, promising me the command of a ship as soon as I should be eligible for it. This was a very tempting offer, as there was no service equal to it, or more difficult to get into, requiring great interest.

It was the practice of the Company in those days to charter ships from their owners; these vessels were especially built for the service, and were generally run for about four voyages, when they were held to be worn out, and their places taken by others built for the purpose. About thirty ships were required for the Company every year. There was never any written engagement on the part of either the owners or the Company as to the continuance of these charters, but the custom of contract was so well-established that both parties mutually relied upon it, and considered themselves bound by ties of honour to observe their implied customary engagements. When, therefore, a ship's turn arrived to be employed, the owner, as a matter of form, submitted a tender in writing to be engaged, and proposed a particular person as captain, and this tender and proposal were always accepted. Thus the owners of these East Indiamen had everything in their own hands, and the favour of one of them was a fine thing to obtain, leading to appointments of great emolument. The post of captain of a ship was usually sold, and not given away. The actual shipowner was termed the ship's " husband," and he, as the phrase went, " sold the ship " to the captain to whom he offered the command, often obtaining as much as £8,000 or £10,000 for the appointment. After the sale the command became the transferable property of the captain who had bought it, and who, if he desired to resign, was considered to have an undoubted right to sell the command to the highest bidder; or, if he died, the same right passed to his heirs.

A few years afterwards this custom was abolished, as it occasioned in a great degree the high rates of freight paid by the Company. A compensation was given to the captains then in the service, and after this it became out of the power of money for a person deficient in the qualifications requisite for the situation to obtain the command of a ship, although previously such persons had often held the appointments.

The position was a most lucrative one. The captain of an East Indiaman, in addition to his pay and allowances, had the right of free outward freight to the extent of fifty tons, being only debarred from exporting certain articles, such as woollens, metals, and warlike stores. On the homeward voyage he was allotted twenty tons of free freight, each of thirty-two feet; but this tonnage was bound to consist of certain scheduled goods, and duties were payable thereon to the Company. As the rate of freight in those days was about £25 a ton, this privilege was a very valuable one. Of course much depended upon the skill and good management of the individual commander, the risk of the market, his knowledge of its requirements, and his own connections and interest to procure him a good profit. In addition to the free tonnage, he further enjoyed certain advantages in the carrying of passengers; for although the allowance of passage money outward and homeward was arbitrarily fixed by the Company, there being a certain number of passengers assigned to each vessel, and their fares duly determined, ranging from £95 for a subaltern and assistant-surgeon to £235 for a general officer, with from one and a half to three and a half tons of free baggage, exclusive of bedding and furniture for their cabins, yet it was possible for captains, by giving up their own apartments and accommodation, to make very considerable sums for themselves.

In short, the gains to a prudent commander averaged from £4,000 to £5,000 a voyage, sometimes perhaps falling as low as £2,000, but at others rising to £10,000 and £12,000. The time occupied from the period of a ship commencing receipt of her outward cargo to her being finally cleared of her homeward one was generally from fourteen to eighteen months, and three or four voyages assured any man a very handsome fortune.

It will be perceived, therefore, that Mr. Axe's offer to me was no ordinary one, but unfortunately there was a regulation of the Company that proved a stumbling-block in the path of my advancement. And this was, that before any one could get the command of a ship it was necessary that he should first make a voyage as fifth or sixth mate, then another as third or fourth, and finally a third as first or second mate. The junior officers in the service were moreover unable to live on their pay, and it required a private capital of at least five hundred pounds to enable a man to arrive at the position of second mate, which was the lowest station wherein the pay and allowances afforded a maintenance. This I could not afford, having now the responsibility and expense of providing for a wife, and I therefore decided to decline Mr. Axe's proposal (much to my mortification, for it had always been my ambition to enter that service) and to accept instead the offer of an appointment of chief mate on a vessel bound for the West Coast of Africa.

This vessel was named the *Fortitude,* and was of three hundred tons burden. She was bound on a somewhat strange voyage, her charter being to discover a certain small bay between the equator and latitude 15° north on the West Coast of Africa. About five years before, a Guineaman, having filled up with a cargo of slaves for Jamaica and put to sea, found herself so crank that she was forced to put to land again for more ballast, and she happened to anchor in this particular bay. The ballast she loaded was found, on examination in England, to contain particles of gold, and also a stone or substance that produced a substitute for vermillion. But on her voyage to the West Indies, the infection of a malignant land fever having seized the ship, it carried off the captain, the mates, half the crew, and more than half the slaves during the passage, the surgeon of the ship alone surviving to bring her into port. He returned to England, but so ill from the effects of the same disorder, that it was three years before he recovered his health. He then began to seek for some merchants to entertain his proposal to fit out a vessel for the purpose of discovering this bay and bringing home a cargo of the ballast. But he was only able to give such an indistinct account of the place, that it was a long time before he could persuade any one to enter into the scheme. At length his persistency and apparent earnestness of belief was successful, and he induced a firm of merchants to attempt the venture. Our ship, the *Fortitude*, was the one taken up for the speculation. She was put under the command of Captain Ross, a clever and prudent man, who very wisely insisted (in view of the hazardous nature of the undertaking) that a whaling crew and equipment should be shipped on board, so as to prevent a total loss in case of disappointment attending our search for the bay.

After a few brief weeks of happy married life, I left my young wife and sailed away to sea. The night before we started, the surgeon of the Guineaman came aboard, very drunk. He was an exceeding tall, thin, cadaverous-looking man, with a sallow complexion, and a peculiar wild look in his eyes in moments of excitement. He was sent with us in order to recognize the bay when we came to it, and to test the ballast, so that we might load none but what was of the best quality. He brought with him several chests, which he said contained microscopes, chemicals, and his medicines, but which we presently discovered were filled with spirituous liquors, chiefly rum, the drinking of which continually, and in immoderate quantities, he excused on the plea of his constitution being shattered by the fever and requiring a constant stimulant to assist the action of the heart.

We had fair winds down channel, and made a

quick voyage to the Cape de Verde Islands, where we anchored off the one called Sal for water, our supply having proved very putrid. Here we sent our boats ashore, and whilst the men were filling the kegs, Captain Ross and I started out in the hopes of shooting some wild goats, which it was believed were to be found on the island. After three or four hours' walking, during which we saw no signs of such beasts, we set out to return to our boats. When nearing the beach I espied a small animal at a short distance, squatting down behind a bush. My musket was loaded with swan shot, and I fired, and nothing retreating from the spot, I ran up and found, to my intense mortification and to Captain Ross's vast amusement, that the quarry I had killed was a tabby cat, which distressed me greatly. A little way further on we saw two or three others, so I suppose some vessel must have been wrecked on the island, from which these creatures had found their way ashore and bred. The island was uninhabited, but frequented by thousands of sea birds, and we gathered a great quantity of their eggs, which proved excellent eating if sufficiently peppered to disguise the strong taste.

Leaving Sal, we ran straight to the African coast, and having sighted Cape Verde, hauled close in shore and headed south to begin our search. All day long we sailed slowly on with two boats out examining the coast, whilst we tacked on and off so as to keep their company. At every small bay we reached we dropped anchor or hove to, and made a dilligent search, the boats landing and bringing back specimens of the sand. The task was one full of danger, for there was a prodigious sea-swell setting in shore, and frequently a great surf raging, which made landing impossible until it had subsided, and thus we would be detained several days at one spot before we could effect our purpose.

As for the surgeon of the Guineaman, he did nothing but sit on the poop all day long, under the shade of a sail, with a telescope on his knee, a pipe of tobacco in his mouth, and a glass of rum and water at his elbow. Here, hour after hour, he talked and muttered to himself with his eyes fixed on the distant coast, and never turned them away. I cannot but admit that he displayed a full and perfect belief in the existence of the bay we were in search of, and professed himself confident that we must sooner or later find it. But his mind seemed affected and his memory gone— whether from the fever he had suffered, or from the liquor that he drank, I cannot say. There was scarcely a watch but he would at some time or other suddenly start up and cry aloud, "Ah! thanks be to Heaven, here it is!—I recognize that forest of trees;" or, "That headland yonder is familiar to me. Praise be to God, we have reached our goal!" or denote a bend of the coast, or the mouth of a river, or a range of inland hills, or anything that was out of the common. Then he would insist on heaving to or anchoring, and signalling to one of the boats to go ashore (he never went himself, for fear of catching the land fever again); and during the time the boat was so engaged he would pace up and down the deck in a sort of mad frenzy, swinging his arms round and round, and talking of the glorious success of our search, and the magnificent fortune in store for the expedition, and the splendid reception we should meet with on our return. When the boat reached the ship, he would seize a handful of the sand and, carrying it down to the cabin, examine it; and presently return with a very dismal face, and say that by some strange mischance he had been mistaken, and we must resume our search. "For we must persevere. We must never give in!" he would always add, "The bay cannot be far off now! The Golden Bay! Make sail, Captain Ross; make sail. We shall soon arrive at the place!"

This lasted for at least a month, during which we had carefully examined six hundred miles of coast, though long before that time had elapsed every man on board the *Fortitude* conjectured that the Golden Bay existed but in the mad fancy or besotted brain of the surgeon. Still, we were under his orders within these fifteen degrees of latitude, as regarded our search, and obliged to be guided by his directions so long as a reasonable hope of success remained.

At length we had sailed all along that part of

the coast where it was likely or possible that any Guineaman, bound for Jamaica, could have touched, and had done everything in our power to fulfil the terms of our charter, but without discovering the bay. The surgeon alone was unconvinced, but on the contrary seemed to grow more hopeful, and continued to daily recognize the Golden Bay, and to pace the deck, swinging his arms and prating of fortune achieved, and with each fresh disappointment appearing to become more sanguine of success. Until at last it became very evident that his reason had completely gone, and that he was nothing else than a babbling madman.

And so one morning Captain Ross called me aside and said:

"I now consider I have fulfilled my orders with regard to this voyage of discovery, and done my duty to my owners' wishes and intentions, and much against my own judgment. How they could ever have put any faith in this mad fellow, whose gold only exists in his frenzied imagination, I do not know. But I am fully determined to discontinue this search, and, in order that we may in some measure redeem these wasted weeks, to at once sail for the whaling grounds. I should, however, like to have your independent opinion upon the course I intend to pursue."

I told Captain Ross frankly that I, and indeed all the ship's company, had long been of one mind, namely, that the surgeon was mad, and that it was folly to continue on the wild-goose chase we were engaged in. So far from resenting the candour of my reply, Captain Ross seemed pleased at it.

"I have long been of the same opinion myself," he answered, "but. I had my duty towards my owners to consider. They had faith in this man, who, when he was ashore, was sober enough, and very earnest, and indeed eloquent in his conversation, as I had frequent opportunities of observing. You will bear me out that I have done my utmost to secure success, and have continued longer at this thankless task than many others would have done. And now follow me."

He led the way to where the surgeon was sitting, looking with a fixed stare at the distant coast.

"Sir," said Captain Ross, addressing him, "I must now ask you to consider yourself my passenger. For I have determined to discontinue the search for the Guineaman's Bay we had hoped to find, and to proceed at once to the whaling grounds."

Hearing which, the surgeon became all in a moment frantic, and had I not seized him, would, I believe, have struck Captain Ross. First he stormed and swore and threatened all manner of things, demanding how we dared desert our duty. when we were just on the eve of discovery. But finding this had no effect, he began next to beg and pray to us to persevere for one week more, or even one day more, kneeling down upon the deck.

But Captain Ross would not consent. Finally the surgeon lost all control of himself, and raved so wildly that Captain Ross was obliged to order the watch aft, and cause him to be conveyed by force to his cabin, and there kept in restraint for several days. After about a week he recovered, and becoming quiet, was permitted to walk on deck again. And after that we had no more trouble with him, for his stock of liquor being all finished, and the captain refusing to supply him with any from the ship's stores, he presently grew strangely silent and moody, and would stand all day long on one spot, leaning against the taffrail, gazing at the horizon, as if he expected his Golden Bay to appear in sight. But it never did; and about a fortnight later he was discovered to be missing one morning, and there was no doubt but that during the night the poor gentleman had cast himself overboard.

Meanwhile we had proceeded to Walvisch Bay, which is situated in latitude 22 South, for the fishery, it being the season for the whales to come in to calve. It was here that for the first time in my life I saw the Hottentots, or negro inhabitants of these parts. We were at anchor in the bay, and I had gone ashore one day to explore the country, which was sandy, but with some low hills a short way inland. Towards these I bent my footsteps, and after about a mile came across a company of Hottentots, and joined them under tokens of friendship. They were very friendly, and lent me a lance to try the throw of it, showing me how to use it. They themselves were most expert with the weapon, being able to bring down a bird upon the wing. These Hottentots were a very black people, strongly built, and quite naked, but with faces good-natured enough. They appeared pleased at my attentions, and especially with the gift of a few trifles that I had with me. After resting a short time, and endeavouring by means of signs to obtain some information from them, I left them and set out to return to the beach, where my crew were waiting for me. And now I observed another party of these blacks, whom I thought hostile in their manner and attitude; so much so that I became alarmed, and as I approached the sea, there being a large sand hillock between us which hid me from their view, I took advantage of the start this gave me, and began to run towards the shore as quick as I could. Directly they caught sight of me again, they set up a shout and followed. They were much fleeter of foot, and I had only time to throw myself headlong into the boat, which fortunately I found in a position to enter, and push off with all speed, when they reached the water's edge, and would have boarded us, had not one of my men discharged a musket above their heads, at the smoke and report of which they all recoiled, and so enabled us to out oars and make way. Seeing which, the blacks recovered their courage, and rushing into the water, flung several lances or spears at us, and had we been but a few yards nearer would certainly have wounded if not killed some of us. My men desired to shoot down the leader for a punishment, but this I would not permit. The adventure had the good effect of making us more cautious for the future, never landing without being armed and with six or eight in company. I learnt afterwards that about three months before the time of which I am speaking, a party of these very Hottentots cut off a boat's crew, and murdered every man of them.

Fish at this bay was in the greatest abundance. We had only to land at one of the inlets and throw our seine, and catch enough for the whole of our crew for a couple of days. Bream and mullet constituted the best varieties.

A few days after my escape from the Hottentots whales were observed spouting, and we put out in pursuit of them. I was in command of the foremost boat, and discharged the harpoon at the whale we were in chase of, by privilege of my position as chief officer of the ship. I made a good strike, inflicting a mortal blow, which caused the whale to spurt blood; but her revenge had nearly proved fatal to us all, for lashing round with her tail, she dashed the boat to pieces, and for ten minutes we were all swimming in the water, and it was a mercy we escaped her rage. The fury of a whale on receiving its death-wound is something awful to behold. It rises perpendicularly out of the water, lashes the waves in its flurry with its tail, then darts off suddenly with the greatest speed, and as suddenly stops and rolls about. But this seldom lasts long, and when about to die, it turns upon its back, and floats a huge mass upon the water.

Several other boats being round us, we were in time taken up, but I felt my first achievement in harpooning a whale sufficient to satisfy my desires in that direction for an exceeding long time.

Having secured the whale, it was towed alongside the *Fortitude*, and made fast. Then began the process of cutting her up and extracting the blubber and bone. Two officers stood on the sides of the ship, with spades in their hands, ground as sharp as razors, and with poles of ten feet in length for handles, with which they cut a hole through the blubber to the body. Two large tackles being fitted to the main-mast head with a four-inch rope, and immense large hooks at the end, one of them was inserted in the body of the whale so that it obtained a firm purchase, and then its tackle was taken to the windlass and hove in until the body was sufficiently raised up. The two officers then cut the blubber about four feet broad, and whilst the windlass was turned, they carved the carcase as the whale worked round. When they could get no further, a second hole was made in the whale, and the second hook inserted, and the tackle heaved taut. Then they cut off the first piece of blubber, and lowered it down between decks, and set to work in the same way for the second piece, and so on until they got the whole of it on board.

The blubber peels off a whale the same as the skin does off a beast. After the blubber, the head, which contains the whalebone, is fastened to one of these tackles, and a man stands upon it with an axe, and cuts off the large bone with the whalebone sticking to it, and this is hoisted aboard. The tongue is likewise hoisted up in the same way, and the carcase is then set adrift, and appears almost as large as it did before the blubber was taken off. Thousands of sea birds are attracted to feast on it as it floats away.

The work now begins on board. In the centre of the ship, directly under the main hatch, there is a place built with two large 90-gallon pots, fixed with every precaution against fire, so as to bear a large furnace below them. A part of the crew are employed between decks to cut off all the flesh from the blubber, which is very fat according to the size of the whale, being from eight to fourteen inches thick. This being cut into pieces each about two feet long by six inches broad, they are thrown into large pots placed at hand. Here two men are employed cutting these slabs into slices of about one inch thick, not, however, altogether detaching them, but leaving the corners uncut so as to hold the whole together. These are finally thrown into the boilers, and the oil soon boiled out and transferred into the tubs standing by, where another man, armed with a long-handled ladle, removes the oil to a large copper cooler which holds about one hundred and twenty gallons. After it has cooled down it is filled into casks, which are securely closed and then stowed away in the hold. This work goes on night and day without cessation, until the whole whale is finished. A good whale will make about sixty barrels of oil.

The captain and officers of these whaling vessels were paid by shares, instead of monthly wages, and this made them alert and ever on a sharp look-out. The ships were all from the port of London, and the employment was a very creditable and profitable one, there being a large demand for the oil for the purpose of lighting the streets. The different varieties of whales are recognized by their spouting; a Spermaceti whale—by far the most valuable—having only one spout hole, and that at the very end of its head, and large, so that it makes a thick spread, like a brush, and spouts very regularly, and for twenty or thirty times, which is different from all other whales. The oil obtained from the head of this species contains more than double the quantity of spermaceti contained in the rest of its body. The other variety is the " Right " whale, which is like the Greenland whale, and has two spout holes far back in the head, and expels the water like a fork, very high and straight up, and not more than five or six times before it goes under again. This species is found in large shoals between the West Coast of Africa and the East Coast of South America, but it is at those seasons of the year when they come towards land to calve, that they are most profitably hunted.

We were very successful in the fishery, and soon filled up with oil, and set sail for England. But stopping at St. Helena, Captain Ross, who had full powers, sold the *Fortitude* to a French gentleman, taking in part payment a very fine American-built brig. This he loaded up with oil, and proceeded to Martinico in the West Indies, hearing there was a strong market there. Having disposed of it to great advantage, he loaded a cargo of tobacco as freight for Dunkirk, where he sold the ship, and he and I returned to London together in one of the Dunkirk traders, after a voyage which was as prosperous in its ending, as it had been disastrous and unpromising in its beginning.

Landing at the Tower, I hurried to the house in which I had settled my young wife, impatient to clasp her in my arms again. But alas, she whom I had left so young and beautiful, and full of life, was dead and lying in her grave, and by her side the little son whom I was never permitted to see.

In my sore affliction I received many tokens of kindness and sympathy from my wife's parents, and especially from her uncle Mr. Axe; and prostrated by the blow, I remained at home for some weeks, until out of very weariness of sorrow I roused myself from the state into which I had fallen, and determined to return to my profession again.

CHAPTER IV.

MY late wife's uncle having renewed his offer to assist me to enter the service of the Honourable East India Company, I now gladly accepted it. When I first went to sea it was in an employ so inferior, and a position so humiliating, that nothing but the custom of the times, and my resolute determination to become a sailor, reconciled me to it. But in the Company's service everything was very different. No finer fleet sailed the seas than that which was directed from Leadenhall Street. The ships were always saluted on their arrival in port in India, and their captains ranked as Members of Council, and were complimented with thirteen guns when they landed, the guard turning out to them as to a general officer on their entering or leaving the Fort. There was, in short, a distinction conferred by belonging to such a service second only to that enjoyed by the officers of the Royal Navy. The Company's ships were each commanded by a captain, and from four to eight officers, who all wore uniforms, and under whom the duties on board were carried on with the same strictness as on a man-of-war.

Owing to the rules of the service I was unable to ship in a higher capacity than that of fifth mate, this being my first voyage to India. But through Mr. Axe's interest I obtained a private permission to leave the vessel at Bombay, if I desired to do so. The ship I sailed in was called the *Barwell*, and was commanded by Captain John Welladvice, a good seaman and a kind gentleman of whom I have always retained the most friendly recollection. There were seven officers on board, and they were one and all gentlemen by education and family. The second mate was a Mr. Kent, who afterwards became my brother-in-law.

We sailed from Portsmouth in January, 1792, but the wind shifting, were obliged to put into Falmouth, where we were detained, weather-bound, for a week. Here, one day, two of our seamen ran away in the jolly-boat while we were at dinner. I was immediately despatched in pursuit by the chief officer, who said he would follow me. A large sailing barge being alongside, which we employed to bring off our water and provisions, I jumped into her, and gave chase. There were a number of vessels in the harbour, which kept hiding the jolly-boat from our view, and the two men having got a long start reached the shore some time in advance of me. The place where they landed was exceedingly shallow, and my barge drawing a good deal of water grounded, and I got wet up to my waist in landing, and in this condition began to run after the deserters. They having dry legs got clear away, and after a long search I gave them up. But when I was returning to my boat I descried a number of people in a field, and going to see what they were about, found one of the men I was in search of, hiding in a ditch with about a foot of water in it. He had a stout stick in his hand, which he was flourishing about, and swore if any man attempted to take him, he would knock him down. Disregarding his threat, I jumped into the ditch and made at him, and he immediately levelled me to the ground with a blow on my head. Fortunately at this moment the chief officer came up to my assistance. He was a very stout man, but powerful, and together we seized the sailor and began to drag him towards the boat, amidst the yells and hoots of the populace, who were all against us, fearing their own husbands being pressed if they acted in any other way. We had desperate work to get to the beach, and having arrived there, a lieutenant with some sailors intercepted us, and took us on board Admiral Waldegrave's flagship, which was at anchor in the harbour. Here the runaway was entertained for his Majesty's service, and so after all we lost our man. The other sailor escaped clear away. He was a clever young fellow, of good family, and had been at Mr. Lalterel's boarding school with me, but by his vicious habits had reduced himself to the necessity of shipping as a common sailor.

Three days after this, the wind changing round, we set sail again, and had a fine weather passage all the way out to India. But despite the kindness of Captain Welladvice to me personally, I found the position I was placed in irksome, after having been accustomed to one of much greater power and responsibility, and I soon made up my mind to avail myself of my private permission when the voyage came to an end, and seek employment more congenial to my spirit.

When, therefore, in June, 1792, we reached Bombay, I made inquiries, and was told that the country service in a merchant ship was amongst the best in the world. I therefore went to Captain Welladvice and requested his permission to quit the *Barwell*. On hearing this, he seemed much surprised, and endeavoured to persuade me to remain, saying very handsomely that he had noticed my merit, and was certain I should rise to a command at no distant date, by which my fortune would be secured at an early period of my life. But although this was very flattering to my self-esteem, I nevertheless declined the advice, and we consequently parted company, though remaining very good friends.

I had brought out with me a letter of introduction to a gentleman at Bombay named Wales, who was a portrait-painter, and a man of considerable influence in his way, for he knew every one and his services were in constant request. He very kindly interested himself on my behalf, and procured me the appointment of second officer on board the *Hormuzeer*, a country ship commanded by Captain Meeks, which was then loading a cargo of cotton and opium for China.

It was in this vessel that I obtained my first insight into the method of delivering cargo to the inhabitants of the Flowery Land. The people of Canton are more shrewd than their unintelligent faces would lead a stranger to suspect. On our arrival at that port, the chief mate being ill, his duty passed to me. It was the custom in those days to weigh off to a standing beam, a most laborious and slow operation, not to mention the scorching heat of the sun. In delivering the cargo, English weights were first used, and afterwards turned into Chinese *peculs* and *catties*. There being a pound draft allowed on each weighment in India, in addition to the turn of the scale, I was expected to show a good surplus on invoice weights. Luckily I had the gunner of the ship to assist me, a man who had been many years in the trade. It was proposed by the mandarins that we should weigh off in scales brought by them from Canton for the purpose, but when Henderson (the gunner) saw these, he at once advised me to reject them, pointing out that the beam was slightly longer on one side than the other, whereby the natives hoped to gain an advantage : and that there were certain extra holes, or notches, on each end of the beam, to one or other of which the scales could be moved by a pressure of the fingers, when again we should suffer. I therefore erected our own scales and began to deliver the cargo. But when it came to the point, I was well nigh driven out of my wits by the haggling and jabbering of the mandarins, who, discovering how exact I was determined to be, insisted upon the scales being kept on balance for half a minute or more, and doing everything in their power to exasperate me. Had the work continued in the way it began, it would have taken a year to weigh out the cargo. But in this predicament Henderson again came to my aid.

" Sir," said he, whispering behind his hand, " these here pig-tails will argufy longer than you on an empty stomach. Just broach a bottle of rum, and settle them down to that and a mess of sweetmeats, for that is the custom in these waters, and can't be done otherwise."

I was only too glad to profit by this advice, and invited the mandarins to refresh themselves. Upon which, they at once went down to the cuddy, and the result was that I delivered my cargo within a week, and was greatly complimented by Captain Meeks on the surplus over invoice weights that I was able to show.

From Canton we sailed back to the Nicobars, a group of islands in the Bay of Bengal, very low and level, and looking in the distance like groves of cocoanut trees rising from the sea-line. The people were inoffensive, and lived in houses raised upon wooden posts about ten feet from the ground, and shaped like large thatched beehives. The cocoanuts here were reckoned the finest in the world, and we bartered for a cargo, giving in exchange coloured cloth, hatchets, and hangers, the latter being in great demand for the purpose of cutting down the cocoanuts. In these islands money was quite unknown, and coins only valued for the purpose of ornament. The Nicobars are a very Garden of Eden for fruits, and the pigs reared there are exceedingly fine and sumptuous, being fattened on the cocoanuts, which impart to their flesh a truly delicate flavour.

Having filled our ship we sailed to Rangoon, where the cargo was disposed of advantageously. Here there was a fine vessel of nearly one thousand tons burden on the stocks, which was to be commanded by a Captain Newton, who was part owner of her with a Parsee named Dorabjee Byramjee. Captain Newton was a great friend of Captain Meeks, who introduced me to him, and as he was constantly on board the *Hormuzeer*, I soon came to know him very well, and we grew to be excellent friends. This turned out to my advantage, for it resulted in his offering me the situation of chief mate on board his new ship, and persuading Captain Meeks to allow me to leave the *Hormuzeer*.

I took up my new appointment at once, the duties of which were very arduous, as the ship was still on the stocks, and, excepting the builder's business to launch her on the water, wanting all equipment, and without any other officer engaged. It fell to my lot, single-handed, to superintend the making of all the ship's sails, to mast and rig her, to keep an account of her stores, and in addition to overlook the work of a hundred native carpenters, who required more watching than can be readily believed. I had also to account for a large cargo of timber that was being loaded. For six weeks I had scarce a moment's rest, and I believe no man could have made greater exertion, or undergone more fatigue, than I did: yet I never grudged the labour, for it was a delight to me to see the beautiful vessel gradually approaching completion under my hands, and I felt each day an increasing pride in her. She was christened the *Lotus*, and was a spendid full-rigged ship, with a most graceful appearance. No expense was spared to fit her out in a superior style, and when at length she was ready to go to sea, I considered myself fully rewarded for all my exertions, by the universal praise she received from those who visited her, and by the appreciation of my owners.

In January, 1793, we sailed for Madras, with a cargo of teak. Proud as I was of my ship when she lay at anchor in harbour, I was soon still more proud of her at sea. The north-east monsoon had broken heavily, and we experienced a very bad gale, but no vessel could have weathered it better than did ours. We had a dry deck from port to port, overtaking and passing every ship bound on the same course as ourselves, many of them labouring very badly, whilst we were running free. No ship could have behaved better than the *Lotus*, and her splendid sailing qualities made me rejoice in the hard weather that proved her superiority over every other craft in sight.

Conceive, then, my mortification when, about a week after our arrival at Madras, Captain Newton informed me that he had sold the vessel! I do not ever remember to have experienced such disappointment as when I heard of this transaction. I had put all my best work and energies into the ship, never sparing myself day or night. I had rigged her from truck to deck, and fitted her from stem to stern, and knew every yard, and mast, and rope, and plank in her by heart. She was a beautiful craft, and I had taken an exceeding great pride in keeping her clean and neat and taut and trim, so that she might easily have passed for a sloop of war. And now I had to give her up! I believe I would at that time have consented to serve in her a twelvemonth without pay, rather than make her over to a stranger. But I had no choice in the matter, and with a heavy heart was obliged to carry out the order for her delivery to her new owner, a most respectable old gentleman of Madras, who had formerly been the captain of an East Indiaman.

As part payment for the *Lotus*, Captain Newton received an old American-built brig called the *Pesouton*, of 450 tons burden. She was a rotten craft, and in such bad and crazy condition, that we were delayed a month patching her up to cross the Bay back to Rangoon. But now came a compensation to me for my recent disappointment. Another ship offering very cheap, owing to the death of her owner, Captain Newton purchased her, and, to my great surprise and satisfaction, gave me the command of the *Pesouton*, he taking charge of the other vessel.

The appointment was only an acting one for me, but it made me a master when I had only just completed my twenty-first year; whereas I saw around me scores of older and more experienced men who had to content themselves with mates' berths, and many of whom professed no hopes of rising higher. Captain Newton and I sailed back in company to Rangoon, where he gave his ship over to Dorabjee Byramjee, and, as previously agreed upon, took charge of the *Pesouton* from me, but only for the purpose of going up to Calcutta, where he was engaged to be married to a lady who lived there, after which I was to obtain the command again.

Having loaded up with another cargo of timber, we sailed in the early part of August, 1793, the south-west monsoon being then at its height. From the very start we made a hard passage, and when half-way up the Bay of Bengal, encountered a series of gales. The *Pesouton* was a crank craft, and too deeply laden, and she laboured heavily, and finally sprung a leak and filled on the afternoon of the fourth day after the commencement of the gale. The well being sounded, and our position proved to be critical, Captain Newton ordered me to cut away the masts, to prevent the ship rolling over, which she seemed like to do at any moment. This afforded temporary relief; but the storm increasing, and the *Pesouton* being now like a log upon the water, our situation became more and more perilous, and it was only the fact of our being loaded with timber that kept us from sinking. The cuddy and fo'castle were three feet deep in water, so that it was impossible to remain below, and all hands and passengers—sixty-five in number—were forced on deck and huddled together under the lee of the galley.

In this condition we drifted for three days at the

mercy of the winds and waves, no sun being visible during that time, and it being impossible for us to ascertain our position. On the third day the gale increasing to a hurricane, our rudder was carried away, and we expected every moment that the ship would fall side on to the heavy sea that was running, and turn bottom upwards, since we could only keep her head up by a single sail set from the stump of the foremast, which appeared likely to carry away at any moment. And this actually occurred towards sunset, whereupon, as a last hope, I was ordered to make arrangements for getting out the long-boat which was stowed keel upwards in the centre of the ship, and the only one left to us, the captain's gig and the jolly-boat having been washed away from their davits. It was a forlorn hope, for it seemed impossible to launch a boat in such a sea as was running, or, if launched, to keep her afloat.

Calling the gunner to help me, I made my way down into the gun-room, under the greatest fear of the ship turning over, to obtain some provisions for the boat. But scarce had we reached the bottom of the companion-way, than the crisis we had been dreading occurred. Although in the dark below, I was immediately able to realize what had taken place by the altered motion of the vessel, and calling to the gunner, we hastily scrambled back to the cuddy door, and had just got through it when we saw a huge mountain of water cresting over us, and in another moment were washed overboard like straws in a mill-race. Fortunately the main-brace had fallen athwart the cuddy door, and we both managed to catch hold of it and cling on. When I came to the surface, after an immersion for some seconds, I let go the rope and struck out with might and main for the ship, and she, providentially heeling towards me as she lifted to another sea, enabled me to catch hold of a rope that was hanging over her side, and so haul myself on board to a position from whence I was able to assist the gunner back also.

The sea was now raging with the greatest fury, and breaking over the *Pesouton* in torrents of foam, and with a force that made it almost impossible to hold on to our precarious positions. The ship was a dead wreck, floating upon her larboard side, whilst we clung upon the outside of her starboard bulwarks, catching hold of the ropes and stays that encumbered them, and anticipating every moment that she would shift keel upwards. It was nearly night, and the light was fast fading from the dull grey sky, whilst all around stretched the desolate expanse of angry sea. Black vapoury clouds floated low down in the heavens, their dark shapes moving sullenly along. At frequent intervals there came heavy tropical squalls of rain, with a suddenness that was startling, and accompanied by thunder and lightning, that seemed to add a supernatural terror to the scene, as the vivid flashes lit up the firmament and revealed to us the desperation of our situation. To add to our misery it was intensely cold for the season of the year, and as we lay on our bellies, clinging for dear life to the wet slippery side of the ship, the waves constantly broke or washed over us in torrents of blinding foam.

As I summed up our chances of deliverance, it seemed to me that life was to be measured by minutes. No one spoke, every soul being struck dumb by the paralyzing fear of imminent death. From time to time some breaker larger than the rest would wash away one or two, whose despairing cries for help rose above the howling of the storm with a weird supernatural shrillness, till they were engulfed and lost for ever in the roaring sea. The gunner, a most respectable, good man, who had left behind him at Rangoon a wife and seven children, was next to me, and presently he moved and coiled his leg round mine. And although this seemed to somewhat weaken my hold, yet there was such a sense of companionship in his mere touch that I suffered it to remain. And so we all of us lay huddled like a cluster of limpets on a rock, the wreck rising and falling with a dull, lifeless motion, and great surfs breaking over her with sharp concussions, and sending the foam and spray flying high into the air.

After about an hour the third mate, Mr Richardson, a fine handsome young man, began to discover signs of failing, being weak and debilitated from a recent illness; and he cried out to me and to the second officer, entreating us to show the crew an example by jumping off and putting an end to our misery. I can recall the ghastly look in his face as I saw it lighted up by the flashes of lightning, and with the agony and sweat of death upon it, when he called hoarsely out :

" This is worse than death, Mr. Eastwick. This is worse than actual death! There is no hope left; and if there were, I would not prolong another hour of this horror to secure an existence of years. Show us how to die, sir. It is but a plunge, and it will be all over."

I considered what he said, and then replied, " Richardson, our duty teaches us to do all in our power to preserve life. It is truer courage to endure our present danger than to succumb to it voluntarily. I for one will not seek to cut short my own life, even for a moment. We are in God's hands. Stand firm, man, to the end, if the end is coming. I beseech you keep heart. We may yet be saved by the mercy of Providence."

As I spoke, I observed an enormous crested wave approaching. It seemed the retort of Fate to my speech. I called to all around me, and especially to my friend Captain Newton, to hold on fast, and then I shut my eyes, tightened my grasp, and bending my head, cowered close down.

As the wave broke I felt I was undone. The rope I had hold of was dragged through my grasp, and in another moment I was carried over the bulwarks, and, by the suction of the water, under the shrouds, which were still standing, and into a position from which I could not extricate myself. I felt the bubbling water swirling round me, filling my eyes and ears and nostrils and mouth with a cruel salt suffocating sensation, whilst instantaneously my memory seemed quickened, and there flashed in review before my mind a thousand scenes and incidents of my past life.

Then I knew by a sort of instinct that I was a drowning man.

In a few seconds I should have been gone, for I had no strength left to extricate myself from the trap in which I was caught. But at this moment the ship gave a lurch, which partially righted her, and then rolled back, so that I· floated clear, and the next thing I remember was being pulled on to a couple of spars, upon which were two sailors, one of whom caught me by the arm as I drifted past.

When I recovered myself and had got the salt-water out of my smarting eyes, I found we were still quite close to the *Pesouton*—not more, in fact, than half a cable's length, and her great black hull loomed up against the sky. I hailed her and asked if there were any left alive. Captain Newton heard me, and called back that he and ten companions were still there, and besought me to try and rejoin them, as in his opinion it was the safest place. I perceived the spars on which I was floating gave but a poor prospect of escape, and I therefore urged the men who had succoured me to try and regain the wreck. But this they declined, saying it was impossible for a human being to make any way in such a sea. I determined, however, to attempt the task, and throwing off a flannel jacket and a pair of drawers which I was wearing, and which was the only covering I had, I commended myself to God, and plunging into the sea struck out for the *Pesouton*, and getting into the comparatively smoother water under her lee, at length managed to reach her.

Here I found that poor Richardson, and Russell the second officer, and a Portuguese woman who had been a cabin passenger on board, together with seven of the crew and about thirty deck passengers, had all been carried away by the huge wave, and were gone for ever. With great difficulty I gained a place next to Captain Newton, and by his side I clung for the next four hours, during which the hurricane raged as furiously as ever.

At last poor Captain Newton's strength began to fail. " Help me, dear Eastwick," he cried, two or three times, in a weak voice; "lash me on. I cannot hold any longer ! "

I was benumbed with cold and fearful of leaving go my own grip, lest my fingers, in which there was scarce any feeling left, should refuse their work again. Still I could not in humanity resist the appeal, and I moved towards him with the intention of trying to pass a rope round his body, when a wave larger than the rest broke over us, and as it resurged I saw Captain Newton's hands go up with a sort of despairing gesture to the heavens above, and a moment after he was swept over the side, and sank immediately.

It was all so sudden that I could hardly believe it at first. I craned my neck forward, hoping to catch a sight of him, to throw him a rope, or even to jump in to his rescue, but he never came to the surface again. And then, all of a moment, I realized that he was gone, and that I had lost my best and dearest friend; and in the revulsion of feeling that overcame me, naked though I was and cold and hopeless in the middle of that stormy sea, a great gush of tears came irresistibly into my eyes, and, forgetful of the danger of my own condition, I found myself weeping like a child for the good man that was taken away.

About an hour afterwards another wave carried overboard the ship's steward, who was a Parsee and like a fish in the water. His greed of lucre had well-nigh done for him, for he had tied round his neck a bundle of silver plate, in a towel, worth a few paltry pounds at the outside, yet, in his anxiety to save it, he had not hesitated to so load himself. He chanced to come to the surface just in front of me, and the day having now broken, I was able to see him plainly. First he endeavoured to tread water, with the view, I imagine, of gauging his position and swimming back to the ship; but the weight of the silver carried him down. Then he tried to swim towards the wreck, but he could not keep his face above water; so he began to fumble at the knot behind his neck to untie it, and his head kept slowly sinking lower and lower, until his feet were kicking into the air. Then with a great effort he righted himself, his hands now wildly clutching and tugging at the knot. But to no purpose; the cloth was wet and would not yield. It had become a desperate fight with death. I caught a glimpse of his face, and it was so trans-figured with fright and agony that I hardly recognized him. With convulsive efforts he kept coming to the surface for a second, or perhaps two, during which he breathed in great gasps of air, and then the weight of the silver dragged him below again. At last he deliberately dived down head foremost, and I believed him gone for ever, when in about half a minute he came up again, having by this expedient slipped the noose over his head. Being now relieved from the weight, he struck out swimming, and regained the wreck, where he immediately began blubbering at his ill-fortune in having lost his silver plate, as though it had been wantonly sacrificed at the value of his life!

About this time the stern part of the ship, towards which end we survivors had collected, began to sink lower in the water, and we were forced to shift our position and make for the fore part. This was a most dangerous undertaking, the footing being insecure and exceedingly slippery, not to mention the rolling and lurching of the hulk. However, we all succeeded in crawling forward, and reaching a position of greater safety, and shortly after this, about the hour of sunrise, the gale considerably abated. In a little while the thick atmosphere began to clear away, and two hours afterwards the sun broke out through the clouds, and almost at the same moment the gunner cried out, "*Land! land!*" and, to our unspeakable joy, the blessed sight of it appeared to eastward.

There was a heavy swell setting in shore, and the wind was still strong, so that we were carried along in the direction of the land, and about midday grounded on a bank with such force that the ship's stern frame gave way, and this formed an excellent raft, on which, of the eleven remaining alive, seven sprang, leaving myself and three others on the wreck. After some hesitation I determined to follow, as I saw they were floating well and drifting straight for the beach.

Pointing this out to my companions, I urged them to join me in the attempt; but they feared the risk, and I had to leave them, bitterly lamenting their fate, yet fearful to put it to the touch with one bold effort.

I had an arduous struggle to reach the raft, owing to the distance to which it had drifted, but the tide was flowing, and this together with the heavy swell carrying me on, assisted me more than my own labours, which were chiefly directed to keeping myself afloat, guiding my course, and avoiding the breaking of the waves. Having reached the raft, I was soon assisted on to it, and we floated rapidly along towards the shore, which was about three miles distant, helped by both wind and tide.

But all the time there was a very heavy surf running, which continually broke over the raft. Perceiving that the two gun-ports, which were very large, were open, and seemed from the position they were in to form a sort of breakwater, I got behind one, securing myself by a small rope that was attached to it. The poor gunner crawled near to me, but was so exhausted by this time that he said that if he was again washed off he must certainly perish. And true enough, before we had gone a third of the distance this occurred, and he was carried away astern, and I saw him no more. He was an excellent, steady, good man, and his last thoughts were for his wife and family. Almost directly after this, the hinges of the port, behind which I was sheltered broke, and knocked me into the sea, but I regained the raft, and getting to the other port, I secured my position there, and this remained fast until we neared the land.

And now the last difficulty of all presented itself, which was the landing through the surf. As we came close to the beach we perceived that the waves were dashing in great breakers some considerable way from the shore, and that it was probable that our raft would take ground some distance before we reached shallow water, and that we should have to trust to our own efforts to gain dry land.

We had not much time to consider, for almost

immediately the stern frame grounded, and a wave catching her as she did so, she turned a complete somersault, pitching us all off into the boiling surf in front. It was now a case of each man for himself, and grim death against us all. I was the first to reach shore, being carried along by the same wave that toppled us over, and which stranded me on the beach. I immediately rose to my feet and did all in my power to assist those less fortunate than myself, and in this way was able to help the other six, who were upon the raft, to land in safety.

Our sentiments of thankfulness to Providence when we realized that we were safe, were such as only those who have escaped similar perils can understand. After the succeeding horrors of a week of tempest, of the final hurricane, of the buffetings of the waves, of the cold and hunger and thirst, of the long, dark, terrible night, and of the dread scenes of horror we had passed through, when so many of our fellow-beings were snatched away from our sides by the remorseless hand of death and consigned to a watery grave in front of our eyes—after all these tribulations, the sodden, desolate shore, and the black jungle fringing it, seemed an actual Paradise to us shipwrecked mariners, and we gave no immediate thought to our destitute condition in the all-satisfying joy of feeling mother earth beneath our tread again.

Of the sixty-five persons who formed the crew and passengers of the *Pesouton*, there were but seven of us who reached land. The spot where we came ashore was near Poreen Point, which is situated on the Arracan coast, north of Cape Negrais, and not far from the mouth of the Bassein river. Of these seven, one man and one boy were so exhausted that they threw themselves down above high-water mark, and lay as if dead, and we were quite unable to rouse them from their condition. My other four companions were hardly better situated, and we were all of us perfectly naked, and almost famished for want of food and water, which we had not tasted for three days.

Hunger impelled me to immediately go in search of assistance, and the four men said that they would come after me when they could, but that at present they felt unable to proceed, so I set forward by myself. I could only follow the shore line, and so I struck southwards. On my right was the sea, filled with ground sharks, and on my left the jungle, that ran parallel with it, and was the certain resort of wild beasts and venomous snakes. The forest was, moreover, too dense to attempt to enter, the thorny nature of the undergrowth making it impossible for a naked man to penetrate even a few paces. There was nothing left but to plod along over the heavy sand. Before starting I arranged with the others to return with help if I could find any, and that they were to remain at the place where we had landed, or to follow in my footsteps.

The clouds had by this time cleared away, and the sun was shining fiercely, which I found extremely trying. In order to protect myself from its rays I broke off the leafy branch of a tree to serve me for an umbrella, and especially to shelter my head. I soon began to be consumed with a great thirst, whilst my feet became sore, and blistered from the burning sand. Having thus, with pain and difficulty, proceeded a couple of miles without discovering any signs of a habitation, I suddenly observed a great rhinoceros in the way I must pass, which so took me aback that I threw myself down in some long grass to hide, and there, overcome with fatigue and exhaustion, immediately fell into a deep sleep.

After about an hour, the four of my crew whom I had left behind, not liking my parting with them, after first vainly endeavouring to arouse the man and the boy from their slumber, came along, and as they passed by happened to observe one of my feet sticking out of the grass, from which they conjectured I had been killed by some wild animal and dragged there to be devoured. Whereupon, they set up a great shouting to scare the supposed wild beast away, which roused me from my sleep, and my mind being full of the rhinoceros I had spied, I at once concluded that the alarming sounds issued from that monstrous beast. Accordingly I, in my turn, set up a loud clamour, and so for some seconds we roared back at each other like bulls of Bashan, until we discovered each our error, and so concluded this singular performance with a hearty laugh, which I think did us all much good, and formed an excellent jest for the rest of the day.

We now continued our journey together until, after traversing about four or five miles, we were stopped by a river of some forty yards in breadth. In its waters we gluttonously quenched our thirst, the same having been much augmented by the intense heat of the sun, the rays of which, striking upon my naked skin, were so powerful, that before long the whole of my back became one large blister.

It now being near evening, and the amount of water we had drunk making us disinclined for exertion, our care was how to pass the night, and we therefore set to work to build a bower of boughs, and also tore up the high grass to make beds to lie upon, and to cover us as some protection against the inclemency of the weather. For towards sunset heavy black clouds again began to gather to seaward, and I knew that during this season of the year the spells of fine weather were never of long duration, and that we might shortly expect a return of the rain. After an hour's work we succeeded in making a sort of shelter capable of containing us all.

Into this we crept and lay down, and for supper chewed roots of grass, which tasted exceedingly salt and bitter, but yet beguiled us into all sorts of pleasant imaginations that we were eating food. At length we fell asleep, but early in the night were awakened by the bursting of a violent storm of wind and rain, which in a moment blew away our bower, and left us exposed to its full fury.

It was now too dark, and the force of the wind too great, for us to make any effectual effort to repair the disaster. The rain was so heavy that in a short space of time it lay in a sheet some three inches deep upon the surface of the ground, whilst the gale blew in great gusts that seemed to cut us to the bone.

The misery of that night was dreadful; yet not so bad, we all felt, as that of the previous one, when we were clinging to the wreck of the *Pesouton* and momentarily expecting our death. For now, at least, we were safe on land, and free from the constant fear of destruction; and in this reflection we sought and obtained a considerable comfort, and were enabled to exercise patience and await with hope the coming day.

My own distress was, however, very grievously increased by the breaking of the blister on my back, through an accidental jostle in the dark from the man next me, by which the whole surface of the skin from the neck to the loins was excoriated. The pain I suffered was so intense, that I feared I should be seized with a fever, and it was a relief to me when dawn broke to start forward on our march again, since this distraction gave me something to do, and prevented my mind lingering on the cause of my suffering.

The first thing that presented itself was the river, and although likely to be infested with alligators, there was no help for it but to swim across, or starve, or be devoured by wild beasts.

We therefore waded in, and assisting one another swam to the other side, which we reached in safety. We then had to cross two other rivers, but both smaller, and after passing the last of them, and proceeding a little way, to our surprise and delight we came across two other survivors of the *Pesouton's* crew. These proved to be the same men who had helped me on to the spars, and whom I left to rejoin Captain Newton when he called to me to return to the wreck after the great wave. They had floated on the spars until they were providentially cast ashore. We came upon them as they were standing beside the body of a goat, which had been stranded and just discovered by them. I recognized the animal at once, for it belonged to me, I having purchased it in Bombay for my voyage to China in the *Hormuzeer*, and becoming fond of it, the beast being an excellent milker, had kept it ever since. Poor Nanny was bloated out to an immense size, and was as full of wind as a drum, but neither her repulsive appearance, nor the absence of instruments, deterred us starving men from attacking her, and we immediately set to work endeavouring to tear her in pieces with our nails and teeth. But she was too tough for such poor tools to make any impression on her hide, and so stinking that she soon nauseated us, and forced us to leave her in loathing.

Resuming our journey southwards, we next came across a chest that had been stranded on the beach, and recognized it as belonging to the

Portuguese woman passenger we carried on board. With some difficulty we burst it open, and discovered in it six red petticoats, very fine, and as many of us putting on one each, we drew the ends between our legs, and fixing them in the back of our waists, in the manner of the Gentoos, made tolerable trousers. There were likewise several Madras palempores, of beautiful patterns, that served to cover our bodies, and some red bandana handkerchiefs, which we bound round our heads; and thus equipped, in the true Oriental fashion, we started again on our march.

Our next discovery was a more fortunate one, being a large pumpkin, floating on the sea close to land. We soon fetched it ashore, and, dividing it equally, ate it with a devouring appetite; having scarcely finished which, and proceeded a short way, than, to our joy, we descried in the distance a black man, carrying four or five cakes of beeswax on his head, and with his back turned towards us. Fearing to frighten him, and that he might seek to escape by flight, our party lay down behind a hillock of sand, whilst I crept softly forward, and then, with a dash, rushed in and caught the man by his arm. He was greatly amazed and disturbed, and threw down his load with the evident intention of making off; but I stroked and patted him on the face, and he, perceiving my intentions were peaceful, and the plight I was in, became re-assured, and accosted me with the words, "*Connah Cow?*" which was a joyful sound, although the only Hindustani that I knew, and meaning, "*Do you want to eat?*" I replied by signs that I was famished, and then pointing to where my companions lay hidden I brought him to the place, and he very willingly became our guide, proving a most good-natured savage.

He conducted us back half a mile, and then struck through a narrow path in the jungle, that we had not observed, into an inland country, which was woody and fertile, until we came to a village, where a number of houses were erected upon piles of timber twenty to thirty feet high, with ladders to go up. This was to protect the inhabitants from the numerous wild beasts, and especially tigers, that infested the country, and which it was very fortunate for us we had escaped encountering during our journey from the wreck.

Before we got to the village two of our party dropped from the effects of fatigue, whilst the other five were only just able to stagger on. At the outskirts of the place we were met by several people, who were working in the fields, and who ran forward to see us, evincing the greatest wonder and surprise at our appearance—as they might well do, since we were the first Europeans that had ever been seen in that country. We were by them conducted to the house of their chief man, after which they dispersed to bring what rice they had ready cooked from their various houses. The chief asked several questions of our guide, and then invited us within. He was a fine-looking old man, with a grey beard, and perceiving that I was the leader of our company, took me to his own house, whilst my men were carried to an adjoining one. In a few minutes a steaming platter of rice and fish was placed before me, which was a delicious sight, and I immediately attacked it without further ceremony than making a *salaam* to my host.

Presently the two men who had fallen down were carried in, and at the sight and smell of the food, recovered sufficiently to partake of it. After this we explained that two more of our party (the man and the boy) had been left behind on the beach where we landed, and four men were at once despatched with food for them, and to bring them in, which they did two days afterwards. The boy happened to understand a little of the language of the country, and I arranged, through his interpretation, for our departure on the third day for Bassein, which place was about two hundred miles' distant from the village.

We started in a large canoe, after thanking the chief man for his hospitality, and promising to send him a present of money later on—which we did by his crew on their return, together with a musket, a supply of flints, and some powder and shot, which he represented to us were the things he most desired. We sailed or paddled and rowed the whole way, our men working by day, and the natives by night. I cannot describe the torture I suffered from my back, which now began to fester,

and over which I could scarcely bear the passing
of oil with a feather. We were four days on our
passage, and when we reached Bassein were rejoiced to find not only an English resident there,
Mr. Blackwall and his wife, but also a ship just
about to sail for Rangoon. The kindness of the
former gentleman knew no bounds. He took us
all into his house, killed the fatted calf for us,
supplied us with clothes and advanced us money,
whilst his good wife, with her own hands, dressed
my back and attended to my misfortunes.

I may here mention that, a few days previous
to our arrival, the captain of the ship which was
anchored there, and his mate and two men, went
out shooting in the neighbouring jungles, and
coming across a young elephant calf, very foolishly
fired at it, and severely wounded it. Whereupon
it set up a shrill trumpeting that at once brought
its mother and some others of the herd to see the
cause, and the captain and his companions, to
avoid the danger, were obliged instantly to climb
a tree. Luckily they chanced to hit upon a large
and strong one, for the elephants scenting them,
and being enraged by the injury done to the young
one, immediately began to try to tear the tree up;
but after a very long time they were obliged to
desist, still continued about the spot for the whole
day, and obliged the rash sportsmen to remain
where they were for twenty-four hours.

So soon as the ship was ready to sail, we all
went on board, after saying good-bye to Mr. and

Mrs. Blackwall, and a week afterwards we reached Rangoon.

Such is the story of my first shipwreck. I have been in many dangers by land and sea since then, but the horrors I endured on the waterlogged hulk of the *Pesouton*, and the hunger and thirst and pain I suffered after reaching land and until I got to Bassein, have always remained in my mind as the most dreadful circumstances I have ever been placed in. That nine of us escaped the dangers and difficulties I have described, has always seemed to me a striking proof of the mercy and power of that Omnipotent Hand that can lift the seemingly doomed sailor out of the tempestuous ocean and bear him safely to dry land.

CHAPTER V.

WHEN I arrived at Rangoon, my back was in
such a state that I had to take to my bed at
once, and was confined to it for a fortnight, and
it was some weeks before the hurt was completely
healed, during which time I could only move about
in a doubled-up state, and with the assistance of

two sticks. Almost directly after my arrival, the Parsee, Dorabjee Byramjee, came to see me. He was poor Captain Newton's partner in the *Pesouton*, and at this time one of the wealthiest Parsee merchants in the place. His concern and sorrow at hearing the shocking details of Captain Newton's death were very sincere, and evinced a true kindness of disposition and sentiment that inclined me towards him; as did also the lively interest he displayed in my own adventures, and his congratulations at my escape. Nor did he confine himself to mere empty words, but sent me the most beautiful presents of fruit, flowers, vegetables, sweetmeats and fish every day, with many *salaams* and compliments. This giving of presents is a common act of courtesy in the East, where it is considered rude and ill-bred to appear without offerings in the hand, and the custom is practised by all from the highest to the lowest, yet not without the hope of receiving back in return a gift or favour of greater, or at least of equal, advantage to the one offered.

What little property I had, to the value of perhaps three thousand rupees, was all lost in the *Pesouton*, and when I arrived at Rangoon I was the poorest man in the place, for I had absolutely nothing at all that I could call my own. I was therefore rather surprised at first at Dorabjee's attentions, for he came to see me every day, clothed in the most spotless white garments, and sat by me for an hour at least, asking after my health and desiring to know if there was anything I wanted. At last he disclosed the reason of this civility, for when I began to regain my strength, he asked me to proceed to Madras for the purpose of recovering the insurance money due on the *Pesouton*, whereby he would be saved much delay and expense. He might have commanded my services without all the trouble he took to discount them, for I very willingly agreed to what he wished, the work being especially suited to my state of health, as not requiring that exercise of physical exertion which would have been requisite in the following of my ordinary profession.

I took passage in the *Anna*, Captain Gilmore, and having reached Madras, carried the matter through so successfully and expeditiously that I was back again in Rangoon within six weeks, and so pleased Dorabjee, that of his own accord he gave me the command of a beautiful ship of 1,100 tons burden, that he had just purchased, and which was called the *Rebecca*.

This was a brilliant appointment for a young man of twenty-one, and equal to at least £4,000 a year, for, in addition to pay of five hundred rupees *per mensem*, I received two and a half *per centum* commission on all freight, goods, and passengers consigned to my care, which was an exceedingly profitable arrangement, as all my voyages were short ones between Rangoon, Calcutta, Madras, and the Straits, carrying a constant succession of cargoes and many passengers. I continued in command of the *Rebecca* from the end of 1793 to the middle of 1795, when she was sold to a Portuguese, and the command of another vessel was offered to me.

But during these two years I had saved some money, and the experience I had gained in the service of others showed what immense profits were to be made by those who judiciously invested their means in shipping. I therefore declined Dorabjee's offer, and proceeding to Calcutta, purchased a fine ship called the *Endeavour*, and took over the command of her. With this vessel I continued running in the same trade, making several short voyages at very high rates, all of which yielded me exceedingly profitable returns.

There was of course a considerable risk to be run in this new undertaking, because since the declaration of war with France in 1793, and our hostilities with Holland, which began in 1795, the Bay of Bengal and the Eastern seas were rendered unsafe to merchant ships by reason of the great number of French and Dutch cruisers and privateers that infested them. Our own strength in these waters was very inadequate to protect our commerce, and in addition to this we suffered some naval disasters which neither redounded to the credit of our seamanship nor the gallantry of our navy. Of the French men-of-war opposed to us, the *La Forte*, *La Prudente*, and *Preneuse* created the greatest devastation, scouring the whole of the Bay of Bengal, and from

time to time putting in to the Isle of France to
refit. General Malartic, the Governor of that place,
was a most energetic, able man, who in addition
fitted out a large number of privateers to prey
on British shipping. These were all fast sailing
ships, well manned, well armed, and splendidly
commanded, and they very soon became a terror
to our trade, for they were all such fast sailers,
that if once sighted it was all up with heavy laden
merchant vessels. The two most notorious were
the *Confiance*, Captain Sourcouff, of 22 guns and
250 men, and the *General Malartic*, commanded
by Captain, or as he presently called himself,
Citizen, Dutert. She was armed with 14 guns
and carried 156 men, and was a brig, and a
beautiful vessel, fitted with long sweeps, by means
of which, even in calm weather, she could approach
her victims. In consequence of the presence of
these hostile vessels all freights ruled very high,
and had it not been for the equally high rates of
insurance which had to be paid, enormous fortunes
might have been made. There were some shipowners who ran the risk themselves, but this
brought ruin to so many, that I insured my own
ship as long as I could, and until the premiums
demanded became so heavy that I was unable to
afford to pay them. But of this I shall have more
to say later on.

During one of my visits to Calcutta, I happened
to meet Mr., now become Captain, Kent, the same
who was second officer of the *Barwell*, East

Indiaman, in which I came out to Bombay. He had left the Company's service, and purchased a ship called the *Eliza*, which he brought out to India in 1796 under Danish colours. Amongst the passengers he carried on board were two young ladies, the Misses King, sent out by Mr. Thomas Morris, who had married their elder sister, to join another sister, Mrs. Esther Bellasis, at Bombay. On the voyage out, Captain Kent had fallen desperately in love with Miss Elizabeth King, and was married to her by the Consul at Madeira. He and his wife and her younger sister were temporarily lodging at Calcutta when I met him by accident. He was very glad to see me, and, taking me to his house, introduced me to his ladies, and my fancy was at once attracted by the younger, whose name was Lucy. She was one of seven sisters, daughters of Mr. John King of Puttenham, near Guildford, in the county of Surrey, who were all famous for their beauty, as their portraits in oil colours do to this day testify. To a lovely face and figure, Miss King added a disposition most amiable, and a grace of manner that immediately commanded admiration. Her hand had often been sought in marriage, and especially by a gentleman in England who afterwards became a celebrated painter,* but she had

* There is a story connected with this gentleman which is worth relating. His name was Thompson, and he was a favourite pupil of the artist Opie. He fell in love with Miss Lucy King about the year 1795, when he was taking her portrait, and proposed marriage to her, but was refused. He thereupon declined to finish her portrait,

hitherto declined all offers of marriage. I enjoyed many opportunities of meeting her, and addressed myself with great earnestness to the task of paying my suit to her. The courtship was a brief one, as must all sailors' courtships be, but the more necessary in my case because of Captain Kent's intended early departure for Bombay, where he had promised to safely deliver his sister-in-law. I therefore declared my suit, and was accepted, and on December 17, 1796, I was married to one who for twenty-eight years was the most faithful wife, the most fond companion, the truest and the sweetest woman that ever made a man happy. The witnesses of our marriage were Sir J. Cox and Messrs. A. and F. Vansittart, both of the civil service in Calcutta.

Shortly after we were married, I obtained a freight for Bencoolen, and my young wife accompanied me. I had the large stern cabin of the ship fitted up most elegantly for her, and she

and took the canvas away with him, determined never to see her again. Twenty-five years afterwards, Miss King, then Mrs. Eastwick, was walking in London one day with her son William, when she passed Mr. Thompson, and at once recognized him. She immediately requested her son to run after him and stop him, as she desired to speak to him. Mr. Thompson retraced his steps, and when he discovered who it was that had sent for him his eyes filled with tears. After the first greeting, during which he was much agitated, he told Mrs. Eastwick that he still possessed the picture he had painted of her, and which he had finished from memory, and that it had never left his room. But he did not think he had any right to retain it now, and that if she and her son would accompany him he would give it to her. They went to his house, and in a recess, with a curtain drawn across it, was the picture. It is now in the possession of a member of the family.

took as much pride and delight in it as she could have done in any home ashore. Being favoured with fine weather, the passage down the Bay of Bengal was a veritable holiday voyage to me, cheered and enlivened by a companionship as delightful as it was novel.

I stayed some time at Bencoolen discharging my cargo, and was then taken up by Government to bring in pepper from the southern ports with which to load two ships bound for England, and I sailed for the small settlement of Old Croee, a place celebrated for those edible birds' nests so largely exported to China, and which were gathered from caves situated about four miles up the river that runs into the bay. Here we were able to obtain excellent turtles at a cost of about a dollar each, and a small species of deer, not larger than a rabbit, at about twopence each. Larger deer, the size of a sheep, were sold for half a dollar, and were excellent eating; whilst fish, cocoanuts, plantains, pineapples, water melons, jacks, pumpkins, yams, and a vast variety of vegetables could be obtained at the most reasonable rates. It was, in short, a very excellent place to be anchored near.

Our ship was berthed between a small island called Pisang and the mainland, and abreast of us was a small field of paddy, about an acre in extent. One morning, to our surprise, we found that the whole crop had been reaped and carried off during the night; and inquiring the cause of it, we learnt from the owner that it was the work of the baboons, which are common in these parts. A company had come down during the night and ravaged the crop. The way they did it was this: they pulled up the rice first, and tied it into bundles; then they formed a line, and with great quickness tossed these bundles from one to another until the whole was removed; and so stretching out in line again repeated the operation, till stage by stage all was carried off, and taken to their hiding-places in the adjoining jungles. Nothing could have been more sagacious or expert than their action in this theft. These baboons, or apes, are of the largest kind, very bold and savage, and stand as high as a tall boy. The natives were afraid of them, especially the women, for it was asserted they would carry off to captivity any female they came across.

Along this coast the Honourable Company had for its protection a Malay corps, officered by Malays, and whilst here I made the acquaintance of a very fine young man, a lieutenant in this force. He told me that once, late at night, when he was returning from inspecting an outpost, on nearing Croee, he had reason to suppose that a tiger was following him, and that it was dangerous for him to proceed. In consequence of this, he made all the disposition he could to meet the expected attack. He had a sword by his side and a creese in his belt—the Malay creese being a weapon like a sharp dagger, and the one they most trust to. Having scraped away the earth so as to give him a firm footing, he knelt down upon one knee, and kept a sharp lookout, for he knew that the beast was near. He soon perceived the tiger, by its glittering eyes, creeping towards him like a cat. As it came within distance, all in the dark, it was an awful moment; but the young Malay was not at all daunted. The brute made its spring, but its charge was received on the creese, which went through the breast of the animal, stabbing it to the heart, so that there and then it fell down dead. But in its dying struggle it clawed the brave young fellow very badly, and he lost a large piece off one of his arms, the wound of which he showed me. This was the second tiger he had killed. He did not seem to consider that he had done anything of special merit, but only that he had been fortunate to escape an ordinary danger to which any one was liable in that wild country.

Having taken in all the pepper ready for shipment at Old Croee, we started for another port, a little to the north of it. The service on this coast was most dangerous, for not only was it very badly surveyed and mapped in the chart, but there were French and Dutch cruisers constantly here, whom we might meet at any time. At this place, when two of my officers and half of my crew were ashore, a sudden gale of wind came on, and blew with such violence that it forced me to put to sea without them. It was very deep water, and having weighed the anchor from the ground, the ship's head off shore, I considered we should safely weather a reef of rocks that lay just outside the anchorage, and from which I apprehended danger. But as we headed out to clear them, the anchor, not having yet been hoisted on board (although we had way on owing to the violence of the squall), took a rock, and catching, began to bring the ship's head round into a position which must have ended in our destruction and all have perished. In this extremity I seized a hatchet, and in a moment cut the cable just in time to save us. It was a great mercy that we escaped, and I do not ever remember suffering so much anxiety as I did for about five minutes whilst we beat out with the gale in our teeth, a swift current setting landwards, and the reef within a cable's length of our lee side. Inch by inch we struggled past it, and at last gained sea room. No young woman could have exhibited greater fortitude than my wife showed on this occasion, who, being aware of the danger, kept her place on deck, yet never uttered a word or so much as asked if the peril was past, being content (as she told me afterwards) to gather her information from the varying expressions of my own face.

Having made the open sea, we were driven towards and through the Straits of Sunda by a succession of gales, and when they abated, and we were beginning to comfort ourselves that all danger was over, we were sighted by two Dutch brigs of war, who were guarding the straits, and immediately gave chase to us.

We had lost nearly all our sails when this occurred, and had not been able to bend on new ones, so that we were taken at a disadvantage. Directly I saw that the cruisers were in pursuit of us I spread all canvas I could, and stood to northwards, but I soon perceived that the enemy, with a complete rig of canvas, were gaining rapidly, and that without more sail we had no chance of escape. Had we been taken, Batavia would have been our destiny, and for my wife to have been landed at that pestilential place as a prisoner of war would have been a fearful thing.

In this extremity we began to hurriedly bend on new sails to replace those we had lost, our only hope of safety lying in the despatch with which we could accomplish the task. It was morning, and my wife had come on deck, and stood with my glass in her hand looking at the two brigs, whilst I had myself taken the wheel so as to spare every man on board for the urgent work aloft, we being very short-handed on account of having left so many of our crew on shore when we beat out. It was a glorious fine day after the storm, with a fresh wind blowing, and every minute I kept glancing back over my shoulder to see the position of the enemy. They had every stitch of canvas spread, and were sailing three feet for our two, the spray dashing up from their stems showing what a pace they were making. As I saw this a great feeling of despondency came over me through the helplessness of my position, when I thought of my young wife, standing there in front of me, and of the fate that might be in store for her. And then, to increase the danger, the brigs opened fire, and a shot came skipping after us, but fell short. In another few minutes they opened fire again, and now it was plain we should soon be in range, and I called to my wife to go below. But she refused to do so. Then, as another shot came closer to us than any previous one, I shouted out to my crew up aloft to redouble their exertions, but they, unable to cope with the work in hand, answered that they wanted help.

There was only myself left who could aid them, but I dared not leave the wheel, for we were sailing close to the wind, and any deviation from our course might throw our sails all aback, and be our ruin.

My wife perceived my extremity. During the voyage from Calcutta to Bencoolen she had three or four times, in a spirit of pastime, amused herself by taking a short trick at the wheel. This gave her confidence for the occasion, and without a moment's hesitation she ran to my side.

" Give me the wheel, Robert," she cried, " and you go and help. I will do my best to keep her head up ! "

There was no time to remonstrate, and indeed her assistance came like aid from Heaven above.

With a blessing for her pluck, I handed the helm over to her, and darted up the shrouds. As soon as the crew saw what had occurred, the noble example seemed to animate them with a new vigour, and they gave vent to a lusty cheer, and when I joined them, and was able to assist as well as to direct, we managed with our united efforts to complete the bending on of the foresail. The shots from the bow-chasers of the Dutchmen were coming fast and thick now, but hope was in our hearts. Sail by sail, we got a splendid spread of canvas on the *Endeavour*, and as each fresh one began to draw, we first held our own, and then gradually left our enemy behind, and when, after an hour's hard exertion, I returned to deck, we were practically out of danger.

Then one of the men took off his cap and called for three cheers for the captain's wife, and never, I think, did any lady at sea receive such a rare compliment as burst from the throats of those rough men, whose best instincts had been appealed to by the brave deed they thus spontaneously applauded.

By nightfall the Dutchmen were hull down on the water, and the next morning I swept the horizon in vain to sight them. I carried the signal of alarm—an ensign flying at our main top-gallant mast-head—all along the coast until I reached Bencoolen, where I found the rest of my crew and officers, who had been brought there by another ship which had observed the signals of distress that they displayed.

For my conduct in this affair the Government
made me a present of five hundred dollars, and a
new anchor and cable (worth a thousand more), to
replace the ones I had lost ; and also complimented
me with a letter of thanks for my public service.
It was, of course, most gratifying to me to receive
these acknowledgments, but I hesitate not to say
that it was my wife who deserved the rewards, for
without her noble behaviour at the moment of
peril when we were so desperately pressed, we had
been lost. Her pluck and presence of mind on
that occasion not only saved me my ship, which
was my entire fortune, but the Government a
valuable cargo of pepper, which we had almost
completed taking on board when we had to slip
and beat out to sea.

Having completed my charter by transferring
my cargo to the *Queen*, East Indiaman, Captain
Craig (the same ship which was the next year
burnt off the coast of South America), we left
Bencoolen for Calcutta. But ill-fortune seemed
to follow us, for on the second day, when passing
the island of Para, we were sighted by two large
French frigates, who at once gave chase to us.
There was nothing to do but to keep on our course,
and endeavour to outsail them until nightfall, so
I continued on with my stun-sail booms out and
everything ready. But they proved to be fast
vessels, and got so close to us before dusk, that
they kept sight of us all through the night, burning
blue lights from time to time ; and despite all my

manœuvres to escape, they tacked after me, and when daylight came were so close that I gave up all hope, and contented myself with expressing a desire that they would delay taking over charge for a couple of hours, so as to avoid startling my wife who was asleep in her cabin.

The wind having dropped, a gun was fired across our bows as a hint for us to haul our colours down, and we could hear the distant shouts as orders were given for the boats to be lowered to board us. My wife being awakened by the report of the cannon came up from below, and seeing the frigate so near, asked me if all hope of escape was over, to which I could only reply that I feared such was the case. Overhearing this, my chief mate, Mr. Swinton, a very silent fellow but an excellent seaman, whose gaze had for some time been fixed upon the horizon, observed, " I wish that squall would come on," and asked if he might hoist the topmast steering sail. I must confess in my anxiety I had not noticed, as I should have done, the particular look in the sky, which now became apparent with the breaking of the day, and indicated wind, but my attention being thus drawn to it, I saw at once that there was a squall gathering, and that if it only headed our way we might yet escape. I at once complied with the chief mate's request, and whilst the crew were engaged in carrying it out, the squall rushed right upon us with the swiftness so common to those latitudes, and in a moment we were enveloped in a thick atmosphere, with blinding rain.

And now I determined upon a manœuvre which would, I felt certain, save us if I could carry it out. Knowing that the squall must have struck the French frigates at the same time it did us, and feeling sure that they would run before it, I ordered the helm to be put hard down, and steered directly for the direction in which we had last seen them, keeping the wind full on the beam, although the force of it sent us heeling bulwarks under. Seeing this my officers became alarmed for the masts, but these I knew to be good ones, whilst the sails were old. I therefore carried on at all risks, and by the course I steered must have passed astern of the frigates at a very short distance, yet entirely hid from their sight by the thickness of the atmosphere.

It was impossible to predict how long the squall would last. If it blew over soon it might leave us still in sight of the Frenchmen, who, with the whole day before them, would certainly capture us. I therefore determined to make the most of it whilst it held out, and I carried on without taking in a single sail. It was an exciting time, during which the *Endeavour*, that had never before made more than nine knots an hour, was now going upwards of twelve, and sending the foam high over her bows as she slashed her way through the water, whilst I stood on the weather side of the poop, my eyes fixed on the straining masts, from which I saw sail after sail blown away.

I had asked my wife to go below directly the

squall overtook us, but this she refused to do, and catching hold of a rope, clung by my side, not saying a word, but taking in every incident of the scene. Such spirit as she displayed is not often found in woman. I have sailed with many, but I never met one, saving my wife, who could resist the necessity of asking questions in moments of extreme peril and urgency.

The squall, as it happened, lasted about four hours. When it was over we had lost most of our sails, and also a couple of boats which had been washed away from the davits, but the two French frigates were nowhere to be seen. They had, in fact, as I had anticipated, run before the wind, whilst I continued to cling to it, and so obtained the weather-gauge of them. I may here mention that I learnt afterwards, when I was a prisoner on board one of these ships, that they were the *La Forte* and *La Prudente*. They had been cruising about Ceylon, and then sailed for Sooloo Bay in the Straits of Bally in search of some China ships, and when they fell in with me were making their way back to the Bay of Bengal, where shortly after this they captured the *Rosenberg*, the *Greenwich*, and the *Elsigneur*.

We soon bent on new sails, and in ten days reached Calcutta without further adventure. I was proud of the ship that had behaved so well, and given the slip to Dutchmen and Frenchmen one after the other; but prouder far of my young wife, who, whether under the fire of one enemy steering the ship as skilfully and courageously as any man, or whether tearing away from the other with masts bending like reeds, sails torn and flapping with a report like cannons, and bulwarks under water, always remembered that she was a sailor's wife, and never spoke a word of alarm, nor changed the colour of her cheek for a moment.

CHAPTER VI.

THE risks I had encountered during my last
voyage, and the great anxiety I had suffered
on three occasions, convinced me that it was wrong
to expose my wife to such dangers, and I therefore

determined not to take her to sea again, but to settle her in a house of her own. She was very much opposed to this, declaring there was nothing she desired so much as to accompany me, loving both the manner of the life and the excitement connected with it. But I could not find it in my duty to assent to her wishes, however much I admired her spirit; so I rented a house at Entally, near Calcutta, small but exceedingly pretty, and surrounded by a large garden, and in this she went to reside when I departed for my next voyage.

Having obtained a freight for Bombay, that port was my destination. After rounding Ceylon and sailing some distance up the Malabar coast, I fell in with a fleet of nine pirates belonging to the Angria State, which is a native territory situated just below Bancoot and not far from Bombay. These pirates had many fastnesses along the coast, the chief ones being Severndroog Island and Gheria, both exceedingly strong forts. For a century they had committed the most audacious depredations upon the commerce of all countries. They were afraid of nothing, and had met and defeated the attacks of English, French, and Dutch men-of-war sent specially to punish them, actually capturing their enemy's ships in some cases. Thus the *Jupiter*, a French frigate of 40 guns, had to haul down her colours to these sea-robbers; and the *Restoration*, a Company's armed ship of 20 guns, was also taken by them in fair fight, besides three Dutch men-of-war. It was not until a regular expedition was despatched against them by the English that they were subdued, their strongholds broken up, and their territory handed over to the Mahratta Peishwa. For some years there was a cessation of their piratical acts, but by degrees they built new fleets of ships and cemented their strength, and in 1798 were in full vigour again and constantly capturing European vessels.

Fortunately for me, the squadron I fell in with was in doubt about my appearance. For it had happened in the previous week that the *Centurion*, 50 guns, Captain Romer, being in the same waters, they had mistaken her for a merchantman, and having approached her under darkness of night, successfully accomplished their favourite tactic of wedging the rudder. They then surrounded the ship and made their attack; but although taken by surprise, the frigate soon had her guns loaded and brought to bear on the pirates, and with two or three broadsides so punished them that they were only too glad to sheer off, many in a sinking condition, and take to flight, with the aid of their long sweeps to hurry them.

Had it not been for the *Centurion's* rudder being wedged, and she thereby prevented from steering, many of the pirates must have been captured or sunk, but as it was they escaped. This adventure made them unusually cautious, and when they sighted the *Endeavour* they suspected the ship, and would not approach close to her during daylight, but kept hovering on and off just out of gun-shot in a way that convinced me they had designs upon my vessel. I therefore caused the guns to be loaded, distributed small arms to the crew, and made my dispositions to repel the expected attack. When it grew dark, after some consultation amongst themselves, the pirates burnt blue lights as a signal, and, getting out their sweeps, began to approach me. Closer and closer they came, till the regular plash of their rowers could be quite distinctly heard. Just then a strong land breeze sprang up, and taking advantage of it, I hoisted all sail and stood out to sea, discharging my guns at them as a parting salutation, and this evidently frightened them, for they made no attempt to follow.

It was but a few months before this that Captain Haig, in a country ship, having been driven past Bombay, and running short of water, sent a boat ashore with some casks to get them filled. The men were allowed to land and roll their casks up to a tank, when a gang of these pirates made a swoop upon their boat, which was left in charge of a man and a boy, and easily captured it. They then filled it as full as it would hold with armed pirates, and pulling off to Captain Haig's ship, easily obtained a footing on board in the dusk, and overpowered and captured the vessel, which was then run into a creek and plundered. Captain Haig and his crew were made slaves, and he was very barbarously treated by the master to whom he was allotted. But his mates were more fortunate, in consequence of their good looks, and being smiled upon by their master's wives. I do not know of what the cargo of the ship consisted, but it was all landed, and a grand to-do about the spoils. During the quarrelling consequent upon the division of the plunder, Captain Haig, the two mates, and half a dozen of the men, having laid a successful plot, made their escape, and got safe away into the interior, where, falling in with a large caravan, they joined it, and so reached British territory safely. It is difficult to suppose that at so late a date the country close to Bombay could be in such a disordered state, but I know the occurrence to be true, for Captain Haig gave me the report himself.

There are three kinds of craft in the fleets of these Angria pirates, viz., gallivats, shebars, and grabs. The first have in general two masts, and are decked fore and aft, being rigged in the European fashion, with square top-sails and top-gallant-sails. The shebars are also two-masted vessels, but are not decked, and have shoulder-of-mutton-shaped sails, extending on single yards several feet higher than the top of the masts. Many of these are over a hundred tons burden, and sail very swiftly and exceedingly close to the wind. The grabs are rigged in European manner. These fleets belong to the Rajah of the place from whence they sail out. Each ship carries eight or ten small guns, and from sixty to a hundred men.

CAPTAIN EASTWICK IN 1805.

(After a Drawing.)

The pay of a pirate lascar is about two rupees a trip, and the serang, or head man, receives eight. In addition to this, they are all given food to support themselves and their families. They seldom stay out at sea more than fifteen days, after which they put back to port again; and if the cruise has been a good one, each lascar gets three or four rupees extra as prize money. The plunder taken at sea becomes the sole property of the Rajah, who fits out the squadrons, pays the men, feeds them all the year round, and runs all risks of failure or success. Sometimes these pirates board their victims by stratagem. Having hailed a ship, they obtain a footing on deck under some excuse, and the serang engages in conversation with the captain while his followers estimate the strength of the crew. If they think they can master them, one of the pirates picks a quarrel, and then calls to his companions to help him. At once a struggle ensues, weapons being produced which were previously hidden from view, and in a few minutes it is all up with the vessel. The pirates then plunder her, and, having taken all the valuables out of her, generally let her go free.

A few days after my escape from these Angria rascals, I reached Bombay. Having discharged here, I was taken up by Government to proceed to Bancoot, and load bullocks to be landed at Calicut for the use of the Bombay army going up against Seringapatam. The fort at Bancoot was under the command of Captain Morris, a connection of my wife, and he received me most kindly in his comfortable residence.

This place is noted for its horned cattle, of a particular breed, large and very good, and which can be purchased for about ten rupees a head all round, and are far superior to those sold in Bombay. A curious incident happened here, while we were taking our bullocks on board. My ship, the *Endeavour*, was flush-built, with high between-decks and a door communicating to the steerage, and another to the great cabin. At the entrance of the latter my chief mate, Mr. Forrest, was standing superintending the work. One of the bullocks having been lowered down on to the main-deck and taken out of his strappings, caught sight of Mr. Forrest, and instantly charged him. The mate, to save himself, slipped behind the door, and the bullock, passing through the cabin, head downwards and at full gallop, went clean overboard through the stern window, which was about three feet from the deck level, and happened to be open. It surprised every one to see an animal of so large a size leap through the aperture with the rapidity and precision with which it was done. We soon got the bullock on board again, and having filled in our full complement of two hundred animals, set sail, and landed them safely at Calicut.

From this place I proceeded to Madras, where I learnt of a sad misfortune that had overtaken my wife's brother-in-law and my own good friend, Captain Kent. On his return home in the *Eliza*, after my marriage, he sold that ship and invested his entire fortune in a splendid vessel of 1,200 tons burden, called the *Malabar*, and brought her out to Madras, where he loaded her with a cargo to return to England. He also secured all the passengers he had accommodation for, so that the prospects of the voyage could not have been finer. But the day before he was going to sail, as a cask of rum was being hoisted on board for the use of the ship's company, it broke away from the hooks when it was being lowered into the hold, and a man happening to be carelessly standing by one of the hatches with a lighted candle in his hand, the spirit caught fire, and the ship was immediately in a blaze. Nothing was saved but the lives of those on board, and before his eyes Captain Kent saw his splendid ship consumed and no one able to do anything to save her. He was obliged to return all the passage money, which amounted to twelve thousand pounds. His only dependence now lay in the insurance, which he had always trusted to his agents, who were also his first cousins. He immediately left by the first ship sailing for England to recover the money. Judge, then, of his misery and surprise, upon his return, to find that his agents had neglected to carry out the insurance. I fear these people, knowing Captain Kent's careless habits, had trusted to his good fortune to return home without loss, and, like many other dishonest characters, to pocket the premium, which in this time of war was exceedingly heavy. This has, I suspect, been too often done. I was told afterwards that these persons had always charged his account, as a matter of course, with the cost of insurance, and without his having ever seen the policy, he being one of the most frank, trusting men on earth, and totally unable to suspect any one. There was no occasion why his agents should have omitted the insurance for this voyage, and had I been in his place I should have brought the case to trial without any doubt about the issue. But poor Kent was a broken man after this, and never looked up again, but gradually relapsed into a settled melancholy and not long afterwards died.

At Madras I was introduced by Captain Malcolm, the town major of Fort St. George (afterwards Sir John Malcolm), to Colonel the Honourable Arthur Wellesley, or Wesley, as he then called himself, the same who became the famous Duke of Wellington. Colonel Wellesley was very anxious to get to Calcutta, where he was proceeding in order to meet his brother, Lord Mornington, who was expected out as the new Governor-General, and he requested me to give him a passage, mine being the first ship bound for that port.

At that time I was not in the habit of taking passage money, nor was I disposed to charge the Colonel anything, although he had two horses with him—the usual freight for which was one hundred and fifty rupees each—and several servants. But he was brother to the new Governor-General, and although a poor man then, yet an officer of great rank and reputation. I therefore acceded to his request, and having done so, determined within myself that he should want for nothing on board my ship, but be suitably entertained. In consequence I laid in a large stock of luxuries for the cabin table, and especially some very choice claret, for which I paid sixty rupees a dozen. But this outlay proved unfortunate for my pocket, for being further persuaded into carrying some other passengers, by the time we reached Calcutta they had consumed all my expensive supplies, especially the claret, whereof Colonel Wellesley drank but sparingly. So that I had nothing left when the voyage was over, except the empty satisfaction of having gained a reputation for keeping a generous table. Indeed, they all spoke very handsomely concerning my treatment of them, drinking my health, and the ship's health, very regularly every day, after the King's, and then their own healths, one after another, and paying me the compliment of saying they had never sipped finer wine.

I found Colonel Wellesley a most agreeable and frank man. We had many long conversations together, and he told me of his being with the Duke of York in Flanders, and afterwards in Admiral Christian's fleet, that suffered so much in the prevailing gales at that time. After which, his regiment, the 33rd, having been ordered out to Bengal, he sailed as a passenger with Captain Pulteney Malcolm in the *Fox* frigate. On his arrival at Fort William he stopped but a short time,

and then embarked for the Manilla Expedition, in
the *Daedalus*, thirty-two guns, Captain the Honourable G. Murray.　Going out in a gale of wind,
the *Daedalus* struck on one of the sandheads at the
mouth of the Hooghley, and was nearly lost.　The
Manilla Expedition was never carried out, and I
think Colonel Wellesley returned from Penang to
Madras, whence, after a short stay, he sailed with
me to Calcutta.

When I became acquainted with him he was a
very spare man (as indeed he remained ever afterwards) most conversable and sociable, and without
more pride than he ought to have.　His behaviour
towards ladies was exceedingly courteous.　My
second officer, Mr. Ross, was married, and had his
pretty young wife on board, and Colonel Wellesley
admired her very much, and constantly walked
the deck in her company.　One day I happened to
show him a miniature of my wife, and his first
exclamation was : " Surely she is not so handsome
as this ! "　His living was plain, and he drank but
sparingly, and this at a time when hard drinking
was considered fashionable.　His wants were very
few, and it was amazing what little sleep he
required.　Whenever I was on deck, late at night
or early in the morning (and in those days I never
slept more than two or three hours at a stretch), I
always seemed to find him pacing the quarter-deck.
There was one relaxation of which he was very
fond, and that was a game of high whist, which he,
the two Messrs. Simpson (who were passengers

on board) and myself played regularly every evening.

I remember a story Colonel Wellesley told me about a sergeant in his regiment, the 33rd, which shows how each man is best suited to his own station in life, and should learn to be contented therein. After the declaration of war with France a great number of volunteer regiments were raised in England when an invasion was apprehended. Amongst others there was one recruited at the India House, and this sergeant of the 33rd was selected to drill it. One of the volunteers was Sir Hugh Inglis, who was a Director of the Honourable Company, and he was so pleased with the man that he gave him a cadetship to Bengal. The sergeant having arrived in India, took up his new appointment, but soon found himself out of place, being quite unaccustomed to mingle with gentlemen. When he heard that Colonel Wellesley had arrived in the *Fox* frigate, he obtained leave and came down to Calcutta, and calling upon the Colonel explained his dissatisfaction with his position. " Sir," he said, " I am tired of being a gentleman, and desire to be degraded back to my former post. In fact, to leave this country service and return to the king's in my old regiment. For to become sergeant in the 33rd again would be promotion to me ! " Colonel Wellesley was too glad to have so smart a man back to offer any refusal, but still, in the man's interest, he considered it right to remonstrate with him. So he told him that having attained the position of a gentleman, he should strive to become worthy of it, and recommended him to return to his duties for a few months. The sergeant, however, would not listen to this advice, but bluntly replied, " Saving your presence, sir, a gentleman is a d—d poor thing to be. It is like being under continual arrest. A man may not do that which he desires, or which comes natural to him, but must always be a-thinking of his behaviour, and if what he does is in accordance with the custom of his station. I would sooner be a private in the line, and master of my own actions when off duty, than colonel of the regiment and pestered with trying to act the gentleman !" It ended with the man returning to his old place in Colonel Wellesley's regiment.

On our arrival at Diamond Harbour, the tide being against us, we were obliged to drop anchor, much to Colonel Wellesley's disappointment, he being anxious, as he told me, to save his monthly allowance, to do which it was necessary to report himself at the Presidency the next morning. I therefore proposed that we should endeavour to reach Calcutta by boat, and he readily accepted the suggestion. Leaving Mr. Forrest, my chief officer, in charge of the ship, with orders to bring her up the river when the tide served, Colonel Wellesley, the Messrs. Simpson and myself proceeded ashore to the Master Attendant to ask his assistance.

This man turned out to be a blunt, rude fellow,

who, in spite of all my expostulations, refused me
the use of his boat and crew, which was what we
required of him. We then went to the Company's
agent, who was a man of quite an opposite character, but though lavishly promising everything,
could perform nothing. All the time I perceived
Colonel Wellesley was growing more and more impatient at the delay, although he said not a word.
But he was essentially a prompt and determined
man in his actions, and could not brook anything
approaching to opposition. I now proposed to him
that we should again try the Master Attendant, and,
in short, compel him to give us his boat ; but this
the Colonel would not sanction, saying that he
was not travelling on the Government service, and,
moreover, that he did not care to subject me to a
repetition of the man's rudeness. I answered as
far as that was concerned it made no matter to me,
and I added that if he would not accompany me,
but let me make another trial by myself, I had
hopes of succeeding. To this Colonel Wellesley
consented, and going to the Master Attendant, I
explained to him the rank of my passenger, and
warned him that if he still refused his assistance
he would certainly hear more of the matter from
his superiors, as I was fully determined to report
his conduct when I got to Calcutta.

Hearing this, the man altered his tone, and told
me (surlily enough) that I might have his boat as
far as Fultah. Here a Mr. Gammage resided, who
kept a beautiful tavern of entertainment and ac-

commodation boats for travellers, and whom I knew well, having spent many a day at his house. I was thererefore satisfied that, once arrived at Fultah, we should have no difficulty in getting to our destination.

Colonel Wellesley was much gratified at my success, and getting into the Master Attendant's boat we rowed up to Fultah, where we obtained the refreshment we required, but found that Mr. Gammage had let all his boats out. In this dilemma, and as a last resource, we had to engage a *paunchway*, which is the most common kind of craft on the river, and only used by the poorest natives, and squatting in this, the future conqueror of Waterloo proceeded to the Presidency.

On our arrival at Garden Reach,* Colonel Wellesley invited me to land with him at the house of his friend Mr. Ledley, whose beautiful mansion was built close to the river's bank; but I excused myself, and, together with the Messrs. Simpson, proceeded without delay to the city, being most anxious to get home, as my wife was in a delicate state of health, and all by herself.

A few days afterwards Colonel Wellesley sent me a very kind note, with an offer to serve me should it ever be in his power at any future time,

---

* "The *Endeavour*, Captain Eastwick, arrived in the river on the 3rd from the coast. She left Madras on the 10th April.

"Passengers on the *Endeavour :* Honble Colonel Wesley, brother to Lord Mornington, James Simpson, Esq., George Simpson, Esq., — Aufrey, Esq., Civil Service, Madras Establishment, and Mr. Heathcote, Cadet."—*Calcutta Monthly Journal,* May, 1798.

and enclosing an order for three hundred rupees for his passage up. This letter was lost in 1825, when I was absent in China. I had several other letters from him at various times, but they are all lost excepting his answer to one I wrote him after the battle of Waterloo, which I have amongst my papers and prize very much.*

Many years afterwards, in 1814, I was at a public banquet given at the Guildhall, London, in honour of the Duke, after his return from the Peninsular War. When dinner was over and healths were being drunk, as was the custom, a message came to me : "The Duke wishes to take wine with you, Captain Eastwick." I at once rose to my feet and looked towards the Duke, whose recognition of me I had not been prepared for. To my amazement he called out to me down the table, "Have you accomplished that hard business of yours, yet, Captain Eastwick?" Not understanding what he referred to, I was quite at a loss how to reply, and every eye in the room being turned upon me I felt covered with confusion. Whereupon the Duke added, "Cutting sticks with a wooden hatchet, I mean." And then, in an instant, it recurred to me that this had been a favourite phrase of mine on board ship when I had cause to reprimand any man for being slow, and would say to him, in sailor fashion, "What is the delay, you lubber? Are you

---

* A diligent search has failed to discover this. The only document found bearing on the subject is an empty envelope, addressed to the narrator, and franked by the Duke.

cutting sticks with a wooden hatchet?" The expression had remained in the Duke's memory all those years!

I arrived at Calcutta early in May, 1798, and on the 1st of June following my wife presented me with a little daughter, whose arrival completed the happiness of our home. By the end of July she was well and strong again, and I had the *Endeavour* ready loaded for another voyage, when one morning I received a letter from Mr. Farquhar, who had just been appointed Governor of Penang, and wrote, saying he heard that I was going to Madras, and as he had business at that place before proceeding to his appointment, he would consider it as a favour if I would give him and my old passenger, Colonel Wellesley, a passage in my ship, the latter being ordered to the siege of Seringapatam, and desiring to reach Madras in advance of his regiment, which was to sail in about a fortnight's time. To this I readily agreed, but when about to start, very alarming news of French privateers in the bay was received in Calcutta, and they gave up their intention.

These privateers were the famous *Malartic*, Citizen Duterte, captain, and *Confiance*, Captain Sourcouff. The former had captured the Company's ships *Raymond* and *Woodcot*, and her presence occasioned nothing less than a blockade. She eventually took the *Princess Royal, Surprise, Thomas, Joyce, Lord Hobart*, and many other merchantmen, before she was herself captured by the Company's ship *Phœnix*, Captain Moffatt. Such importance was attached to her capture, that Captain Moffatt was publicly presented with a sword of honour. The *Confiance* was an even more destructive vessel than the *Malartic*. She attacked the *Kent*, East Indiaman, off the Sandheads, and after a tremendous engagement, in which she killed or wounded sixty of the *Kent's* crew, she forced that vessel to haul down her flag. Immediately upon this news reaching Calcutta, the Company's frigates *Nonsuch* and *Bombay* were despatched in pursuit of the privateer, and coming up with her made certain of capturing her. But the *Confiance*, though only armed with 22 guns, was commanded by a captain of the greatest gallantry and determination, who at once gave fight, and after sustaining a desperate action, escaped by press of sail. The *Kent* was, however, recaptured and brought into Calcutta. The *Confiance* was a remarkably beautiful ship. She sat very low upon the water, and had black sides with yellow moulding posts, and a French stern, all black. She carried a red vane at her maintopgallant masthead, very square yards and jaunt masts, upright and without the smallest rake either forward or aft. Her sails were all cut French fashion, and remarkable, having a great roach and steering sail, very square. There was not a ship in those seas that she could not overtake or sail away from. It was the custom of her commander, Captain Sourcouff, to ply his crew with liquor, and they always fought with the madness of drink in them. It was not until three or four years later that this formidable vessel was captured.

The presence of these two privateers caused Colonel Wellesley to give up his passage with me, preferring to accompany his own regiment in the *Earl Fitzwilliam*, which was a heavily-armed Company's ship. But he met with nothing but misfortunes * in her, and had better have trusted to the *Endeavour* again. First of all she went aground off Saugor, and narrowly escaped destruction. If it had not been that the sea was calm and the weather fine, which was most unusual at that season of the year, she must have gone to pieces, and every soul on board perished. She was got off by the exertions of the troops on board, who hauled her into deep water by cables made fast to anchors laid out astern, after the ship had been lightened by throwing overboard the greater portion of her cargo. She reached Madras (where I saw her) in a crippled condition. To add to Colonel Wellesley's troubles, the *Earl Fitz-william* was supplied with unwholesome water,

---

* The following passage occurs in one of the Duke of Wellington's letters, printed among his "Despatches," and dated from on board the *Fitzwilliam* on August 19, 1798 :—

" Tell —— that I conceive it to be very inconsistent with the principles of the Christian religion to give people bad water, when he had notice of the probability it would be so. You may likewise say that a Gentile could not have done worse than give us a bottle of good rum by way of muster, and fill the casks with the worst I ever saw."

which led to a great sickness amongst the 33rd Regiment, and the death of many men during the short voyage.

From Madras I was freighted to Bombay, where I obtained a cargo back to Calcutta, and sailed for that port again, little suspecting the great misfortune that was now about to overtake me.

CHAPTER VII.

I HAVE mentioned how dangerous was the Bay
of Bengal in these days, owing to the French
men-of-war, and privateers that were continually

cruising about in search of our merchant ships.
It was computed that within a single twelvemonth British shipping to the value of not less
than two millions sterling had been captured or
sunk.   There were three notorious frigates which
every one had learnt to dread, the *Preneuse*, the
La Prudente, and the *La Forte*.   It was from the
latter two ships that I had escaped when returning from Bencoolen in 1797, and by a strange
coincidence they were both captured in the
month of February, 1799, though at points many
hundreds of miles apart.   The victory over the *La
Forte* I shall presently relate.   Her companion
ship, the *La Prudente*, on the 16th of the same
month, was sighted early one morning off the
south-east coast of Africa by the *Daedalus*,
Captain Ball, who immediately gave chase, and
by midday brought her into action, and in fifty-
seven minutes forced her to strike.   She was
returning to Europe from the Isle of France, and
had three hundred men on board.   In the next
year the *Preneuse* likewise met her fate off the
same coast, being run ashore and burnt by her
own captain in order to escape capture at the
hands of a British squadron that was in pursuit
of her.   But before these three frigates were
taken their presence had paralyzed our Eastern
trade, and the rates asked for insurance were so
prohibitive, that at last I was totally unable to
afford the premiums demanded, and on the voyage
I am now describing I remained uninsured.

During my passage to Bombay I had been most fortunate, not having sighted a single hostile sail, and on my return had arrived as far as the Balasore Roads, close to Juggernauth Pagoda, and in the waters where the Bengal pilots are always cruising, without encountering any of the enemy, so that I was already congratulating myself upon my good fortune, when at the eleventh hour I found myself all undone.

For towards evening, while we were becalmed and on the lookout for a pilot, a large ship was sighted in the offing, which, on a breeze springing up, stood towards us. As she came near I felt sure she was a man-of-war, and the cut of her sails soon indicated a French one. My belief was presently confirmed by seeing her fire a shot to windward at another vessel of my own size that chanced to be passing. As, however, her chase was after me, she did not alter her course, so I crowded on all sail and endeavoured to escape. But I soon found the frigate was faster than I, for she overhauled us rapidly, and after a time brought her bow-chasers to bear, and sent a shot after us. It showed that we were within her range, for the ball went clean through our main and fore sails, making great holes in them, and carrying away some of the rigging. In this extremity I altered my course, and stood in towards a sand-bank in the Balasore Roads, with various soundings from ten to four fathoms, and considered dangerous to large ships. The Frenchman evidently had this feeling and redoubled his fire, his aim being very accurate, and the shot going over our deck, and through our sails and cutting away our rigging. The man at the helm was so alarmed that I was obliged to threaten him to keep him at his duty, but with the effect of making him steer very badly. It now became a stiff breeze, and the enemy having drawn quite close, evidently with a view to ending the matter, made disposition to give me a broadside. As such would have sunk me, or at any rate occasioned great loss of life, and it being evident that to hold out longer was only risking the safety of those on board, and that there was no alternative but to strike, I threw my sails aback. And so at 9 p.m. on the last day of February, 1799, I was forced to haul down my colours and surrender my ship.*

* *The Times* of August 3, 1799, has the following leading article referring to the incident mentioned in the text:—

"Advices have been received at the India House of the capture of the following country ships in the Bay of Bengal:—*Recovery*—McKinley; *Yarmouth*—Beck; *Earl Mornington*—Cooke; *Chance*—Johnson; *Endeavour*—Eastwick; *Surprize*—Moore; and two others, names unknown. The first has been sent to Madras as a cartel. They were captured by the *La Forte*, frigate.

"We have the satisfaction to state that the *Sybille*, frigate, Captain Cook, afterwards fell in with and captured *La Forte*, after a severe engagement. The French frigate did not strike her colours till after she had lost her captain and all her officers. When the ship struck she was in possession of a boy. *La Forte* mounted fifty guns, and was full of men. We consider her capture to be fully an equivalent for the loss of all the ships she had just before taken.

"The *La Forte* was commanded by the famous Admiral de Serci, a pupil of Suffreins, and certainly the most active and distinguished officer in the French service. Whilst the East India Company have to rejoice at getting rid of so formidable an enemy, every man must

I cannot describe my feelings of mortification as I saw the boarding party put foot on my deck, and heard the officer summon me to give up my vessel. It was the first time I had ever been placed in such a position, and although there was no disgrace in being captured by an enemy so superior, still my spirit rebelled at having to strike my colours to a Frenchman.

lament the fate of a very brave officer. He had the character of great humanity towards those whom the chances of war threw in his path.

"Captain E. Cook, who commanded *La Sybille*, is likewise well known in the service. He is the son of the famous navigator of that name, and the officer who undertook the hazardous negotiation between Lord Hood and the magistrates of Toulon, previous to our fleet taking possession of that town and harbour. We are sorry to learn that he is dangerously wounded in both arms. Our loss is very small as to men."

On the 5th of August, *The Times* gives further particulars of this action :—

"The following are some further particulars respecting the capture of *La Forte* frigate. Captain Cook on arriving at Madras in *La Sybille*, 44 guns, received information that *La Forte* of 55 guns, 24-pounders, had taken several of our ships, and was cruising in the Bay of Bengal. He instantly went in search of her. They met in the night near Ballysore. *La Forte* mistook *La Sybille* for an Indiaman, and fired some random shots to bring her to, one of which unfortunately killed Captain Davis, aid du camp (*sic*) to Lord Mornington. Captain Cook approached without showing any lights, and first undeceived the enemy by a broadside. During an action of an hour and a half, the French officers did everything that was possible to keep their people at their guns, but our fire was tremendous, and the slaughter great. All the French officers were amongst the killed before a lad, who had for some time commanded, finding further opposition fruitless, struck his colours.

"The *La Forte* was laid down for a 74, and is perhaps the largest and finest frigate in the world, carring her guns four feet higher than the *Victorious*. Admiral De Sercy (*sic*), on returning lately from Batavia, married a Creole lady, with whom he obtained a large fortune."

Having placed a prize officer and crew on board the *Endeavour*, I and my chief and second mates were taken as prisoners to the frigate, which proved to be the famous *La Forte*. She now put about, and proceeded to chase, and soon captured, the vessel at which she had first fired, and which was the *Mornington*, Captain Cooke, with a valuable cargo and sixty thousand dollars specie on board. On this capture they put a prize master and a very considerable body of men, and also a commissary with an additional crew to secure the money. The two prizes were then told to keep within signalling distance until further orders were sent them in the morning, and all the ships were hove to for the night.

Captain Cooke and Mr. Mackerel (a passenger on board the *Mornington*) were brought prisoners on board the frigate, and sent to keep us company on deck, where I had seated myself behind one of the guns. I was previously acquainted with the former, and we were comforted to meet, even under such distressing circumstances. He, like myself, had lost his entire fortune with his ship, and we mutually condoled with each other upon the unlucky fate that had robbed us of our all just as safety seemed within our grasp.

There were several other English prisoners on board the *La Forte*, from whom we learnt the treatment we might expect. Their food was salt beef, boiled in vinegar, to which was added boiled peas, as a substitute for bread. Only one quart of water was allowed *per diem*, and not a glass of wine or spirits.

As for the discipline of the ship, it was very slack. It was not at all unusual to see one of the foremast men, with his beef in his hands, eating it while walking the quarter-deck, and claiming an equal right to do it with the commanding officer, thus, I suppose, demonstrating the claims of liberty, equality, and brotherhood. Nor was any scruple made of playing cards on the quarter-deck. The lieutenants generally came on deck with only trousers and an open shirt, often a check one, so that it was almost impossible to distinguish them. The men, however, went through their duty with alacrity, and were obedient to orders.

Amongst the prisoners were two officers of the 28th Light Dragoons. They had been in charge of 107 men of their regiment, who were being conveyed on board the *Osterley* from Madras to Calcutta, when that ship was captured, about a week previously to us, by the frigate. An exception had been made in their favour, for they were most courteously treated, especially by Captain Beaulieu La Loup, the second in command on board the *La Forte*. Whilst we were sitting talking about these matters, a message was brought to us that Captain Cooke, Mr. Mackerel, and myself, were required aft. We immediately went to the quarter-deck, where we found the Admiral, a fine old man and a very distinguished officer. He told us that he was sorry for us, as he was informed that we were the owners, as well as the commanders, of the ships he had just taken, but that we must console ourselves by the reflection that it was the fortune of war, and that, seeing what a loss we had already sustained, he would give us our liberty, and also allow the passenger, Mr. Mackerel, to accompany us, and that in the morning a long boat and all our personal property would be placed at our disposal, and permission granted us to make our way ashore.

The French Admiral's reference to the "fortune of war" was soon to find another illustration; for at the very time he was speaking there was a fine English man-of-war within a few miles. This was the *La Sybille*, of forty-four guns, and commanded by Captain Cook, one of the best officers in his Majesty's service, and a son of the great Captain Cook, whose ships the *Resolution* and the *Discovery* I had once seen when a boy. Captain Cook, of *La Sybille*, had made an extraordinary quick passage from Madras in search of this very Frenchman who had taken us, having been informed that *La Forte* was creating the utmost havoc upon our commerce at the head of the Bay. On arriving at the Sand Heads he had cruised about for three days, but failing to sight *La Forte* had almost given up all hope of meeting her, when the flashes of the bow-chasers fired at me were observed by his sailing master, Mr. Douglas, who at once gave it as his opinion that they proceeded from the firing of cannon, although on account of the great distance no reports were heard. Captain

Cook was of a different opinion, considering the flashes were caused by sheet or summer lightning on the horizon; but he yielded to his sailing master's opinion, and stood towards the direction indicated, and soon found that the enemy he was in search of was discovered.

The *La Forte* was a frigate of fifty guns, 24-pounders, and was 170 feet long and 45 feet beam. Her admiral and captain were most distinguished officers, and their conduct towards us personally was, I must admit, both kind and generous. But they had sent so many men away on board the various prizes they had recently captured (of which there were at least seven or eight) that their crew was very much diminished, and they were left badly manned, having not more than three hundred souls on board, all told.

The English frigate had, on the contrary, more than her full complement of men, there being, in addition to the sailors, a company of the Scotch brigade on board, who had taken the place of marines, the strength of these latter having been much reduced by deaths consequent upon a fever contracted by them when a large force was landed for some time at Calcutta. These soldiers were under the command of Captain Davis, an *aide de camp* of Lord Mornington, who had volunteered for the service.

In addition to this, the *La Sybille* was commanded by a captain as gallant as any that ever stepped, and, fired by his spirit, the whole crew were determined to wipe away the stain that the many recent naval disasters we had sustained had brought upon the British flag in those seas.

It was a brilliant moonlight night, with light winds and calm sea. Captain Cooke and I, having retired after our interview with the Admiral to a corner of the quarter-deck, were sitting talking, and congratulating ourselves upon our promised liberty, when our attention was suddenly drawn to a strange sail making towards us, and distinctly visible in the moonlight. She was a large vessel, and there was a curious fact about her, that she did not display a single light, but sailed serenely on with all her canvas spread, and yet without any signs of life on board. The French officers actually mistook her for a merchantman " with the watch asleep," and about to be delivered into their hands. They had enjoyed such a career of good fortune during the last month, that they were ready to accept this new ship as only a further instalment of the luck that seemed to be theirs.

Nearer and nearer came the strange sail, as calm and stately as if she had the entire ocean to herself, and no other vessel in sight. Such confidence amounted to audacity, for the display of lights from the French frigate marked her as a man-of-war. As the approaching ship continued her course and came within range, the Captain of the *La Forte* began to exhibit some doubts about her, and ordered a few shots to be fired at her. But these eliciting no response, he commanded the firing to cease, observing in my hearing, " She will prove another *Bon Prix !*" Still, as a matter of precaution, every man was kept at his quarters, though in a careless way, and the guns were all loaded and pointed at the stranger.

We prisoners were now ordered to retire below, and were shown into the officers' berth-place, the door of which was locked upon us. This did not, however, altogether prevent us from obtaining a view of what was going on, for there was a small port-hole, through which we peered in turn, and tried to conjecture who or what this vessel might be that came on in such a masterly manner and appeared to anticipate no danger, although she was sailing into the very teeth of one of the strongest frigates afloat, and one which had proved herself to be a terror in those waters.

Suddenly, having got into a proper position, and as the moment of action arrived, all the tarpaulins which had covered the lanterns and hidden the lights on board of the *La Sybille* were removed as if by magic, and an illuminated large English ship exposed to view. She was now within two cables' lengths, and luffed to the wind on the starboard tack, and the next instant the whole broadside of a well-directed fire was poured into *La Forte.* Then edging down, after the discharge, before the wind, the *La Sybille* came fairly alongside.

And now occurred such a scene on board the French frigate as I can find no words to describe.

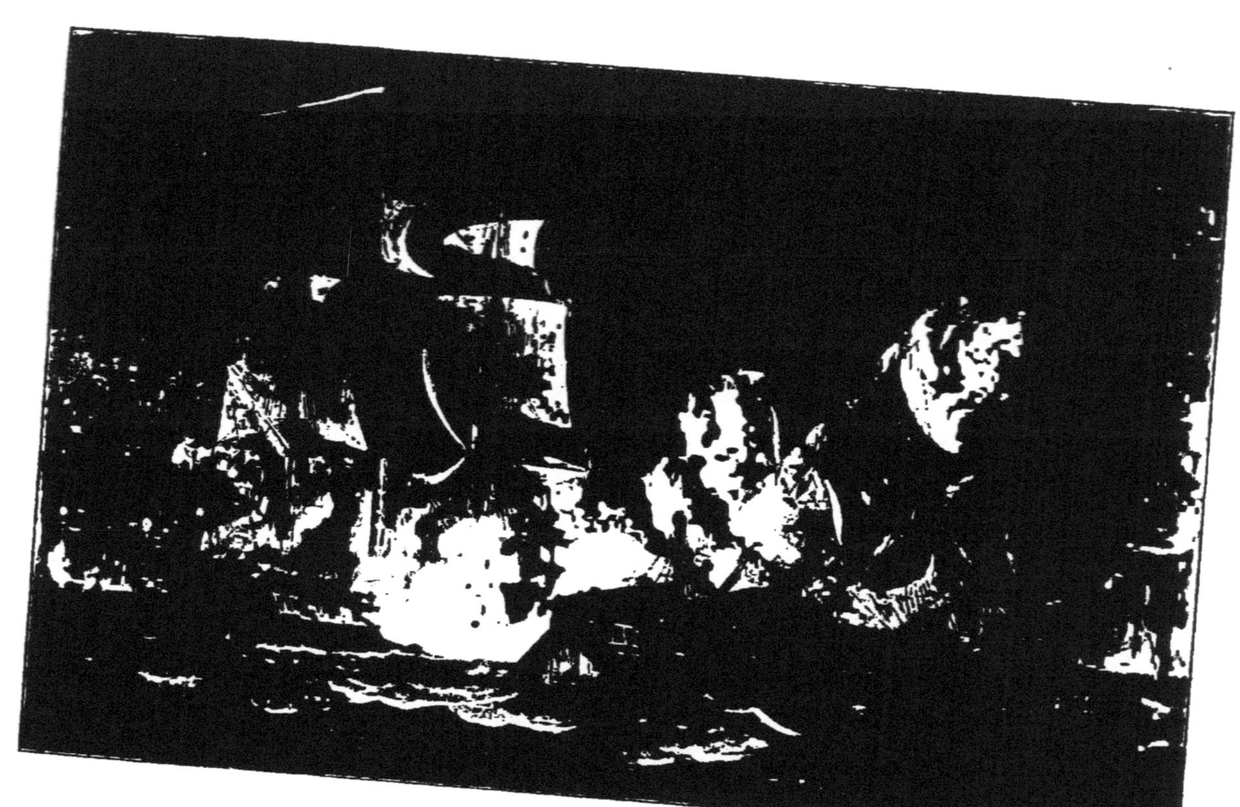

THE ACTION BETWEEN LA FORTE AND LA SYBILLE.

(*After a plate in "The Naval Achievements of Great Britain. London, 1804.*)

Her decks had been raked with the small grape-shot that came like hail from the 24-pounders of her opponent, and in a moment all was shouting and noise and confusion. Whistles were piped, orders were cried out, and the crew were hurried up to serve the guns, urged on by their officers. The admiral was killed early in the action, and the captain fell next, as gallant a man as could be desired. He was cut in half by a chain-shot whilst trying to rally his crew, who, having been fairly caught a napping, were all in alarm and confusion. The execution wrought amongst their ranks by the sudden broadside was dreadful, and the whole ship resounded with the shrieks and groans of the wounded, making a noise that was sickening to hear. Still a gallant fight was kept up, despite the demoralizing effects of that deadly fire. The musketry rattled, and between the thunder of the guns, as broadside after broadside was returned, there came the lesser but constant discharges of the brass swivels mounted on the quarter-deck. There was, however, one great disadvantage that the *La Forte* suffered; owing to her enormous height she could not depress her guns sufficiently to fire with proper effect at her opponent, because of the close quarters at which the action was fought, whilst the *La Sybille's* shot told with disastrous results at each discharge.

After fifty-five minutes' hot fighting, the French-man, finding she was beaten, desired to escape, and attempted to make sail. But this the *La*

Sybille was determined to prevent, and altering the aim of her guns, the *La Forte's* shrouds were presently shot away, and soon afterwards her masts went by the board one after another with an awful crash, carrying all the top hamper with them, until the deck became an inextricable mass of tangled rigging, and the frigate lay a helpless cripple upon the water.

Meanwhile we prisoners below had long since resigned our position by the port-hole, and sought safer quarters at the further end of the berth-place. When we heard the crash of the falling masts, we thought the *La Forte* was being boarded, although we could not at all understand the situation, being at the time unaware that the ship we were in conflict with was a British man-of-war, but rather believing it to be one of the Company's vessels. Though not engaged, we were most dangerously as well as uncomfortably confined, and being denied the satisfaction of assisting in the fight, could not have been more cruelly situated. The cabin we were imprisoned in was about thirty feet long, and ten feet above water, and during the engagement at least thirty shots passed through it. One of these went so close to us, as we were sitting on a chest together, that we were induced to shift our position, and scarce had we done so than a cannon-ball struck the chest itself and demolished it altogether. There was only one dim lantern burning in the cabin, and the gloom and obscurity seemed to increase the sensation of danger from which, since we had been locked in, there was no apparent escape.

I had rather be in a dozen actions face to face with belching cannon, and exposed to the full fire of the tops, than experience again such another hour as we passed through. The din and noise were awful; the great ship shook and quivered under every discharge of her guns; a suffocating smell of gunpowder smoke pervaded the whole vessel, we being to leeward; and every second or third minute there came a great crash, most startling in the dark, and we heard a shot go rioting through the prison we were confined in, and did not know whether the next might not carry us all off. From overhead came the trampling of feet, the cries of the wounded, the crashing sounds of falling· spars and top hamper, heard between the thundering of the cannon and the lesser roar of the small arms. The excitement of action was wanting, which assists men to face fire, and at times hardly to heed it. And added to all was the terrible sense of uncertainty as to what was happening, with whom we were contending, and whether the *La Forte* was winning the day or losing it.

After the tenth or twelfth shot had penetrated the berth-room, Captain Cooke swore he could stand it no longer, and that it required more courage than he possessed to sit still and be shot at, like a rat in a hole. He therefore began groping about to find a means of exit, and came across an aperture in the bulkhead, made by the starting of the timbers consequent on a shot striking the place. Through this, being exceedingly spare in person, he managed with great difficulty to squeeze his body, and so got further below to a place of comparative safety, from whence he called to us to join him.

The advice was excellent enough in its way, but the thing was to carry it out. Mr. Mackerel attempted the task first, I, at his request, aiding his exertions. But unfortunately he was a very fat man, and got fairly wedged when half-way through, so that he called out violently to be hauled back. This was no easy matter, and accomplished with such difficulty that the ludicrous effect of the scene has never passed from my memory, and critical as our situation was, I could not refrain from laughing aloud, when, in my endeavours to pull him back by the legs, his pantaloons first began to peel off, and when I transferred my grip to his feet, one of his boots gave way in my hand, and sent me sprawling backwards.

Mr. Mackerel was mightily indignant at my levity, and upbraided me for it in solemn and measured language, after I had at last managed to extricate him. He then very soberly laid himself down flat on the floor, observing, with a groan, that it was safer than standing; and as this seemed sensible, and I did not like to desert him, I followed his example, jestingly thanking him for the extra protection his ample person afforded me—a joke he was in far too much consternation to relish.

There we lay for half an hour, Mr. Mackerel saying not a word, but breathing very hard, and whenever a crash was heard, turning instantly on his side, so as to present his back to the attack if it should come, and then giving vent to a groan, by way of thanksgiving, when he found himself unhurt.

At last the action began to draw to a close. The discharges of cannon were less frequent, and the *La Forte's* men being all engaged in trying to set sail, the rattle of musketry on the quarter-deck above our heads almost ceased. Very nearly the last shot fired was one which, in penetrating the berth-place, was so checked, that it came rolling slowly towards us; upon which Mr. Mackerel jumped up and made a clean bound over it with an agility that would have done credit to a goat. As I scuttled out of its way, its size showed me it came from a twenty-four pounder, and I knew it must have been fired by a Man-of-war. But before I had time to acquaint my companion of this joyful discovery, and bid him take heart, a great number of men (the *La Forte* having now struck) came running down below to secure the valuables plundered from the various prizes, and tie them round their persons, and one of these unlocked the door of the berth-place, with the object, I conceive, of appropriating some of the dead officers' property, and this enabled Mr. Mackerel and myself to get out.

I immediately went on deck, where the second captain, who was quite a lad, caught sight of me.

The tears were in his eyes, and he was greatly agitated as he asked me to hail the British frigate and say we had struck. Young though he was, the command had devolved upon him through the death of all the senior officers. Still, if he had been a veteran of a hundred fights, it would not have been in his power to continue the action any longer, nor could he have shown more proper feeling at the unfortunate position in which he was placed.

I ran to the side of the *La Forte*, and shouted out that she had hauled down her colours, and then through the thick cloud of smoke, that hung over and almost hid the vessels from each other's view, there came back such a ringing English cheer as few are privileged to hear. I have never in my life, before or since, heard any cry like it. It filled the welkin with a glorious sound that recorded the accomplishment of a great deed, and I felt my heart beat faster, and my blood go rushing through my veins in pride. Then the firing ceased, and in a short while a boat containing Mr. Vashon, the second lieutenant, and Mr. Major, the third, was lowered from the *La Sybille* and came to take charge of the *La Forte*.

The surrender of the French frigate was soon completed. I then went on board the *La Sybille*, which I found in charge of Lieutenant Hardyman, Captain Cook being dangerously wounded. I at once represented the probability of recapturing the *Endeavour* and the *Mornington*, which were still within sight. It was, however, impracticable to do anything then, since it was necessary to attend to the wounded, and temporarily repair the more urgent damages that both ships had sustained. There were many prisoners also to be placed in safety, and these matters occupied the whole night. By morning order was restored on both frigates, and they were brought to anchor off the roads of Ballasore.

At my suggestion the French colours were now hoisted above the English on board the *La Sybille*, and the *Endeavour* lured into a position where her recapture was almost certain. But success depended upon the cant of the frigate : if she canted round one way my ship would have been placed in a situation that would have ensured her being at our mercy ; but if the frigate canted the other way, there was then no room without going past the French frigate and afterward hauling up to windward for a long stern chase. Although his sailing master, Mr. Douglas, recommended the course I proposed, Lieutenant Hardyman, who was a very obstinate man, would not listen to it. The prize-master in charge of the *Endeavour* suspected something, and tacked and stood under the French frigate's stern, where he saw enough to inform him of the true position of affairs, and at once sailed off, giving a signal of warning to the *Mornington*, which wore ship and followed. I then begged Mr. Hardyman to sail in pursuit, but he pleaded the damaged condition of the *La Sybille*, saying that the carpenter had reported her mainyard to be too badly wounded to carry sail. Having a great interest at stake, I earnestly pressed him to reconsider his decision, and urged in seamanlike phrase that crowbars or fishes might be lashed on to the yard for a makeshift, and there being a large property to be recovered it was worth the trial, as the frigate with her mainsail set would certainly keep pace with the *Endeavour*. But he would not listen to me, and I had the mortification of seeing my own ship escape before my eyes. It meant a loss to me of £10,000 in property uninsured, and certainly an indirect one of double that amount by the capture of my vessel at a time when tonnage was scarce, much work to be done, and no other craft to be obtained. The *Endeavour* was a ship of the best class, suitable for transporting troops and just the kind the Government sought for, and there was a certainty, had I recovered her, of my being engaged at a very high freight, for the expedition then being sent to fight Buonaparte in Egypt.

In this celebrated action, according to the returns which I obtained for the navy agent, out of three hundred men on board the *La Forte*, fifty-five were killed, including the fine old admiral, the captain, and the first, second, and third lieutenants, and eighty-five wounded. On board the *La Sybille* there were only fifteen killed and wounded, the fire from the *La Forte* having gone clean over the heads of her crew, and never been brought to bear properly upon the deck. But amongst these were Captain Davis (an *aide-de-camp* to Lord Mornington), who was on board as a volunteer in command of the Scotch Brigade, and who died of the wounds he received ; and Captain Cook, who also succumbed some months later at Calcutta,* and was accorded the honour of a public funeral.   The engagement was one of the sharpest and severest that had taken place during the war, and was begun and ended in one hundred minutes.

As for myself, though not a prisoner of war in the hands of the French, I was in a very sorry plight, having lost my all.   I had nothing to do but to return to Calcutta, and a pilot being wanted to take the *La Sybille* and *La Forte* up the river, Captain Cooke of the *Mornington* and I volunteered to go in the cutter and send one out. There was great fatigue and some danger in this, we being out of sight of land, but we managed it

---

* Captain Edward Cook died at Calcutta on the 23rd of May following.   There is a striking monument in Westminster Abbey erected to his memory by the East India Company.   It bears a fine relief representing the *La Forte* and *La Sybille* in close action, surmounted by a bas-relief of Captain Cook, who is depicted as wounded and supported by one of his men.   This monument, which is immediately behind one erected to the memory of General Wolfe, the hero of Quebec, bears the following inscription:—"Erected by the Honourable East India Company as a grateful testimony to the valour and the eminent services of Captain Edward Cook, commander of His Majesty's ship *Sybille*, who on the 1st March, 1799, after a long and well-contested engagement, captured *La Forte*, a French frigate of very superior force, in the Bay of Bengal, an event not more splendid in its achievement than important in its results to the British trade in India.   He died in consequence of the severe wounds he received in this memorable action, on the 23rd May, 1799, aged 27 years."

successfully, and the *La Forte* was eventually carried safe into port and anchored off Bankshall.* Considering her shattered condition and the unfavourable season, it was very fortunate that she was brought into the river so soon, for it shortly afterwards came on to blow so strong that there is very little doubt but that she would have foundered had she been out at sea. As for the *La Sybille*, her mainyard was fished as I had recommended, and this proved sufficient to bring her up the river, so that if Lieutenant Hardyman had acquiesced in my request, there is no doubt but that he would have overtaken and recaptured my ship.

Proceeding to Calcutta, I only stayed there

* The *Calcutta Gazette* of the 4th of April, 1799, thus reports this occurrence :

"On Tuesday afternoon, the 2nd inst., the public curiosity was gratified by the appearance of the long expected *La Forte*, prize to His Majesty's ship *Sybille*. The salute fired from the battery at Fort William announced her approach, and drew every eye upon her. The numerous boats that attended the splendid trophy, the ruined majesty she displayed as she was seen pulling up the stream (her scanty canvas hardly aiding her tide's way), and spreading her enormous bulk across the river, introduced her to the numerous spectators who impatiently awaited her arrival, with an air of triumph which every British heart seemed to partake of. The three-coloured flag was displayed from the mizen-gaff under the English Jack, and a little after two o'clock she came to an anchor and graced the harbour of Calcutta with her presence. She was soon crowded with visitors, as she has continued to be ever since. When repaired, the *La Forte* will be one of the finest frigates in the British Navy."

It is melancholy to think of the gallant Captain Cook lying on his deathbed close at hand. A long description of his funeral appears in the same journal a few weeks later. The command of the *La Forte* was given to Lieutenant Hardyman, who succeeded Captain Cook when he fell.

sufficiently long to report the capture, the news of which occasioned the greatest possible public rejoicing, and then hurried on immediately to Entally to join my wife. She came running into the verandah to meet me, with our child in her arms. Truly for a ruined man it was a happy reunion, and confirmed by her noble spirit, who, when I broke to her the news that I had lost my all, but yet had escaped with my life and freedom, cried out, with thankful tears in her eyes, " What matters the loss of your fortune, Robert, since you are safe ! " It is such affection and conduct as this that brings sunshine to our darkest hours, and encourages us to rise again when we are cast lowest down.

CHAPTER VIII.

I WAS now too poor a man to be able to remain idle, and I therefore spent only a fortnight with my wife at Entally, and then proceeded to Calcutta in search of employment. While here, I chanced to learn that there was a little brig called the *Harington* for sale, through the death of her owner. I immediately went down to the river to see her, and was vastly taken with her trim and taut appearance, and as I had many friends in the city and considerable credit, I was able to borrow sufficient money to purchase her.

Having obtained a freight for Madras, I left Calcutta towards the end of May, and on the 1st of June (my daughter's birthday) arrived off Fort St. George. Two days afterwards there was a great excitement in Madras on the occasion of the reception of the standards of Tippoo Sultan and the colours of the French Republic, which had been captured a month previously at the storming of Seringapatam by the army under General Harris. The French had formed an alliance with Tippoo, and there were many officers and soldiers of that nation in his service, sent to his assistance by General Malartic, Governor of the Isle of France, and Admiral Serci, who was killed on board the *La Forte*. I heard there were three hundred or more of these Frenchmen taken prisoners, and they were commanded by Citizen Chapuy. They called Tippoo, Citizen Prince Tippoo, and fought under the colours of the French Republic. These men actually formed a Jacobin Club at Seringapatam, and when they hoisted their standard in that capital Tippoo ordered a salute of two thousand cannon, five hundred rockets, and all the musketry, as a mark of the esteem in which he held the alliance with France. These mercenaries never exhibited any gallantry throughout the siege, and at the storming, so soon as Tippoo was killed, retired within the walls of the palace and shut themselves up there till the first burst of violence had passed away. They then asked and obtained quarter. Their appearance, I was told, was exceedingly mean, they being much demoralized by debauchery and riotous living. All of the officers —about thirty in number—bore commissions from the French Government.

Whilst I was at Madras I saw an article which merits particular notice as evincing the extreme and cruel hatred Tippoo bore towards the English. This was a piece of mechanism as large as life, representing a tiger in the very act of devouring a prostrate English officer. Inside the body of the animal was a row of keys of natural notes, acted upon by the rotation of certain machinery, and these produced sounds intended to represent the cries of a person in distress, intermixed with the horrid roar of a tiger. It was, in addition, so contrived that whilst the barbarous music continued to play, the hand of the victim was often lifted up and the head thrown convulsively back, to express the agony of his helpless and deplorable condition. This machine was invented and made under Tippoo's immediate orders and directions, and it was his custom in the afternoon to amuse himself with witnessing the exhibition of this miserable symbolical figure, the tiger being the emblem of his government. The machine was sent to His Majesty the King, and some years afterwards I saw it in the Tower of London.

I heard, from one of the soldiers who had come down with the escort conveying these trophies, an incident of the storming of Seringapatam which is worth recording, as showing the amazing gallantry of an English sergeant. After the breach was made in the walls a forlorn hope was called for, and amongst others who volunteered was a Sergeant Graham, of the Bombay European Regiment. So soon as General Baird, who was in charge of that particular brigade, gave the order to advance, this brave fellow rushed forward in front of his comrades, and mounting the breach, pulled off his hat, and with three cheers called out, "Success to Lieutenant Graham," alluding to the certainty of his being awarded a commission if he survived. But now, anxious to secure himself a still more distinguished honour, he returned to the advancing column, and, by a few words of spirited and soldier-like persuasion, obtained the colours of his regiment from the officer who carried them. With these he rushed to the front again, ascended the ruined breach, and clambering upon the rampart, planted for the first time the British ensign on the walls of Seringapatam, calling out as he did so, "D——n them! I'll show them the British flag!" This act alone, by military usage, entitled him from that instant to the rank of a com-

missioned officer. But just as he had accomplished
the brave deed a shot struck him in the heart,
and he fell dead with the ensign still grasped in
his hand. He left a European widow and five
children.

I remained at Madras for a month, and then
returned to Calcutta, where I was detained until
the month of October by the unusually heavy
south-west monsoon. I then sailed again for
Bombay, and arrived there in December. It so
happened that Captain Malcolm (the same whom
I have mentioned before) was shortly expected at
this place, being ordered on a mission to Persia,
and the Company's frigate *Bombay*, Captain John
Selby, was lying in the harbour ready to convey
him there. But another vessel was also required
for the work, to carry the greater part of the escort,
and I offered the *Harington*, which was taken up
by Government, and sailed in company with the
Bombay on December 29, 1799, for the Persian
Gulf. A few days after leaving Bombay, and
when entering the Gulf of Oman, I encountered
strong contrary winds, and not making any pro-
gress, I thought it prudent to run under the island
of Kishm whilst the *Bombay* went to Muscat to
visit the Imaum of that place, who had formerly
entered into a treaty with Tippoo and the French,
but after the fall of Seringapatam made over-
tures to the Governor of Bombay, and dismissed
the French doctor by whom he had previously
been guided. Captain Malcolm was deputed to

see the Imaum and settle matters with him, and ordered me to proceed to Bushire in advance and await his arrival.

Not knowing Kishm, I cast anchor where the bottom was foul. A large ship was at anchor about six miles beyond me, and it was not long before I perceived a boat from her pulling towards me. This ship proved to be commanded by an officer of the Imaum of Muscat, and that prince himself was on board of her, and had very kindly sent to inform me that the place I was anchored at was not good, and that I had better come closer to him. This I did immediately, and sent an officer to ask when I might have the honour of paying my respects. An audience was fixed for the next morning, when Captain Bailey, of the Bombay Artillery (afterwards General Bailey), accompanied me. On getting on board the *Arab* a salute of three guns was fired, and we were presented to the Imaum, whose name was Syud Sultan. He was a very handsome man, about thirty-six years old, plainly dressed, with sandals and no stockings. I informed him of Captain Malcolm having gone to Muscat with the object of seeing him, and he immediately despatched a person to Ormuz, a large capital town, to give intelligence to Captain Malcolm where he was to be found. There were a great many of the Prince's head men on board, and also his two sons, boys of about nine and twelve years of age. Nothing could exceed the simplicity and courtesy of the Imaum's manner and conduct, considering his position, which was not only that of a ruler over a vast country, but also the highest religious person in it. When we had finished our conversation he invited us to go ashore with him, and on reaching the land he stepped from one thwart of the boats to another, and was the first to touch ground, without military parade of any kind. The people, however, showed him the highest respect, almost amounting to adoration, some of them kissing the hem of his garment. .

The next morning, the wind having changed round, I again made sail for my destination, and safely anchored in the small harbour of Bushire, to await the arrival of Captain Malcolm. On the 1st of February he arrived in the frigate *Bombay*, with his staff, consisting of Captain Campbell, Mr. Strachey, and Dr. Briggs, with several of the Madras Cavalry to be mounted as a guard of honour in Persia. Here he landed and pitched his camp, sending a letter of notification to the Persian king. Having invited me to join him ashore, I experienced his hospitality for a fortnight.

I do not know that I was ever entertained in a more luxurious way than during this period. The camp was pitched a few miles out, on the road to Shiraz, and in the middle of the open country, which in a place where such filthy towns exist as in Persia was a great advantage. The camp equipage was of the most complete description, it being considered necessary to make a great show in dealing with these barbarous people. The anticipated approach of the English ambassador had for some time been the talk of the country, and it was determined that every form of ceremony should be observed. To this end not only was a great state kept up, but endless presents were distributed, in the giving of which Captain Malcolm seemed to take a positive pleasure. Watches, pistols, guns, daggers, spying-glasses, clocks, and the like, were produced and awarded in great numbers, and crowds of Persians of every class flocked round the camp all day long in the hope of coming in for some piece of good fortune.

There was an incident that occurred at this time which I have always remembered. Captain Malcolm had a very handsome black slave as a steward, who had been given him as a great favour by his brother, Sir Pulteney Malcolm, in whose service the man had originally been. This black was celebrated for his enormous strength. One day while we were at dinner he ran in, saying, "You tink me berry strong. But you come see dis Arab man outside." As he was a great favourite, we all got up at once and went outside the tent, and to our great astonishment saw a single Arab walking up with a pipe of wine upon his back. He was stooping down with a half-bent form, and a band round the bottom of the cask and the other end round his forehead. The load must have been at least seven or eight hundredweight.

After staying with Captain Malcolm for a fortnight, by which time my cargo was landed and my charter ended, I took my leave, and sailed to Bussorah, at the top of the Persian Gulf, where I made the acquaintance of Mr. Manisty, the Resident. He lived in a very large house, which was excellently furnished, and more in the Europe style than any I have seen in India. Close at hand was a great range of stabling, and a circus for the exercising of horses, of which he was a great judge, as well as a large dealer, exporting them to India. His house was situated about half a mile from the Euphrates river, and approached by a very nice creek. During my stay I twice accompanied Mr. Manisty on a shooting party, which was always conducted in the most comfortable and satisfactory manner. The previous evening Mr. Manisty would send his servants to the spot he desired to hunt, generally on the opposite side of the river, to pitch his tents and prepare the next day's dinner, which was always the best of its kind. The following morning we started in his beautiful boat, lined with red cloth and well manned. In this we had a fine breakfast, so that on landing we were at once ready to take up the sport of the day, which was generally very good, there being a large quantity of game, and many hogs in the place. The party consisted of Mr. Manisty, his assistant, Mr. Kinloch, who afterwards brought home so large a fortune from Forbes' House, Mr. Milne, the surgeon, since celebrated with the Rajah of Sattara's case, and myself.

Mr. Manisty chartered me to take a cargo of his horses to Bombay. Whilst they were being collected for shipping he recommended a very nice one for myself, I having expressed a wish to purchase one for my wife. He suggested that I should try the paces of this animal, so I rode it out into the desert in company with Captain Bailey and Mr. Kinloch, having an Arab servant in attendance. When at some distance from the town we saw a large flock of sheep, which my companions desired to ride up to, and have some conversation with the shepherds. But to this I strongly objected, not desiring to encounter the barking and annoyance of the shepherds' dogs, who, not liking the European costume, sometimes make sharp attacks upon people wearing it, even to biting the heels of their horses. I felt that my steed's spirit was quite sufficient for me, without this incentive. So I kept apart, and thought the opportunity a good one for trying the qualities of my horse. He was a very spirited animal, and after galloping some way refused to reduce his speed, as I wished him to do, and I very·foolishly dug my heels into him and gave him a sharp cut. Upon this he began to rear, and I pulled the reins at the same time, and over he came upon his back, fortunately without harm to myself. I was so astonished at the suddenness of it all that I forgot to retain hold of the bridle, and while I lay on the ground, a little confused, he, being fretted, set off for the town as quickly as he could gallop. When, after a minute or two, I rose to my legs, judge of my surprise at finding I could see neither horse, nor town, nor any of my party. There was nothing visible but the horizon all round, exactly like being at sea out of sight of land. I did not know what to do, for if I moved I might be walking away from the town. Fortunately the Arab servant observed the horse dashing off without a rider, and, instead of following it, very wisely came the opposite way, and by that means discovered me, and taking me up behind him, we were soon at the gate, where the horse had been stopped. I did not purchase the animal.

Having filled up with a freight of Mr. Manisty's horses, amongst them some very valuable ones, I set sail. Touching at Bushire, I received some specie as freight, and also a fine Persian greyhound, a present from Captain Malcolm to a friend in Calcutta. After leaving this place we encountered the fiercest heat in our passage down the gulf, and were obliged to have the awnings wetted all day long. The horses on board required more than the ordinary allowance of water, and to give them this I put the crew and myself on short allowance, which was almost the first instance in which I had been so reduced. This occasioned a thirst such as I had never before experienced. We had long been out of beer, but one day, thinking I might perhaps find a bottle by looking, I emptied out all the lockers in the great cabin, and to my joy found one half full, which

I at once opened and drank. It was no doubt miserable stuff, but I never relished anything so much. Soon after this we reached Bombay, where I landed my horses in good condition, and obtained a freight to Calcutta.

By the profit of these last four short voyages I was able to pay off all my obligations, and find myself unencumbered with debt, a result I could hardly have hoped to achieve in such a brief period. But freights at that time, owing to the recent vast destruction of shipping during the war, ruled high, and trade was very profitable for those who could supply the markets with the commodities most in demand.

My next voyage was to Penang, where I discharged my cargo, and sailed immediately for the Pedir coast, on the northern part of Sumatra. This was a new and dangerous trade to me, the Malays here being a dangerous set to deal with, instances having often occurred of European vessels being cut off in the roads and their crews put to death. I was anchored off a place called Murdoo, and went ashore daily with one of my sepoys, each of us being armed with a cutlass. Mine was silver-handled and very handsome, and when I used to cross from this town to another about two miles off, I noticed that my weapon attracted the eyes of the natives.

After some parley, I made a good bargain with a native merchant living in a town about nine miles off, and whose character was reputed honest, and whom I was told I might trust. But after having taken my advances, and arranged on a certain date to bring the goods I had purchased, which consisted chiefly of beetlenut, two days beyond the time passed without his presenting himself. Whereupon I went ashore to consult a certain rich merchant from the Coromandal coast, who was established here and whose name was Peer Sahib, and with whom I had enjoyed considerable intercourse. Calling upon him, I mentioned I was disappointed in the man whose character was reputed honest, but who had failed to keep his promise with me, which necessitated my going to find him in his own town. Whereupon Peer Sahib said he was glad I had come to consult him first, as he had that very day learnt something of which he was bound to acquaint me, and had I started without seeing him I should in all probability have lost my life. He began by observing that my silver sword was too rich and handsome to keep me out of danger, but would rather lead me into it, and that it would have been more prudent for me to have armed myself with a ship's iron-handled cutlass, as life was thought too cheap here to prevent its being taken when there was anything to be got for it. He then told me of the following plot which had been concocted against me. The Acheen admiral, with five *praus*, was then lying in the river, and having heard that I had opium on board, and was going to recover my debt from the man who had deceived me, had laid a plan to cut off my ship while I was ashore, and would probably try to do so that very night. The way it was to be done was this, that all should be at anchor near the *Harington*, one of the *praus* being covered with mats, sprinkled with beetlenut on the top, so as to resemble a boat-load (such as I was expecting), but crowded with armed men underneath. That this *prau* was to come alongside as a vessel of the merchant who owed me for the advance, bringing the produce purchased. That having thus dropped into a suitable position, the mats would be suddenly thrown aside, and the *Harington* captured.

It was certainly a clever trick, for nothing could be more plausible or likely to take my men off their guard, although the general dealing at that part was always conducted with the greatest caution, Europeans knowing the danger of the trade, and being prepared to fight at the slightest suspicion. On the *Harington* I had a cannon loaded with grape on each side of the after part of the quarter-deck, muzzles pointed forward, and two sepoy soldiers standing by. Two more stood on each side of the gangway with loaded muskets, and four others were stationed at other parts of the ship, and on the lookout. A very strict watch, with an officer constantly going the rounds, was kept up all night, and never at any time was more than one vessel permitted to lay alongside. In spite of all these precautions we might certainly have been taken in by the trick prepared for me. Of course I thanked Peer Sahib for his most friendly information, and immediately repaired on board my ship to make dispositions in case of attack.

I was determined, however, not to lose my money, and started that afternoon to row up the river to the town where the merchant I was dealing with had gone, but had the good fortune to meet his *prau* bringing the boetlenut for payment before I had rowed two miles, and I escorted it back to the *Harington*, and by nightfall we had the whole aboard. I then weighed anchor and stood out to sea, much to the disappointment of the Acheen admiral, in whose fleet there was a great commotion when they saw what I was doing, whereby it showed that their plot was foiled.

From the Pedir coast I sailed back to Penang, and whilst at this latter place the two annual Macoa ships arrived and departed. Two days after they left, I was privately informed by a merchant of the place that they carried no less than half a million sterling on board for the purpose of buying opium at the Calcutta sales, which they were fearful of losing, having been delayed by bad weather. This information was worth a fortune, and having confidence in the smart sailing qualities of the *Harington*, I determined to follow with all speed, and endeavour to arrive before them.

Fortunately the north-east monsoon immediately broke in with a series of heavy gales, and by carrying on, whilst the great lumbering Portuguese vessels were hove to, afraid to proceed, I overtook and passed them, and reached Calcutta just in time for the sales.

I was the only person in the sale-room who knew the amount of specie the Macoa ships had on board, and that they might be sighted off the sand-heads at any moment, and how anxious they were to catch the sales. This knowledge gave me, I fear, an air of too great confidence, which wrecked my success. For directly the bidding began, I joined in ; whereupon all eyes were turned on me, who was a stranger in that place having never purchased opium before, and it was asked who I was and why I was bidding. Then some one said, " It is Captain Eastwick of the *Harington*, who has just returned from Penang, and consequently knows the latest news from those parts." This at once created a suspicion that I possessed some special information on which I was acting.

. Had I allowed one or two lots to be knocked down at first, without bidding, and so ensured a moderate rate, I might doubtless have bought as much as I could afford later on, and certainly had my share with the parties bidding against me. But I felt so secure in my knowledge of the demand that must presently arise, that I very foolishly showed my intentions at the outset, and offered up to sixteen hundred rupees a chest for that which the previous year fetched only twelve hundred.

At this critical moment a gentleman named Hunter, with whom I had an acquaintance, came up, and catching me by the shoulder, whispered in my ear: "For God's sake take care what you are about ! Do you not know that Laprimandaye ruined himself last year by buying at twelve hundred ? "

This so startled and disconcerted me, that it struck a damp upon my mind, and my courage instantly failed me. It was like baulking a willing horse at a big leap. There only remained at that time two Armenians competing with me, and one of them named Sarkies bid rupees sixteen hundred and five. Whereupon I rose and left the room in a great state of nervousness, willing to go on, yet choked off by the insidious whisper in my ear.

At sixteen hundred and five rupees Sarkies took as many lots as he required, and then the other Armenian, Malcus, took up his biddings, and went on for as much as he wanted. Other native and English merchants, feeling satisfied that there was some cause for this high price, went on when Malcus was finished, and the price was sustained through the whole sales.

As for myself, I never so much as bought a single chest, though I had been the cause of increasing its price by a third, whilst those who speculated cleared large profits, the two Armenians making twenty thousand pounds each within a month, whilst I did not make a sixpence. When the Portuguese ships arrived they had to buy what they wanted at enormous prices. The high stake was too desperate for me, but to the Armenians it made but little consequence, they being very wealthy men, and fond of commercial speculation.

I have often since that day reflected with shame on my timid disposition, that could be frightened by an idle breath into forfeiting such a certain fortune, and leave the reaping of it to men who were bold enough to venture on the mere expression they read on my own face when I began my bidding. But I have always been over-cautious in money matters, knowing what it is to lose hard-earned money, how easily it may be done, and with what toil and trouble retrieved.

About this time my wife, after repeated solicitations, determined to pay a visit to Bombay, where three of her sisters happened to be living. There was no suitable accommodation for her on board the *Harington*, and I therefore sold the ship to Mr. Campbell, and accepted the temporary command of a large Portuguese vessel for the express purpose of giving my family a comfortable passage to Bombay.

The *Harington* was a little craft, but she yielded me a greater profit on my outlay than any vessel I have ever owned. She was a very fast sailer, and would make three voyages while many other ships were completing two. I was grieved to part with her, for I never experienced such an exhilarating feeling as when standing on her deck, with the wind on our quarter, we overhauled and passed ship after ship, as we always did.

My wife and I were very sorry to break up our pretty home at Entally, but her health was not satisfactory, and I thought that a change of residence to Bombay might restore it. We had a fine passage to our destination, and received a warm welcome from my wife's sisters, Mrs. Bellasis, Mrs. Gordon, and Mrs. Watson, who were all living in a large house in Nesbit Lane in the Fort. Captain Bellasis, who belonged to the Bombay army, and was one of the handsomest men in India or elsewhere, showed me the greatest hospitality. He told me that he was at the storming of Seringapatam, and on the day after we had captured the place a most violent storm of thunder and lightning and rain occurred, such as passed description, and continued for some hours. During the height of the storm the lightning frequently struck parts of the city, and two British officers of the Seventy-seventh Regiment were killed, as well as many natives. Captain Bellasis had a marvellous escape of his own life, the lightning striking the exact spot where he was quartered, and killing all his servants, horses and dogs, he himself being so much hurt that it was at first thought he was dead, but after some time he recovered. The natives attributed the storm to the wrath of Heaven, but it is probable it was caused by the heavy firing of the previous day collecting clouds in the sky.

My own stay at Bombay was brief, the calls of my profession taking me back to Calcutta. Shortly after I left, Captain Bellasis was involved in a duel with Mr. Arthur Mitchell, and the latter was shot through the heart and dropped down dead immediately. Captain Bellasis and his second, Captain Byne, were arrested, and a trial ensued, when a verdict of murder was brought against both, and Captain Bellasis sentenced to fourteen years' transportation to Botany Bay. There was very great indignation at this unheard of severity, and a petition was drawn up and signed by every officer in the Bombay army, and sent to His Majesty the King, begging that the prisoner might be pardoned. But meanwhile he, and his second, who was sentenced to seven years, were transported to Botany Bay, and Mrs. Bellasis determined to accompany her husband. All this was so distressing to my wife, that her health gave way, and she was ordered home at once by the medical man, and sailed in the *Skelton Castle*, Captain Isaacs, without my having the chance of seeing her again. She arrived in London at the end of 1801.

As for Captain Bellasis, having reached Port Jackson he was at once emancipated, and appointed to the artillery of the Colonial force,* as

---

* The following are extracts from "The General Standing Orders of New South Wales," a book especially interesting from its being the first ever printed at Sydney :—

"Mr. George Brydges Bellasis is appointed to act as Colonial artillery officer. January 16, 1802."

a lieutenant. In 1803 both officers received His
Majesty's unconditional pardon, without any slur
being left upon their character, and returned to
Bombay, where Captain Bellasis rose, in time, to
command the artillery in the Peishwa's dominions.
His noble wife accompanied him to New Holland,
and returned with him.

At Calcutta I resigned the command of the
Portuguese ship, which was a lubberly craft altogether, but amazing comfortable in the great cabin.
I was then offered the command of the *Betsy* by
my friend Mr. James McTaggart, who was one of
the leading merchants in Calcutta, and to whom I
have been indebted for many a kindness. This I
accepted, and she was chartered by Mr. Basil
Cochrane to take a cargo of rice to Madras. I
also carried three passengers on this trip, of whom
one was a Mr. Haldane, who was, I conceive, the

"H. E. the Governor has been pleased to appoint Mr. George
Brydges Bellasis to a Colonial Commission as Lieutenant of Artillery,
and to rank as such in the Colony, being charged with the inspection
and direction of the batteries and cannon in this settlement, and also as
Commandant of the Governor's Body Guard of Cavalry. October 14.
1802."

Not bad as the commencement of a convict career! Six months
later the following appears:—

"June 5, 1803. Sydney Cove. The Royal Standard having been
hoisted for the first time in this territory, on the anniversary of His
Majesty's birth, His Excellency is pleased to extend the Royal Grace
and free pardon to Colonial Lieutenant of Artillery and Engineer
George Brydges Bellasis. By command of His Excellency. W. N.
Chapman, Secretary."

In the severe verdict recorded and sentence suffered, Captain
Bellasis seems to have been made a scapegoat for the sin of duelling
so common at that period.

greatest epicure in India. When we landed he requested me to order a good dinner at one of the taverns, which I did to the best of my ability. Never shall I forget the horror and disgust he evinced when he joined us at the table, owing to the manner and style in which the meal had been served up. Without tasting a morsel, though there were some excellent dishes prepared, he laid down his knife and fork, and putting up his hands with an air of appalling solemnity, ejaculated, " My God! that I should be brought to this!" He then instantly left the place, and went to the house of a Mr. Kenworthy, whom he had not seen since they came out to India, thirty years before. With this gentleman he remained two months, and, as I learnt afterwards, died of a surfeit on his passage back to Calcutta. He was a kind, warmhearted man, and a commercial resident in two places, with an income of Rs.10,000 per mensem. I only mention this anecdote to show the evil of giving way to the unrestrained indulgence of the appetite.

From Madras I proceeded to Bombay, where I first learnt of my wife's departure for Europe, which was a great disappointment to me, for I had fully reckoned on seeing her. The letters acquainting me of her sudden intended departure went by a direct ship to Calcutta, and consequently missed me.

After having discharged my cargo at Bombay and shipped part of another for the return voyage,

Governor Jonathan Duncan sent for me, and said he wanted my ship to sail immediately on a short expedition. This was to take troops to Demaun in company with the frigate *Cornwallis*, Captain McKellar, there having arisen the necessity of making an exhibition of our power there. I consented to this proposal, but without coming to any terms, supposing they would be made by Captain Anderson, the Superintendent of Marine. In the course of the day a note was handed me, informing me that I was not to do anything without written orders from Government, which would be sent me in due time. I had a long-standing engagement to dinner that night with Mr. Fawcett; who had invited me to meet General Bellasis, a connection of Captain Bellasis, and a party of friends, previous to my sailing to Calcutta (as had been intended) the next day. I now begged to be excused, but Mr. Fawcett would accept no denial, saying he would have a *peon* in waiting to bring any Government order that might arrive. I therefore went to the dinner, and no message from Mr. Duncan being brought me by midnight, I concluded there was no chance of my being required till the next day, and consequently slept at my brother-in-law's, Colonel Gordon's, house. Very early in the morning I was awoke by a servant, who gave me a letter from my chief mate informing me that the troops had been sent on board the previous evening, and that on refusing to sail without me, Captain McKellar, of the

Cornwallis, had ordered one of his officers on board to take charge of the *Betsy*, and had got under weigh and sailed.

This proceeding I could not understand, but I rose and went immediately to Government House. Mr. Duncan was in bed and asleep, and no one dared disturb him ; but the case was too important for me to desist, and he was awakened and came out in his dressing-gown to see what was wanted.

I told him Captain McKellar had run away with my ship.

"And what is the reason you were not on board her ? " he asked very sharply.

"Your own letter, sir," I replied. "Here it is," and I handed him the one in which he wrote and told me I was not to do anything without written orders from Government. "I have received no written orders, nor has my chief officer, but only verbal ones from Captain McKellar, whose authority I refuse to recognize."

Mr. Duncan read the letter, and then admitted the propriety of my conduct in causing him to be awakened, for, when he first came out to see me, he was very angry at being disturbed.

He then considered for a short time, and said that, saving for the treatment I had received, he was not sorry that this had occurred, because he had a squadron of Arab dhows with a number of troops on board, intended to join those that had gone on in the *Cornwallis* and my ship, but that he had no marine officer to send, and begged I would take charge of them until I should reach Demaun and regain my own ship.

I said I was ready to go at once, upon which he replied he was very glad to observe my promptitude, as despatch was everything, and I must immediately go on board and sail, and even though wind and tide might be against me, I was positively not to drop an anchor until I reached my port. At this moment Major Broughton, the commander of the troops, came into the room to inquire for orders, stating that all the soldiers had been embarked. "This is Admiral of the Fleet Eastwick," said the Governor, with a laugh, "He is in charge of your squadron, and is going on board immediately; follow him!" And so without even a change of clothing I went direct from Government House to the harbour, and within an hour had weighed anchor and was standing out to sea.

I made a quick passage to Demaun, keeping close in shore and getting the full benefit of the land breeze. When I arrived there I found, to my great surprise, no other ships in the harbour, and it was not until the next morning that the *Cornwallis* and *Betsy* came in. I instantly repaired on board the frigate to say I was ready to take command of my ship. An officer went to tell Captain McKellar, and after waiting about twenty minutes, the great man came on deck. I was standing close by when he turned round and asked the officer, " Where is the man ? "

"If you mean the captain of the ship you took away without his leave, I am that person," I said. "I left Bombay in these Arab dhows a day after you, and I got here a day before you."

He could hardly believe that I was actually the same who had been left behind in Bombay, and the fact of my having outsailed him, when the matter was one of such urgency, was a rebuff to him in front of his officers. He grew very red in the face, and asked me what was the reason I was not on board my ship when she put to sea.

I replied it was from the simple fact that I did not consider the charter completed till Government had come to terms, which had not been done. And furthermore, because of a letter from Governor Duncan, in which he told me I was not to sail without further written orders, and these I had never received.

"I don't understand these things from the master of a merchant ship," replied Captain McKellar, in a high tone, "and I shall not let you resume charge."

At this I was very indignant, and felt inclined to express myself strongly; but remembering the respect due to the quarter-deck of one of His Majesty's frigates, I restrained my wrath, and simply answered, "Very good, sir. I shall return at once to Bombay, first going ashore to send you my written protest, and to throw the ship and cargo on you and your Government's responsibility."

Hearing which he changed colour again, and would have spoken; but I would not remain to listen, and immediately left the ship and rowed ashore. Just as I sat down to write my formal protest a lieutenant arrived, who had been sent after me by Captain McKellar, to request me to take charge of the *Betsy*. This, after some parley, with explanations and apology, I consented to do. The next day I sailed to Diu, and there being no further need of my services, I was sent back to Bombay, where I reported the whole matter to the Governor. In the end, I not only received my freight at the highest rate payable, but was honoured with the thanks of Government for the fast voyage I had made in the Arab dhows, and thus I gained a complete advantage over Captain McKellar.

This officer arrived at Bombay a few days afterwards, and resumed charge of his own ship, the *Terpsichore*, a small frigate. The same evening Colonel Gordon gave a large ball, to which all the captains and officers of the men-of-war in the harbour were invited excepting Captain McKellar. He was told the reason of this slight was his conduct to me, which greatly mortified him. He was a most tyrannical man on board his own ship. A few days after this he sailed for Madras, and during the voyage it came on to blow hard, and it was necessary to take a reef in the topsails. But in doing this he ordered his first lieutenant, for no reason whatever except to assert his authority, only to lower the yards down sufficiently to have it done. The lieutenant, a fine, dashing young man, and a *protégé* of Lord St. Vincent (then First Lord of the Admiralty), remonstrated against the danger of having so many men on the yard without being supported by the lifts. A short altercation ensued, which ended in the lieutenant being ordered to his cabin under arrest. The danger he had apprehended took place, the tie breaking and the yard coming down with a jerk on the cap, by which two men were thrown off and one drowned. The next morning the lieutenant was ordered to resume duty, but he refused until he had been tried by court martial, which took place at Madras. Captain McKellar was broke and sent home to England, but the Duke of York, who had raised him, got him reinstated after great delay, and put on the bottom of the list. This was more than he deserved.

From Bombay I sailed to Madras, where I was charted by the house of Harington and Company to proceed to Port Jackson in New Holland, near to the recently established penal settlement of Botany Bay.

CHAPTER IX.

THE voyage to New Holland I was now about
to undertake was to a country quite new to me.
Nothing of moment occurred on the way, except
the discovery of an unmapped rock off Wilson's
promontory in our passage through Bass's Straits,
upon which we narrowly escaped striking. When

SYDNEY COVE, NEW HOLLAND.

From a plate in " An Historical Account of New South Wales.")

nearing Botany Bay, my first officer, Mr. Jones, who had been here before, was deceived by the appearance of a fine harbour, and declared it was Port Jackson, which he said he knew very well. I consequently stood in, but the soundings being shallow, I soon felt sure he was wrong, and came to an anchor at nightfall. It was lucky I did so, for Mr. Jones proved to be quite mistaken. The next morning we sailed to seaward again, with a fine land wind, and in the course of the day made Port Jackson, which was quite near at hand and easily distinguishable by a lighthouse and two headlands. Being much annoyed at Mr. Jones's error, I stopped his further advice. We soon got a pilot, and sailed up Sydney Cove, and found ourselves in one of the finest harbours in the world.

Having entered my ship and cargo, I was called upon by Mr. Lord, a merchant of the place, who offered me his assistance to dispose of my goods. This I accepted, and a most excellent honest man I found him to be. The settlement was in want of almost everything I had on board, but two ships were daily expected from Calcutta—one the *Buffalo*, commanded by a captain in the navy, and which had been sent to Bengal for Government supplies; the other my old brig the *Harington*, which I had sold to Captain Campbell, who now commanded her. The Government or the *Buffalo* had between them the majority of the settlement in their debt for former supplies, and the house of Campbell had almost all the remainder.

On account of these liabilities, I soon found that the people were restrained from making large purchases from me, for fear of bringing the law upon them for what they owed; for everything purchased from the *Betsy* was so much against the *Buffalo* or the *Harington*. This obliged me to act with the greatest caution, not only in regard to whom I trusted, but how I made my sales. The consequence was that when I came to dispose of my cargo, which consisted of India produce, tea and sugar, I passed a most anxious time. In order to facilitate trade I gave three public entertainments in the colony, which procured me considerable *éclat*, and enabled me to make the personal acquaintance of the people most likely to deal. But unfortunately many of these were also officials in the place, all of whom were interested in business in addition to their duties as Government servants, and they endeavoured to presume on their power as the latter, and this led to one or two pretty quarrels.

For instance there was a Mr. Jamieson, who was senior surgeon there, and in charge of the medical department, and was also an extensive merchant. Shortly after I had commenced business, he purchased a large quantity of goods from me at agreed prices. But some days afterwards, when the *Harington* arrived from India, and made a great bustle in the market rates previously ruling, Mr. Jamieson wished to cancel a great portion of his purchase. This, of course, I declined to agree to, and the matter was taken into court. I pleaded my own case, and notwithstanding that the judge was in league with his medical friend, I gained my cause.

Amongst other things, it was the custom in this young colony to pass a simple I. O. U. for payment of what was purchased. This was considered quite valid, and on leaving the settlement it was only necessary to present all these notes to the different individuals, and they were obliged to take them up, either by payment, or by giving Government bills. In accordance with this recognized custom, I sold a large quantity of goods to Mr. Palmer, the commissary, who, although a very needy man, was yet most extravagant and reckless in his dealings, besides being deep sunk in debt. He purchased two thousand pounds' worth of merchandise from me, in order to sell again, giving me his I. O. U. for the amount. But when it came to settling, he proposed to pay me with his private bills on England, which, considering the distance of that country and the state of his credit in the colony, was very much the same as not paying me at all. I refused altogether to accept anything but a legal tender, and claimed to be paid the amount either in money or in Government bills. We had a suit about it, and it was decided in my favour. Whereupon Mr. Palmer thought to frighten me by appealing to the judgment of the Governor. But whilst describing himself in the preamble as John

Palmer, Esquire, Commissary, in the body of this precious document he came to be Mr. John Palmer, Merchant.

The Governor, Captain King, a most just and worthy man, on perusing this strange appeal, sent for us both, and addressing Mr. Palmer, said: "I am going to speak to you as a private friend; I advise you to withdraw this appeal. For, as Governor, it is impossible for me to receive it, seeing it is presented by you in two characters. You must either sue in one or the other. And if you finally elect to appeal as Mr. John Palmer, Merchant, you can no longer hold the appointment of Commissary of this colony."

Mr. Palmer at once withdrew his appeal, and I received my money in Government bills, he mortgaging the whole of the goods in order to make up the amount.

These circumstances (two only out of a great many) will serve to show how much I had to contend against, and how difficult are the conditions of conducting business amongst young communities before they have learnt to be guide by established commercial customs.

An incident happened to me at Port Jackson which is, I think, worth relating. I was ashore one day at Mr. Lord's store, when a very pretty young woman entered. She was dressed extremely neat, though in the fashion of a servant, but she appeared both from her manner and speech to be of gentle birth and good education.

Her age was about twenty-four, and I seldom remember to have seen so fine a complexion and such handsome eyes and features as she possessed. Approaching me without any diffidence, she informed me that she was maid to the judge's lady, and had been sent to purchase some article for her mistress. I desired her to wait, till some-one should arrive to serve her, there being no one in the store at the time. Whereupon she at once took a seat, and after a moment's hesitation asked me if I had recently been in India.

I replied that I had just come from that country.

Hearing which she evinced considerable agitation, and then inquired, "Do you know a gentleman named M——?"

I reflected a moment, and answered her that I was acquainted with two gentlemen of that name.

"The one I mean," she cried," "is very tall, and with blue eyes like—like my own, I think. He is an officer in the Madras army, and about twenty-six years old."

"Then, madam," I replied, "I know him well. And indeed I met him at Fort St. George, after his return from the siege of Seringapatam, no longer back than last year!"

"Did you? did you?" she exclaimed in great excitement, rising from her chair, and in her agitation coming close to me and clasping her hands. "Oh, sir, tell me all about him. Is he well? Is he happy?"

" He was both well and happy when I last saw him," I assured her. "But why do you ask? "

" Because I am his sister! Because I would give twenty years of my life to see him once again! " she answered, to my great surprise, since the gentleman she alluded to was of considerable position, whilst she from her condition could only be a convict. " Oh, sir," she added, with tears in her eyes, " you have made me so happy to hear that he is alive and well. He is my dear brother, though I am no longer worthy to claim relationship with him."

Then of her own accord she explained to me that, although of good family, she had fallen into the crime of theft in London, and had been unhappily, although, as she allowed, properly, punished by transportation. Her offence was that of shoplifting, being urged thereto by some species of madness which she could not explain, since she had never wanted for anything, being a lady of good family. Having been caught in the act of secreting some article in a silk-mercer's shop, she was apprehended on the spot, and had given a false name, under which she was convicted and sentenced, so that none of her friends knew of her disgrace or where she was. She assured me I was the first person living to whom she had confessed her secret, being surprised into doing so upon my mentioning my acquaintance with her brother. She begged me if ever I met him to inform him of her condition, so that he might know she was alive and well, and to tell him that though she could never hope to see him again, she retained in her heart an affectionate memory of him.

Strangely enough, fifteen years afterwards I did meet her brother at Cheltenham, and gave him his sister's message. He was astonished beyond words, and said that after her sudden disappearance his family had mourned her as dead, if not worse; so that he could hardly credit my statement, until it was confirmed to him by two or three other particulars I was able to mention. He was retired from the army and enjoyed independent means, and he immediately set to work to procure his sister's return to England. But in the meantime she had married in the colony, and risen to a very respectable station, and declined to leave it. She made me promise that I would never disclose her real name to any person other than her brother, and this request I have scrupulously respected, and do so now.

Whilst I was at Port Jackson I had great difficulty with my officers. Before my arrival there I addressed the four of them, and warned them to beware of the expenses and allurements of the place, and offered, notwithstanding that they were in debt to the ship, to advance them two months' pay each to spend at the place, so that they might pay for what they wanted and avoid going into debt. But I warned them that if they did incur liabilities they must take the consequences, as I should then leave them behind. They all declared there was no fear of this, and appeared very grateful for my kindness.

But soon after we were established at Sydney, I noticed, in my daily visits, such extravagances that I could not help reminding them of what I had said. Constantly I observed quarters of mutton, which cost at that time two-and-sixpence a pound, and other luxuries that I did not even see at the Governor's table. At the end of eight weeks Jones, the chief mate, came to me, with great lamentation, for a hundred pounds, as he was threatened by one of his creditors, who at first had persuaded him to buy, and now showed his true colours. " You have only yourself to blame ; " I told him, " I have nothing to say. You must take the consequences." I had heard that he had not been quite correct about the cargo. He was taken to jail. The following week the same application from the second mate. The same result to him. The week after, the third. The same again. I was now left with the fourth mate, a youngster who knew nothing. He was the son of a general officer on the Madras establishment. He had parted with a diamond ring and other things, and these I redeemed. It was with the greatest difficulty that I afterwards recovered payment from his friends.

Another incident which occurred during my stay in the colony will serve to illustrate the barbarous customs of the blacks of New Holland. While I was at Sydney, one of the natives, having climbed a tree, fell and broke his thigh. His companions, after a very brief examination, pronounced him incurable, and then, shocking to relate, collected a great heap of dry grass and wood, and surrounding him with it, set it on fire and burnt him to death, considering it to be an act of mercy to terminate his sufferings.

Whilst I was at Sydney two men were found guilty of robbery and condemned to be executed. They were convicts, and in order that their fellow-convicts might be warned by their example, a large company of them were drawn up at the place of execution. The two condemned men, with their coffins, were brought to the place. The warrant was read, and every appearance observed that could give solemnity to the scene, and impress the minds of the spectators with awe. Then the executioner stepped forward and put the rope about the necks of the poor wretches, and the next moment every one expected to see them dangling in the air. But now came a great surprise. The Provost-marshal held up his hand, and at the same time unexpectedly produced their pardons from his pocket. One of the men seemed much affected, but the other afforded a novel case in the history of grievances. For so far from exhibiting gratitude and thankfulness at his reprieve, he actually began to lament the circumstance, giving as a reason that he could never hope again to be so well prepared for death as on that occasion, and that he was convinced in sparing his life he had been robbed of enjoying the certain blessing of going to heaven!

I have mentioned that my old brig the *Harington* arrived here a short time after the *Betsy*, and that she was commanded by Captain Campbell to whom I had sold her, and who was a friend of mine. He ran her for some years in the trade, and must have made her value several times over, for he had established a mercantile house in the settlement, and did a large business. But about five years after this he lost his vessel by a most extraordinary outrage, the details of which I heard from his own lips when I met him in Madras in 1808. It seems he had brought out a freight of Indian goods, and had anchored the ship in a place called Farm Cove, just opposite to the house he had engaged for himself whilst he was on shore. One morning on waking up he discovered that the *Harington* had mysteriously disappeared. He at once went to the Governor and reported the strange loss, and orders were instantly issued for a muster to be taken of the convicts to see if any had escaped. It was found that a man named Stewart and several others were missing. Upon further inquiry it appeared that a brig had been seen at daylight from the South Head, standing out to sea, from which joint circumstances no further doubt could be entertained but that the *Harington* had been piratically seized and run off with by a body of convict desperadoes. A small vessel called the *Halcyon* was at once manned, soldiers placed on board of her, and

despatched in pursuit, together with a large number
of rowing boats, with military parties in them
which towed the *Halcyon* out.   Unfortunately
there was a dead calm off shore, and the ship
could make no way, and at nightfall (the
Harington having been out of sight for many hours)
they all put back.   The next day Captain Campbell's
chief officer, Mr. Fisk, and several of the crew of
the *Harington* arrived in two boats, after having
spent a most arduous night at sea.   Mr. Fisk
reported that about ten o'clock on the night of
the capture, it being Sunday, whilst the brig was
lying at two anchors, and the ship's company
in bed within the steerage, he was suddenly
awakened in his cabin by two ruffians at his bedside, one of whom held a loaded pistol at his
head and commanded him to be silent on pain of
instant death.   Others of the desperadoes proceeded
in the same manner to the steerage and overpowered
the crew, and all the ship's company were presently
put into confinement.   The villains, who were very
numerous, then cut away both anchors, and towed
the vessel out, and making sail steered to the eastward.   The next afternoon, when upwards of twenty
miles from land, they ordered Mr. Fisk and the
crew on deck, one by one, in which order they were
sent into two boats and cut adrift from the ship.
The *Harington* was fully provided for a long voyage,
for when she was run off with, Captain Campbell
was on the point of sailing for the Feejees, and
had provided all necessaries for several months.

A ship called the *Pegasus* was at once prepared for pursuit, and twenty soldiers put on board her, and she sailed carrying Captain Campbell, Mr. Fisk, and the *Harington's* crew. As the felons on board the *Harington* had neither anchors, boats, nor timepieces on board, it was apprehended that to procure them they would commit some fresh enormity, and might probably first sail for the Bay of Islands, and attempt the seizure of the American brig *Eliza*, that had cleared for there the previous week, carrying also, as was generally known, a considerable amount of specie on board. The *Pegasus* was absent for over two months, but discovered no signs of the runaways, and suffered great hardships in addition, from their water and supplies running short before they returned to Sydney. It was not till the following year that the *Harington* was captured. She had made her way to Manilla, when an English frigate fell in with her, and the signals not being properly responded to, a boat was sent on board the *Harington*, and, discovering her piratical nature, took charge of her. But a few days afterwards the brig was wrecked, and the convicts, who had been left on board, again escaped. Their ringleader Stewart had, however, been taken to the frigate, and he was carried to Calcutta and lodged in jail there.

Towards the end of my stay at Sydney, the Croppies, who had been sent out for complicity in the Irish rebellion of 1798, and who belonged to all ranks of society, rose in mutiny one night in the hope of overcoming the colony and gaining their freedom and independence. Hitherto these misguided men had behaved very well. In fact from the time they had surrendered in Ireland, on condition of their lives being spared, they had appeared reconciled to their fate. I had heard a good deal about them from my friend Captain Reid of the *Friendship*, when I met him in Calcutta before this voyage. He had been chartered to convey these United Irishmen (as they called themselves) to Botany Bay from Waterford, and declared that their demeanour on board had been very much to their credit, so that during the whole passage he had no occasion to punish any one; in a word, that such as were before gentlemen, however mistaken and misled, supported by their behaviour on board their claim to that character. In the colony they had been treated with as much consideration as the law allowed, but in spite of this began after a time to find their position intolerable.

They had, moreover, got a fixed idea into their heads that on the other side of the Blue Mountains, which are a little way from Sydney, there was a settlement of white people, and several of them had been so deluded as to concert means for reaching it. Two or three parties had absconded a few months before the time of this outbreak, of whom the greater portion had gone in quest of this imaginary settlement, and many had been starved in the bush after trying to prolong a miserable existence by eating grass. Others had been killed

by the blacks, whilst two at least were known to
have joined the natives to live with them. One
party had returned to the sea-coast, and under
cover of night cut out the schooner *Norfolk*, and
sailed her out to sea, but being followed and
captured were all hung for pirates—to such an
end had their mad and unconsidered undertakings
carried them. But the fate of these adventurers
was no warning to those left behind. The idea
of the white settlement was unshaken, and they
determined to reach it and be free.

It was to achieve this end that they laid a well-
concerted plan by which they obtained possession
of a large quantity of arms, some of which had
been hidden for many weeks, and having chosen
leaders of their own and formed a design of attack,
they collected together one night to the number
of at least a thousand, in formidable resistance to
the authority of the Government.

I was awakened at midnight by the firing of
guns and beating of drums, and could not imagine
what had occurred. Hastily dressing myself, I
sallied out into the street, and was informed by
several people, whose faces were white and scared,
that the convicts were up, and in possession of a
portion of the town. I immediately proceeded on
board the *Betsy*, whose crew I armed, and caused
her guns to be loaded with grape, and gave orders
for a strict watch to be kept, and every precaution
taken to meet and repel an attack. There were
eight soldiers on board, and four of these I left in

charge of the ship, and returned with the other four to my house on shore, to protect a sum of eight thousand dollars that was deposited there. From thence I went on to Government House to learn the cause of the *emeute*, but found that Captain King had gone to Paramatta, having heard that there was a general rising there. His lady, Mrs. King, was relieved to see me, being greatly alarmed at the state of affairs, and begged me to escort her to the Deputy-Governor, Colonel Patterson, which I did, and placed her in safety under his roof, where there was military protection.

I then went back to the jail-house, where the troops were collected. Here I learnt that a large party of prisoners had organized a plan for a general rising throughout the country, so secret that it was quite unknown to any one but themselves. They were to be divided into three parties, and take away the arms from every house, and this night had been pitched upon for them to meet at a given point. One of these parties, led by a stonemason, had to pass one of the quarries in which he was accustomed to work, but it was so dark he lost his way, and not joining the other two at the appointed time, it was thought that their plot was discovered, and many of the convicts dispersed. Major Johnson, who had left Sydney with a hundred soldiers on hearing of the outbreak, met this body under the stonemason, about three hundred in number, and began to parley with them. The stonemason came out to meet Major Johnson to tell his grievance, but was most insolent in his behaviour, and this so aroused the Scotch blood of the officer that he drew his sword and cut him down. The rebels immediately fired, and their fire was returned by the soldiers, and this had aroused the whole town. In a very short time the convicts were routed, and the soldiers, re-forming, marched back to Sydney to protect the town, it being too dark to follow the fugitives. When morning broke the troops searched the place, and took many of the convicts into custody, and before sunset fifteen of the most prominent were brought to a drumhead court-martial and forthwith hung, without benefit of clergy, as an example to the rest.

Soon after this incident I finished my business in this improving colony, and left it, much pleased with the society and the climate, which is, I think, one of the finest in the world. The colonists, in general, appeared to be well reconciled to their situation, and a proof that their minds were not very ill at ease is afforded by the fact that they had a theatre, and, under the patronage of Governor King, gave several representations during the time I was there, all very tolerably acted. Amongst other plays I remember witnessing Farquhar's comedy of *The Recruiting Officer*, and the entertainment of *The Virgin Unmasked*, both affording very excellent amusement.

Having declared my intention of returning to India by the Eastern passage, Governor King chartered me to convey to Norfolk Island a number

of the prisoners implicated in the late insurrection.
As chief mate I engaged, just previous to sailing,
Mr. Lodge.   He was one of the officers of the
Investigator, king's ship, which had been recently
condemned as unseaworthy, and he gladly accepted
the post of mate on the *Betsy*.   As second mate
I secured another man, but he proved an infirm
fellow, addicted to drink.

Upon reaching Norfolk Island I hove the *Betsy*
to, there being no anchorage at this place, and
rowed ashore to call upon Colonel Fovaux, the
Governor, report our arrival and deliver to him
letters from Port Jackson.   After reading these he
invited me to stop with him, and the next morning
asked me to accompany him down to the beach to
see the disembarkation of the prisoners.

Signals having been made to the *Betsy*, the ship
stood in close to land, and the convicts were sent
ashore in boats, each of which also carried a
certain amount of cargo.   This cargo the prisoners
were ordered to convey through the surf, and then
load upon trucks and wheel to the warehouses.
The task was a humiliating one, and I felt sorry
for the poor prisoners, who had suffered so much
from confinement during the voyage that many of
them were totally unfit for the work.

Amongst them was General Holt, a fine handsome gentleman both in appearance and demeanour.   He had been a famous rebel leader in
the mountains of Wexford and Wicklow, and
though only the son of a farmer, gathered around

him a thousand men, and established himself as their chieftain. He and another, whose name I have forgotten, were known as " The Babes in the Wood," from the fact of their strongholds being in a forest, in which they could never be found, and whence from time to time they made daring raids into the surrounding country. Dwyer, who was afterwards High Constable of Sydney, was for some time a member of Holt's band. Finding at last that the French invasion of Ireland, on which they counted greatly, had failed, after the suicide of his friend Wolfe Tone, who was taken on board the *Hoche*, French frigate, Holt, who was very hard pressed by the Government troops and on whose head a reward was set, surrendered on condition of his life being spared, and was in due course transported to Sydney, being the last rebel leader out. Here, owing to his good conduct, Governor King emancipated him, and made him free in this foreign land, but not to leave it. When the insurrection of convicts occurred, he was considered to be implicated in it—more, I believe, on suspicion than on proof—and was consequently tried and judged guilty, and condemned to transportation from Botany Bay to Norfolk Island, and sent thither in my ship.

At this place he was very finely dressed on landing, in a new blue coat with a black velvet collar, like a gentleman should be—which he was, every inch of him—and he sat with dignity in the stern-sheets. On the shore was a large truck waiting, with fourteen prisoners to drag it, who had been landed just previously, and amongst them Captain the Honourable St. Ledger, and some others who had been men of fortune in Ireland. The jailor, standing by them, perceived General Holt in the stern-sheets of the approaching boat, and called out to the coxswain to ask who he was. " General Holt," came the reply. Then the uncouth man cried out, " D—— the General. Let Holt assist to unload the boat; put the biggest bag of sugar on his back, for he appears a big man in his own estimation." This was done, and the General, all in his fine clothes, laden like a common felon, was forced to wade a long way through the water, the boat from its drought being unable to come close to the landing-place.

It was a sorry sight to see so gallant a gentleman submit himself to these vulgar people in authority, and with a silent dignity obey the orders given him. For, after all, he, and many other of the prisoners were gentlemen by birth—such as Counsellor Sutton, Dr. McCullom, Mr. Brannan, who had held the situation of High Sheriff of the County of Wexford, and Mr. Lysight, a man of considerable property in Ireland, supposed to be near two thousand pounds a year, and all forfeited to the Crown. They were persons of refinement, whose only crime was a love of their native island and a desire for its freedom; had they been Englishmen, this would have been highly esteemed. Nevertheless for this feeling, which I hold would do any patriotic person positive credit, they were condemned to transportation and treated as common criminals. I had been in daily contact with them for the last fortnight (for I had berthed them aft in my cabin instead of with the common prisoners between decks), and I never heard any sentiment pass their lips except such as I could commend. They spoke of their wrongs and their disappointed hopes with resignation, but with an amazing eloquence that forced from me the tribute of sincere pity.

The next morning, whilst I was breakfasting with Colonel Fovaux, a petition was sent in from General Holt, in which he begged that he might be put to some less menial and degrading servitude than that assigned to him. I was so struck with pity for his fate, that I could not resist adding my appeal on his behalf, bearing testimony to his admirable conduct during the passage from Port Jackson. Colonel Fovaux was a very strict disciplinarian, and rather resented my interference at first, but it ended, I am glad to say, in poor Holt's petition being granted. Having learnt that I had exerted myself on his behalf, he took an opportunity of thanking me before I left; upon which I told him that what I had done had been dictated by the commonest instinct of humanity, and my regret was that I could not assist him more. I was glad to hear that about twelve years afterwards, having behaved very well in New Holland, he was permitted to return to his native country, and lived there to a good old age.

I stayed a week at Norfolk Island, and I cannot leave it without mentioning the beauties it possessed in all the varieties of the picturesque, both in hill and dale. From sea-line to summit it was covered with verdure and fertility, whilst the climate was exquisite. The waters abounded in fish of the most delicious kinds, especially eels, and the only drawback that detracted from the universal merits of the place was its want of anchorage. The island was one of the most plaguey difficult places to land at that I have ever come across, there being only three spots where a boat could make the shore, and these only during certain favourable winds and in fine weather; and it was not safe for vessels to cast anchor, so that all the time the *Betsy* was there, she was in charge of a pilot who kept her continually, on and off, under sail.

CHAPTER X.

IT was in July, the winter season in those lati- tudes, that I left Norfolk Island and returned to Calcutta. The voyage back to India was as new to me as the one out had been, for I sailed by the Eastern passage, and the navigation required the greatest care and attention on my part. We passed close to New Caledonia, and then sailing up the Sea of Albion, endeavoured to make the passage between New Britain and Ireland. It was here, whilst I was engaged in taking lunar observations, that one of my quartermasters called out to me to see the quantity of fish, and I found we were passing through a vast shoal. In less than a quarter of an hour we had fifty of them lying on deck, each about the size of a cod. Rocks were now seen under the bottom, the water being very clear and transparent, and appeared so close that I feared the ship must strike, but on heaving the lead I found ten fathoms. My chart being a very bad one I did not like my position, and went up aloft to direct the steerage ; but the wind falling and the ship making little way, I wore round and went back the way we entered, and then stood south-west. The next day we passed another unknown rock, like a boat bottom upwards, and the same night entered and passed safely through Dampier Strait.

After this, fair winds carried us along at an amazing rate through the Straits of Malacca, and my voyage from Norfolk Island to Poulo Penang, though a very intricate one, was the quickest ever made, averaging six knots an hour the whole way. At Penang I took on board Mr. Harington, of the house of Harington and Company at Madras, and in September, 1803, I arrived off the Sandheads.

Here I found a letter awaiting me from Mr. Mc'Taggart, to say that he had a most excellent offer of a Government freight to Penang, but he feared it was impossible for me to get the ship up to Calcutta and load in time to sail on the day required. My answer was to send me down some tow-boats and some small anchors, and I promised to be ready. And I kept my promise.

I have already mentioned Mr. Lodge, my first officer, whom I took from the *Investigator* at Sydney. He proved to be one of the best I had ever seen in all the duties of his station, but nevertheless the most extraordinary. He drank a bottle of brandy every day, besides wine and beer, but it had no effect upon him, and his appetite in eating was the most voracious of any man I ever met. He was not very tall, but extremely stout, and such a man at this season of the year in Bengal, where he had never been before, could not be exposed to the sun without the greatest danger. I therefore sent him to his cabin while we were working up the river, and took his duty. I was fortunate in getting to our moorings before I expected, it being about two o'clock, and the heat most fierce. I then called Mr. Lodge, and told him I must immediately go ashore and enter the ship, and I desired he would not expose himself, but see that the men attended to the pilot's orders to place the vessel in safety. Having finished all I had to do on shore, I went to dine with Mr. Harington at half-past seven, and just as

I was sitting down a note was put into my hands begging me to send a doctor, as Mr. Lodge was dangerously ill. He died before a medical man could see him, being struck with apoplexy. His blood and body were in such a state that he could not be kept beyond the time requisite to get a shell to put him in; the heat was too great, the fever burnt him up. It was a sad spectacle to see such a man end his life in this way.

Having loaded with the Government cargo for Penang, I cleared on the day necessary, much to Mr. McTaggart's satisfaction. At Penang I freighted again with Eastern produce for China. We had a slow voyage, the ship's bottom being very foul, and it was not until the autumn of 1804 that I reached the Sandheads again.

Here we took a pilot on board, who carried us up to Saugor, where we were obliged to anchor, as the wind failed us. I noticed the pilot had brought on board with him a very pretty little native girl of about ten years of age, and I asked him who she was, and he told me the following story. He said that he was constantly ashore at this place, and that there was a custom of the inhabitants here which shocked him very much. This was their method of sacrificing human life. Only a short time previously a young man, whose father was dangerously ill, had made a vow that he would sacrifice himself to the sharks if his father recovered. The old man did so, and the son determined to fulfil his promise; but going into the sea his heart failed him, and he endeavoured to return, but was seized and devoured before he was able to get out. The pilot had himself witnessed this incident. Shortly afterwards his attention was attracted by the young girl whom he had brought on board, and who was crying very much, because, her father being ill, she had been forced to make a vow that if he recovered she too would give herself to the sharks. The pilot, a most humane, kind-hearted man, with children of his own, was so affected by her piteous grief that he offered a considerable sum to buy her, and so save her life, and this the cupidity of her mother could not resist, and so he got the girl. She was very pretty and gentle in her manners, and I heard afterwards became an excellent servant to the pilot's wife. On his return to Calcutta he made a report of the whole thing to Government, who were quite ignorant of the custom, and at once put a stop to it.

The next day, proceeding up to Calcutta, we anchored off Mud Point. The channel lies near the shore, and we had a pilot schooner in company with us. While walking the deck I observed an immense tiger come out, and with careless indifference stand looking about upon the beach. My pilot hailed the schooner and told them to put a charge into one of her guns and try and hit the tiger. This they did, and the shot went so near that it dashed the sand all about the beast, who threw up his tail and retreated to the jungle. Some short time before this, the pilot told me, four gentlemen went on shore here from the *Ardaseer* to see what they could shoot. After looking about for two hours they made a fire and. sat round it to take something to eat, and full of jokes concerning tigers, should one pounce upon them. And notwithstanding the fire (which all wild beasts have a great fear of) a tiger actually did come, and carried off a young man of the party, a nephew of Sir Hector Munro. His friends instantly seized their guns and fired at the brute, and wounded it severely, so that it dropped its victim. The young man was carried back on board the *Ardaseer*, but he died a few minutes after they got him on deck.

Having been fortunate in all my pursuits and speculations, and amassed a small fortune of £20,000, and being anxious to join my family in England (the more induced thereto by the receipt of several letters from my wife, who complained of the loneliness of her life), I set about discovering the best means of investing my money to advantage, so that it might yield me a certain and sufficient income. Dorabjee Byramjee, the Parsee merchant of Rangoon, was now established in a large way of business at Calcutta, and had for a long time acted as my agent; and when I asked his advice, he said at once that if I would only continue to leave the management of my fortune in his hands, he would guarantee me a handsome interest for it. I had known him for a long time, and felt great confidence both in his integrity and ability, and so I left with him the sum of one hundred and forty thousand rupees at 2*s.* 8*d.* the rupee, at an interest of twelve *per centum*, he to remit the money home as soon as it suited his convenience. Money at this time was very scarce (the Government paying ten *per centum* for the Decimal loan), and I did not like to put Dorabjee to the inconvenience of drawing out my money which was in his hands at a moment's notice, and having always considered him an old tried friend, I was now proving it.

The *Tottenham Castle*, commanded by Captain Dalrymple, was lying in the Hooghley ready to sail to England by way of Bencoolen, where she was ordered to load Company's pepper. Sooner than return idle, and in order to save the passage money, I accepted the situation of chief officer on board of her. But after I had engaged I learnt that another ship—the *Lord Eldon*, Captain Sweet—was to sail in company with us, and her commander, being the senior officer, was Commodore, and had all the advantage of a first choice of station. In consequence he sent us to load at Poulo Bay, a most pestilential place at that time of the year, the wind blowing over a swamp on to the anchorage. It was nothing but a strict insistance upon having all the ports barred at night directly the land-wind arose, that kept us from losing perhaps the greater portion of our crew.

A short while before we sailed, the *Lord Eldon* also came to this port to complete her cargo from the warehouse there, which would only take three or four days. The first night her long-boat broke adrift and went ashore. The carpenter, caulker, and eight men were sent to repair it, and having slept on shore, they all contracted the fever and died. The steward, a strong hale man, from fear alone took the infection and was carried off, in spite of his having taken particular care of himself. In short, by the disregard of the precaution (which I urged upon their chief officer) of barring the ports, the fever caught hold of the ship's company, and forty-eight hours after our departure the captain, all his officers except one, and nearly half the hands were stricken down and died. We ourselves lost our doctor and nine men, mostly invalid soldiers, who insisted upon coming up on deck to lie at night, in spite of my repeated warnings. It grieved me much to see these poor, foolhardy, obstinate fellows, thus throw their lives away, after they had escaped the dangers incidental to their profession, and when a return to England was assured to them ; but they were not under my orders, and in spite of my advice persisted in the dangerous course that led to their death.

This same ship, the *Lord Eldon*, had a passing strange adventure on her next voyage out to India. She was hove to off the Needles, waiting for some passengers who had been delayed, when a sudden sea-fog came on. Under cover of this, a French privateer approached and took up a position alongside of her, with a view to capture her. The people on board the *Lord Eldon*, considering it was a king's ship intending to press them, all hid, and the crew of the stranger had no difficulty in making their way on board. The captain, hearing the noise and clamour which ensued on the discovery, came upon deck, and to his confusion found his ship in the possession of the enemy. Nothing daunted at so sudden a reverse, he called to his men to repel boarders, and they, flying up on deck from their hiding places, after a sharp fight drove the invaders overboard. The privateer made sail and escaped in the fog, but the captain of the *Lord Eldon* with his own hand killed the Frenchman who had got possession of the wheel, by cutting off his head with one stroke of his sword.

To return to my narrative. Leaving Poulo, we touched at Bencoolen to report and obtain our final orders, and whilst at anchor here four of the crew deserted from the ship in the jolly-boat, and got ashore some four miles down the coast. Next morning, having received information of where the jolly-boat was, I sent a midshipman and the gunner, an experienced man whom I thought would be an additional security, to recover it. But they, attempting to land in a foolhardy way, got upset, whereupon the gunner had no thought except to save a bottle of rum which I had put into the boat for the crew, and did not seem to notice anything about the poor young midshipman, who was a married man, and was drowned. The following day Captain Dalrymple and myself went to see what was best to be done about the boat.

Having landed, we determined to take a small turn ashore, but when about a mile from the beach we suddenly came upon a herd of buffaloes, which proved to be very savage beasts; for on catching sight of my companion, who was some short distance in front of me, they immediately gave chase to him, upon which he turned and fled for the boat. I followed his example, but not being in good health, my strength soon began to fail. Looking back over my shoulder I plainly perceived the savage animals were gaining on me, and almost at the same moment my wind was completely exhausted, and I felt I could continue no longer. By a great effort I managed to reach a clump of grass and thorny bramble, and threw myself into the very middle of it, and, despite the torture I suffered from a myriad prickings, lay quite motionless, hidden from the view of the infuriated beasts, though able to discern them. They appeared monstrously surprised at my sudden disappearance, and at once pulled up short, and after snorting and bellowing and pawing the ground for some time, turned tail and fled in a panic, as quickly as they had charged. It took me a very considerable time to emerge from my hiding place, and I verily believe that I carry about me to this day portions of those thorns that pierced my person. But painful though the spot of refuge was, I felt thankful to have escaped with my life, which would certainly have been sacrificed had I not got out of sight of the beasts.

Leaving Bencoolen, we made a tolerable passage to the Cape. A curious circumstance happened to us in the Bay of Bengal. We spoke the English frigate *St. Forenza*, Captain Lambert, and wishing to communicate brought ourselves alongside. Just as we had done this the wind altogether dropped, but there was a very high swell running, that caused the ships to fall close together, nearer and nearer, until their yard-arms almost touched as they rolled. The situation had become one of eminent danger. Not a word was spoken by either of the crews. Captain Lambert gave his orders on board the frigate, and I mine on board the *Tottenham*. Providentally, with spars and boats, the danger of knocking up against each other was averted, and we managed to sheer off and escape collision.

After stopping à week at the Cape we sailed for St. Helena, where Captain Dalrymple gave a ball to all the gentlefolks on the island. It was a great success, and I was amazed not only at the number of very elegant young women, but also at the fineness of their dresses and the energy of their dancing.

In December, 1805, we arrived in the Downs, and were brought to by His Majesty's ship *Jupiter*, 44 guns, commanded by Captain G. Argles, who had been third officer on board the *Barwell* when I went out to India. I had formed an intimate friendship with him, so that we had exchanged watches in Bombay as a token of it. Captain

Argles sent a boat to board us, and demanded press hands, for whom he offered in exchange ticket hands. Our cook, who was a lame fellow and safe from being pressed, but possessed of a fine humour, played a pretty prank upon this officer, who appeared to be an extremely proud and vain man. He gave him to believe that there were two men stowed away on the pepper in the orlop deck, whereupon the lieutenant, with great parade, taking up his stand at the entrance, roared out to them in the king's name to come out. Receiving no answer, he sent three men in to search, but the pepper being loose they were too much alarmed to remain, and out they came gasping and choking and sneezing, and said there was no one there. The lieutenant, in a pet, called them all manner of names, d——ing them for lubbers, and, pulling off his fine coat, went in himself, and under a minute had bolted out again with a declaration that any man in there must be dead, and the king's service did not require dead men. But what with his coughing and sneezing, and the tears running from his eyes, it took him at least five minutes to express himself; and all the while we, who were in the joke, could scarcely contain ourselves for laughter. He took all the men he wanted, and supplied their places with ticket men, who were hugely pleased at the exchange and the chance of returning home so soon. Captain Argles, learning from his lieutenant that I was on the *Tottenham*, sent me a most friendly note to express his regret that he should distress an old friend, but he did not know I was on board, and if he had, his orders were so strict he could not refrain from demanding the men.

Arriving at Gravesend, we were again boarded by two different press-gangs, one commanded by a press-master from shore, and the other by a lieutenant from a frigate at anchor just above us. There were two of my crew whom I was interested in, and desired to save from being pressed. I therefore directed them to what I considered a safe place, under a large couch belonging to Captain Dalrymple. Instead of following my advice they stowed themselves away in the lockers amongst the bottles, and two others, worthless fellows I should have been glad to have seen pressed, who had heard me give the advice, took the place I indicated. Dinner being ready, I politely invited the lieutenant to join us, for which he thanked me. A little later his men, under the guidance of the press-master and a midshipman, were in full search, and it happened at the same time that the custom-house officers were looking out for smuggled goods. The latter scrutinized every place, and amongst others the locker where the bottles were. Conceive my chagrin on seeing the two men in whom I was interested turned out in the face of the press-gangs and immediately seized. I was so annoyed, I could not help telling the lieutenant that had I known he would have taken our two best men, he should have done so on an empty stomach. They were both married, poor fellows, and their feelings at being caught just as they were going to meet their wives, were miserable. But it was their own fault, for the two other worthless fellows, who had taken the place I pointed out, escaped free.

Just before we anchored at Gravesend a large fleet of colliers was working up the river, and two of them came into collision with us, so that we all three went ashore. Captain Dalrymple, saying he had nothing to do with the ship now, left it with the pilot and me, and started off in a post-chaise, first promising to have another waiting ready for me at Northfleet. We soon got our ship off shore, and were presently up at our moorings, when a vagabond West Indiaman came athwart our bows, and detained us three hours beyond the time I had expected. At last I got ashore, and finding the post-chaise ready started for London. The post-boy drove me over Westminster Bridge to Mr. Cross', behind the Haymarket, where we got fresh horses, and went on to Arlington Street, which we found with great difficulty, it having been newly built, and the roads not properly laid out at that time.

I knocked at the door of the house where my wife lived, and in another moment my dear daughter, now nearly seven years old, ran into the hall and opened it. I knew her in a moment, and rarely have I felt such pleasure as when she asked me, in her pretty manner, " Are you my father ? "

For an answer I took her in my arms and kissed her a hundred times. I will pass over the meeting with my wife, and the happiness of that period of reunion. Nothing could have been fairer than the prospects now in front of me. I was at this time a young man of only thirty-three years of age, and I considered myself settled with an independence for life. I had come back to a happy home, in a house which, though small, was, I thought, the prettiest I had ever seen, with Primrose Hill and all the surrounding fields in front of it, and I felt there was nothing wanting to make me comfortable and happy.

Early in 1806, an old friend of mine, Mr. Hunter, who was a very wealthy man, and had long out of kindness acted as my banker in England, offered me, at a very low rent, a house on his estate in Worcestershire. He owned almost the whole parish of Bewley, which contained about five thousand acres, and was a great man there. Whenever he went from town to this estate grand preparations were made for his reception. On entering the parish, about two miles from the church, the bells would begin to ring. His coach with four of his horses always came first, then his chariot with a pair of horses, and after these a post-chaise with his maids, and about six men servants on horseback. The house he offered me was replete with every comfort, and being on a little hill, commanded an extensive and beautiful view for miles and miles around, whilst there were charming walks everywhere in the vicinity, and the pleasant addition of fine shooting and fishing.

My wife had long been in London, and now desired a change of residence to the country, and so I accepted Mr. Hunter's kind offer. It was a great undertaking, and I had to pack an enormous heap of furniture on a large eight-horse waggon, piled up almost as high as the house, and pay £20 for the journey of 114 miles. We ourselves followed a few days later in a post-chaise, stopping one night at the Angel Inn, Oxford, and after leaving early the next morning, and lunching at Stratford-on-Avon, arrived at Bewley Hall, the residence of Mr. Hunter, in the evening. Here he very kindly put us up until our own house was ready, and all the time we resided there we were welcome guests at the Hall.

One happy year I spent with my family, and then I received news that my agent, Dorabjee Byramjee, had broke and run off to Serampore, and that all my money in his hands was swept away. I will not attempt to draw a picture of the intensity of my feelings at this sudden reverse of fortune. It was a cruel and stunning blow, coming at a time when I was happy in the idea that I was settled for life, and the owner of an established income, which I had worked hard for, and faced many dangers to obtain. At first my heart recoiled at the struggle before me and the doubtful results of a speculative life. But the tender

sympathy and encouragement of my wife soothed
my sorrow and nerved my determination, and,
throwing off my burden of despondency, I commenced the Battle of Life afresh.

CHAPTER XI.

IT was just at this time of trouble and misfortune that my eldest son Robert was born, in the month of October, 1806. Within a week of this event I received a letter from a friend of mine,

Mr. Holloway, who, having heard of my loss, invited me to join him as a partner and proceed at once to Buenos Ayres, in South America, that place having recently been captured by the British troops under Sir Home Popham, who was his brother-in-law. Mr. Holloway had received a private letter from this officer pointing out that there was much to be done by those who were first in the field, and on the strength of this, Mr. Holloway's agent, Mr. Davison, of St. James' Square, had offered to give him a credit of one hundred thousand pounds to establish a house of business at Buenos Ayres and Monte Video; and with this in view, the ship *Anna* had been purchased, and the command of her, together with such a share in the venture as I could take up, was offered to me.

This handsome proposal I could not refuse, even though it necessitated my leaving my wife sooner than I desired. But she herself urged me to go and not lose so fine an opportunity, and I therefore sent a letter by return post to say I would be in London the next day. With a sad and heavy heart I bade my dear ones farewell. My daughter was now in her ninth year, and a most engaging child; as I embraced her and my wife and cast a last look at my little son sleeping by his mother's side, my heart was filled with a great resolution that I must work and retrieve my fortunes, if only for the sake of these innocent ones. It was my duty, and this knowledge gave me a mind to contend against everything that came in contact with it. But it was a bit of grief!

On my arrival in London, I soon had ample work to employ my mind in providing a cargo for the *Anna*, and in this constant occupation found the best physic for the mental anxiety and trouble that harassed and oppressed me. The country I was going to was new to me, and I had not any personal knowledge of what description of goods was best suited for such a market. However, where there are British troops and fighting, there is always drinking, and where there is victory there is toasting, and so amongst other things I laid in eighty pipes of Spanish wine and forty casks of brandy. The person from whom we procured these was named Jones, and his house of business was in Water Lane, Tower Street. He was a very illiterate and eccentric man. Perhaps because of the large purchase I made, or for some other reason, he took a great liking to me, and pressed me to go and stop with him until the *Anna* sailed, saying he had a country house in Saint George's Fields, and another at Streatham, but had no society except a few publicans who dealt largely with him; but this hospitality I could not bring myself to accept.

I had been introduced to him by our broker, Mr. Beddick, of Cooper's Row, Tower Hill, a clever man of fortune. He told me that though Mr. Jones could scarcely write his own name, and certainly not speak English as it should be spoken, he was yet worth half a million of money. One day as we were walking to Mr. Jones' office, Mr. Beddick said to me, "I will have a little joke with Jones, and if you will stop in the anteroom you shall hear what I say and enjoy it." On reaching. Water Lane, Mr. Beddick went into the sample-room, where Mr. Jones always sat, while I remained in the office. He then said to Mr. Jones, "Yesterday I had a large dinner party, and Captain Eastwick was one. Among other things, in speaking of you he said that he had never seen such a man, so clever in his business and so honest in his dealings, and that he thought you the best judge of spirits and wine of any man he had ever met with. As there were several persons at my table, who will be large purchasers in your way, the eulogy cannot fail of doing you good. Now, as Captain Eastwick has been a large purchaser himself, I think you ought to show your right feeling by making him a present of something in your way for the use of his voyage—brandy, for instance."

"Well," replied Mr. Jones, "I should not mind making him a present of a dozen."

"You would not surely be so offensive as to offer him such a trifle?" says Mr. Beddick, in a tone of indignation, well assumed.

"Why, how much do you think I should give?" asks Mr. Jones in rather a sorry voice.

"A hogshead at least, if you wish to do yourself credit."

"A hogshead!" roars out Mr. Jones. "I never gave away six bottles in my life."

Hearing this I entered the room, and asked what they were disputing about so vehemently.

"Oh, nothing," says Mr. Beddick, "only a little argument between Mr. Jones and myself."

"Only a little argument," stammers Mr. Jones. He then took Mr. Beddick aside, and whispered in his ear, "Well, I think I will send him half a hogshead"—which he actually did next day.

Several of my friends were at me to accept Mr. Jones' invitation and spend at least a few days with him, saying he had no relatives but a sister, who kept a gin-shop in St. Giles, and who was one of his best customers. But I could not reconcile it to my position to accept this man's hospitality, though informed he had everything of the best.

Mr. Jones kept two young clerks, smart men, one drawing £200 and the other £150 a year. One day as Mr. Beddick and I were going out, they came to him to ask his advice about leaving the employment, saying they were both married, and their salaries were not sufficient for their means, as they had too much work to do. Mr. Beddick told them by no means to leave. About six months after this, Mr. Jones being one day in his usual place in the sample-room (where he often sat in the dark, to avoid the expense of a candle, his sense of smell being quite enough for him to tell the quality of the liquor), as he was groping from one part of the room to another, having forgotten that a trap-door down to the cellar was open, he fell in and broke his leg, and died in consequence. In his will he left his business and the whole of his stock in hand, worth about £50,000, to his two clerks, and his large fortune went to a variety of persons, with most of whom he had but a very slight acquaintance, and in such a way that some of my friends supposed had I cultivated his acquaintance, I should have come in for a share.

A circumstance occurred in connection with the clearing out of the *Anna* which served to show the nefarious conduct of the custom and excise officers. Amongst our cargo was a vast number of trunks containing printed cottons, on which a drawback was receivable on exportation. These goods are always packed under the inspection of a Government officer, to take account of the number of yards. As we were in great haste to sail, Mr. Beddick entered five hundred yards short of the quantity we intended to take, so that, in the event of any mistake, no impediment should be thrown in the way of our sailing as soon as ready. In packing up one of the trunks, one of our clerks, in his haste, made a mistake, putting in three pieces too few. The excise officer perceived this, and instead of rectifying it at the moment, made his private mark on the trunk. As the shortage was eighty-four yards, the total at a penny halfpenny a yard amounted to only ten shillings and sixpence. The ship was loaded and ready to sail, when to our annoyance and surprise a stop was put on her, and we were charged with an attempt at fraud in claiming a drawback on eighty-four yards that were not exported. The trunks were examined and found to be deficient, and though the clerk was taken before the Lord Mayor to make oath that there were five hundred yards more exported than we claimed drawback upon, and that this was purely a mistake, the fact had no avail, and we were ordered to satisfy the seizing officer, and ten guineas was asked and given him. Such reprehensible extortions were very common in those days.

At last we got away, sailing from Gravesend early in November, and after a very quick passage arriving off the river La Plata on Christmas Day. Here we were spoken by the frigate *Medusa*, Captain Bouverie, who communicated to us the astounding intelligence that Buenos Ayres had been retaken by the Spaniards, and that Colonels Beresford and Park, and all their forces, were prisoners of war. In consequence of this the British army had been withdrawn and concentrated at Moldanado, to await reinforcements; and here we were ordered to proceed.*

---

* It is a curious thing that the recapture of Buenos Ayres was not known in London until the 26th of January, 1807, or five and a half months after it occurred. In announcing the event in its issue of that date, *The Times* writes :—

"Moldanado commands the entrance of the River Plate, by which means several merchant vessels which have sailed from hence to

At this place we found the 38th, 40th, and 47th regiments, under the command of Colonel Backhouse, and many transports and men-of-war under the command of Admiral Stirling, who had superseded Sir Home Popham. As the latter was on the point of starting for England, I repaired on board the *Raisonable*, Captain Rowley, in order to deliver some private letters to him, as I had been desired to do, and the same evening he left in the *Rolla*.

For doing this I was sent for on board by Admiral Stirling, who demanded of me why I had delivered these letters without his sanction, he being then in command. I was taken aback at this question, but after a moment's consideration made bold to ask him, by way of reply, if there were any orders issued against visiting a man-of-war. This he was obliged to own there were not, whereupon I respectfully refused any explanation of my conduct, and so took my leave. Nor did I hear anything more

Buenos Ayres, will be prevented from falling into the hands of the Spaniards."

And on the 19th of February :—

" The *Rolla*, Captain Coffin, having left Buenos Ayres on Christmas Day last, reached Weymouth on the 16th of February, with Sir Home Popham on board, and brought the following news :—Of the vessels sent to Buenos Ayres in consequence of the alluring prospects held out by Sir Home Popham, the following had arrived at the River Plate :—*The Duke of Kent* (Robinson), *Anna* (Eastwick), and *Spring-grove* (Greenwood). They were left with Admiral Stirling at Moldanado when the *Rolla* sailed."

Sir Home Popham was tried by court martial on his return to England, and sentenced to be reprimanded. It was not long, however, before he obtained another command.

of the matter, except that Admiral Stirling was very angry.

At Moldanado I made the acquaintance of Colonel Backhouse, who had come up from the Cape of Good Hope with the 47th Regiment, and now commanded the army as Brigadier-General, and I continued to enjoy his friendship until his death, many years afterwards. He remained at the head of the troops until the arrival of Sir Samuel Auchmuty, who brought with him reinforcements amounting to 7,000 men, and the army then proceeded against Monte Video.

The siege of this place was an operation of great difficulty, there being a vast number of buildings scattered around the city, which required the approach to be made secure by raising batteries. Fortunately this was done with trifling molestation. When the day of the storming arrived, I was able to see the whole of the fight, as my ship was anchored almost abreast of the place. There was a strong picquet of two hundred men, under Colonel Vassell, of the 38th Regiment, sent to hold a particular point. Against them, to drive them back, came a thousand men of a kind of militia, under a Spanish colonel, who was dressed in a very fine uniform. But the brave 38th displayed extraordinary gallantry against these odds, and, in spite of the incessant fire, eventually drove the enemy back with so much fright and confusion, that they jumped off their horses and ran behind the rocks in all directions

to escape the fire directed upon them, whilst their
colonel fell down and expired from positive fright,
there being no wound discovered upon him when
his corpse was searched afterwards. Shortly after
this a breach was made in the walls, and considered
practicable, but no sooner effected than it was
filled up with dry hides by the garrison, and
these formed a most awkward obstacle, affording
no sound footing for the stormers. But, nothing
daunted, a party of the 38th and 40th proceeded
against the breach, headed by Colonel Vassell and
his volunteer comrades, Colonels Brownrigg and
Brown. Colonel Vassell was the first wounded
and his orderly sergeant assisted him to rise, and
notwithstanding one of his legs was mangled beyond
description, he stood upon the other, and waving
his cap, called out, " On ! on ! gallant 38th. Do
your duty ! " The storming party had to pass
four 24-pounders, loaded heavily with canister
musket-bullets, four hundred to the charge, which
created amazing slaughter. But in spite of this,
the gallant fellows pushed on and swarmed through
the breach, only to find themselves enfiladed, and
with cannons facing them from within, all pointed
towards them, and these killed and wounded
many, including Colonel Brownrigg. It was quite
surprising the troops were not beat back, but it
only showed what British pluck can do. In a
short time after this the Spaniards gave in, and
the gates being opened, our army took possession of
the city.

Within a couple of hours of our being masters of the place, an English sailor found his way to the top of the steeple of the great church, and fixed the Union Jack there. I am quite unable to explain how the daring man effected his object, but it was a proud sight to see our flag flaunting high in the breeze, a signal of British victory.

The climate of this part of the world is extraordinary, and unlike any other that I have been in. You might kill as many cattle or persons as you wished, but they never went to putrefaction. The air absorbed everything, and their bodies wasted away without any offensive smell. On the other hand, few people survive their wounds. Poor Vassell, a gallant soldier, whom every one admired, wanted to have his leg amputated, but a surgeon (and a clever man, too) did. not see the necessity of it. Mortification took place, and he died and was buried the following day, with military honours, his band playing the Dead March in Saul. Brownrigg, who was in the same house, asked who was going to be buried. Told Vassell, he replied, " Vassell to-day ; Brownrigg to-morrow." So it was.

The day we occupied Monte Video, there was a deserter, a large-sized Irishman, captured, and being brought to a court-martial, condemned to be hung.. I was quite near, and saw him ascend the ladder to the gallows. When they turned the ladder round to swing him off, the rope broke, and he fell to the ground, where he began to kick his legs in the air. The priests were at his neck in a moment and loosed the rope, and his look of astonishment as he opened his eyes and saw them round him, seemed to indicate that he was surprised at finding them following him to Purgatory so soon, for he exclaimed, "What! You here, too?" He certainly thought himself dead, until they assured him such was not the case. Then he got up and walked with them to the General, who gave him a free pardon.

At Monte Video we became in a short time completely established as merchants, and found a profitable market for our goods. I rented a large house on shore, and fitted it up for our purpose, and there Mr. Holloway, myself, and two clerks took up our residence and met with immediate and considerable sales, so that before General Whitelock arrived we had disposed of much of our cargo.

The General arrived in April, accompanied by General Gore, and the army being now augmented to nine thousand chosen men, preparations were made for the recapture of Buenos Ayres. As nearly the whole force was intended for this purpose, the merchants were formed into volunteers for the defence of Monte Video, and were regularly officered like the militia in England, keeping guard and night patrols, with a watchword.

In April, the army was crossed and landed at Insanardo, about nine miles distant from Buenos Ayres. A more improper place for a base of

TROOPS LANDING AT MONTE VIDEO.

(From a plate in G. E. VIDAL's "*Picturesque Illustrations of Buenos Ayres,* 1807)

operations could not have been chosen, the only approach to the city from our side being through a heavy swamp.

At this time Buenos Ayres did not contain eight thousand muskets nor any provision to sustain a siege, and there were at least ten millions sterling of Government property in the place. Had our troops advanced at once and surrounded the city, nothing could have prevented it falling into our hands. But General Whitelock delayed doing anything for a week, and then ordered the march in divisions, with instructions to meet and form at certain points. He directed, moreover, that all flints should be taken out of the muskets, and if the troops were molested on the march, they were to break into the houses and bayonet the inhabitants. This was a most foolish thing to order, for he had only to examine the doors at Monte Video (which were the same as those at Buenos Ayres, as any one could have told him) to discover that it was the custom of the country to build them so strong as to make it impossible to break them in without great violence and instruments for the purpose.

At half-past six on the morning of the 5th of July the advance was ordered. It was very soon found that the task to be accomplished with unloaded guns was a desperate one.* The immunity from

* "After two or three days' hesitation General Whitelock formed his plan of attack, the most extraordinary, it would seem, that ever entered into the head of a military man. A town inhabited by

fire gave the besieged an additional courage, and the storming of the buildings as ordered was quite impracticable. From the house-tops, and from every elevation of advantage, a murderous fire was poured down upon our brave but bewildered men, killing them by dozens, and leaving them totally unable to defend themselves, and much less to retaliate. Nothing but the high discipline of the troops sustained them through this ordeal. Nearly all the divisions missed their point of formation, and the scheme of action entirely failed. General Whitelock, with a few troops, kept at a distance of two miles, and with him, to his annoyance and contempt, the brave Colonel McMahon, with all the artillery. In short, the folly and incapacity of a presumptuous general caused a disgraceful defeat.

Had our army done what they ought, namely, surrounded the city at a certain distance, with the artillery suitably posted, nothing could have prevented it shortly falling into our hands, and with a very small loss of life on our side. The Spaniards were aware of this, and some of them

60,000 or 80,000 inhabitants, who had several months to prepare themselves and were known to be bent upon a most obstinate resistance, was to be carried by a *coup de main*, and by a force not amounting on the whole to above eight or nine thousand men. The army was to penetrate through a long line of streets, with not a musket loaded, to certain points, occupy the flat roofs of the houses, and then by a simultaneous movement, on a concerted signal, advance against the principal defences of the enemy!"—*The Times*, September 14, 1807.

told me afterwards that General Whitelock was only fit for a picture, not for service.

It is not my object to enter minutely into the details of this melancholy affair, which, owing to its mismanagement, disgraced the British name by forcing the capitulation of nine thousand men to an enemy not much their superior in number, and whom at the beginning of the campaign we thoroughly despised. The result was that we not only failed to retake Buenos Ayres, but lost Monte Video as well, and had to withdraw altogether from South America, thereby missing the opportunity of establishing ourselves in a country which might have more than compensated for the loss of our North American colonies. There was a great bluster of another expedition being sent to retrieve our laurels, but the defeat was never avenged.

When the expedition sailed from Monte Video, Admiral Murray, in the *Africa*, was in command of the fleet, whilst Admiral Stirling remained behind. Mr. Holloway was the only merchant permitted to accompany the army, and had the city been captured, as it ought to have been, our fortunes would have been made. For, in the first place, he took with him twenty thousand dollars in gold to purchase all the hides in Buenos Ayres, which we heard amounted to about two millions, and the price ruling half a dollar each. Being first in the market we should have bought the whole of these in the Spanish way, by paying a deposit, and eventually resold them at one and one-and-a-half dollars each. In the second place, there were at Monte Vido sixty-five ships, prizes of war, that had been taken from the English, and retaken by the fleet, and these were offered by Mr. Blacker, the prize-master, for one hundred and thirty thousand dollars, many of them being only valued at the rate of firewood, and the best ships at merely nominal prices to obtain a sale. Mr. Holloway and I had joined another gentleman in this speculation, and had nearly completed arrangements for their purchase, when the failure of the attack altered all our plans.

When Admiral Murray sailed, it was arranged that on his tender returning with the news of the capture of the city, it was to be signalled by a Union Jack flying at the top-gallant masthead. The day came, and the vessel—the *Aurora*—appeared, but no flag, and the word " stupid " towards the lieutenant commander for forgetting the agreed signal was in every mouth. At last she drew towards Admiral Stirling's flag-ship, and a boat from her boarded the frigate. In a few minutes the barge with the Admiral, the lieutenant, and a midshipman came ashore. Only the former landed, and the lieutenant and midshipman pushed off and had no communication with the shore. The Admiral walked up to Government House, looking very grave, and giving orders to have the north gate shut. All flocked after him to hear the news, and wondering why he did not at once announce the victory. I was there, when I heard my name called to say there was a letter awaiting me at my house, and hastening thither, I found it surrounded by a crowd of persons, anxious to know its contents. Judge of my surprise, and indeed the surprise of all to whom I read .it, when I found it contained the news that the whole of our army was taken, and a treaty made with the Buenos Ayres Government that the English force was to return to Monte Video, and give up that place at the expiration of two months. Of all the defeats we have ever sustained, this was, I think, the most ignoble. The feeling in Monte Video was so intense, that very strong and insulting expressions about General Whitelock, calling him both a coward and a traitor, were written upon the walls of the streets.

Whilst all this had been going on at Buenos Ayres, I was occupied in commercial business. I kept two horses, and very often rode out into the country with Mr. Travers, the Customs' Master. One day, when some distance out, we were pursued by two natives on horseback, and narrowly escaped having the lasso thrown over us. The dexterity of the people in this respect is wonderful. When they want to kill a bullock—of which there are thousands in the country—they select one of a herd, and riding up, throw their lassoes over its horns. This lasso is about the size of a half-inch rope, made of hide, and very strong. One end is fastened to the saddle of the horse, the other end has an iron ring through which the rope goes. They have the knack of winding this, the size of a hoop, round their heads, and then throwing it with unerring skill. After which the horses go out of their own accord different ways, and the bullock is penned and cannot move. One of the men then jumps off, and running up to the animal, puts a knife in the top of its head, and it falls dead, as if struck by lightning.

On the return of the expedition, every one was intensely occupied to sell their goods. We had freighted our vessel with cocoa for the Cape, under charge of Mr. Dalton, one of our clerks, and another vessel, a fine cutter, we had loaded with a similar cargo for England. The whole of the remainder of our goods, to the value of sixty-five thousand dollars, Mr. Holloway, much against my will, sold to Mr. White, an American merchant of the place, taking Jesuit's bark in payment. We subsequently found difficulty in getting freight for this, and had to pay a very high rate. In the end it reached England three weeks after our Privy Council had issued orders that no more bark was to be exported to France, so that an article which had been up to eighteen shillings a pound fell to two, and the whole of the money was lost to the concern by the freight, insurance, and warehouse charges. The cocoa sent to the Cape in the *Anna* was sold to a gentleman named Graves, a friend of the Commissary-General, for the purpose of supplying the army there. But this being without orders from the general commanding, he would not afterwards sanction the purchase. The Commissary-General being, I believe, a party concerned with Mr. Graves, used every subterfuge to do away with the contract, saying that the cocoa did not equal the sample, but a committee of merchants being called, this charge was refuted, and declared unfounded. After this many efforts were made for redress, but nothing could be effected by our agents, and there the money remained, and was lost altogether.

I took my passage home in the cutter in which I had loaded our cocoa for England, and we sailed under convoy of Admiral Murray's fleet. It is impossible for me to describe the character of the man I came home with. He was both owner and captain of the craft, and a great drunkard as well as a coarse, vulgar fellow. He had insured his vessel high, as I happened to know, and the second night after sailing, when lying in my berth, I noticed a very unusual motion in the cutter. I immediately went on deck, and found that the man was making an endeavour to leave the fleet, so as to go home by himself on the chance of being captured, and thereby recover the large insurance he had made on the vessel. I immediately wrote out a protest, and presented it to him by my clerk Mr. Curtis, telling him I would hold him responsible for my cargo. At this he took alarm, and putting the vessel about, rejoined the fleet.

But after this he was very bitter against me,

and there was nothing he did not attempt to make me uncomfortable. He stole my wine and beer, kept my cabin from being cleaned, and, in short, annoyed me with a thousand petty provocations, instigated by the malice of a low and vulgar mind. Being only a passenger, I was powerless to do anything. When we approached the channel, he actually began to sound two hundred miles beyond all soundings, as a means of discovering our position! I had taken some lunar observations, and knew our exact position on the chart, yet I could not make him believe it till we were visited by one of the officers of the navy, who confirmed my statement.

Nearing England, the wind chopped round, and blew hard from the east, and the whole fleet, under orders from Admiral Murray, bore up for Cork. Here this captain actually began to purloin part of the cargo! Fortunately for me, my friend Captain Dalrymple, now commanding the *Marquis of Ely*, was at this port, and directly he heard of my uncomfortable situation, he insisted that I should continue my voyage to London in his ship, and I, for my part, was only too grateful to avail myself of his kindness, and escape from the annoyance and discomfort to which I had been subjected. Having left Ireland, we were soon in the English Channel, and when off Brighton, I hailed a fishing-boat, and in this I was landed.

On my arrival at London, after reporting the treatment I had been subjected to, Mr. Davison strongly urged me to go down to Falmouth, and prosecute the captain of the cutter there. But neither my health nor my inclination could submit to such a journey by coach in the month of January, with the snow deep on the ground, and the roads notorious for their bad state. The man pillaged more of the cargo, after arriving there, but our agent at Gibraltar, where he was ordered, deducted from the freight money all the deficiency, and so he got punished.

I proceeded home to Bewley, where I found my little son Robert dangerously ill with the whooping-cough. He was wrongly treated by an ignorant doctor, and died on the eighth day after my return, and thus I was only blessed with his sight during the first and last week of his brief life. Poor little one! he lies buried under the pew we occupied in Bewley church.

CHAPTER XII.

OUR son's death was a grievous shock to my wife, who was completely wrapped up in him. Nothing seemed able to comfort her, and notwithstanding the beautiful situation of our house and the many advantages we enjoyed, it became so distasteful to her after this bereavement, that I determined to leave it. Accordingly, the next year, we went to reside in Union Street, Somers Town, where Mrs. Kent, my wife's sister, who had recently lost her husband, came at our invitation to reside with us.

My venture in South America had swallowed up the most of what fortune I had left, and ended in disappointment and loss, instead of the brilliant thing I had looked for, and it now became necessary for me to consider what steps I should take to provide an income. In the autumn after my return from Buenos Ayres, I received a letter from my old and tried friend Mr. James McTaggart, the same who formerly owned the *Betsy*. He wrote, saying that, although he did not know the extent of my misfortune, yet he was aware I had met with an immense loss, and desired to offer me the command of a ship he had just laid down, and the building of which would cost ten thousand pounds; and that if I pleased I might take her over with his interest, to pay him when I was able, and from the time she was ready for sea, or, if I preferred it, I might command and sail her for him.

This splendid offer I was obliged, however, to decline, partly because of my wife's state of health, but more particularly because Mrs. Kent, who was a young and handsome woman, had decided to go out to Bombay at the invitation of her brother-in-law, Colonel Gordon, and my wife was most anxious that I should take charge of her. This delayed my departure till early in 1809, just previous to which, on the 15th of December, my dear son William was happily born. Thus, for a second time within the period of a little more than two years, I was obliged to leave my wife with an infant son by her side, and begin battle with the world again, almost as poor in my thirty-seventh year as I had been when I went to sea a quarter of a century before.

In the month of January Mrs. Kent and I left Union Street on our road to Portsmouth, with the intention of stopping on the way at Frimley, where Mrs. Kent the elder resided. After leaving our house, Mrs. Kent went to bid farewell to another sister, Mrs. Watson, who lived in Howland Street, and there she stayed an undue length of time, and the consequence was that our post-chaise did not start till six o'clock in the evening. Mrs. Kent had a good deal of luggage, and her jewel-case with trinkets of three hundred pounds value in it, besides about a hundred pounds in money between us. We had to cross Hounslow Heath, which at this time was infested with robbers. Only a week before, the clergyman of Egham, a most active magistrate and well known, on returning home from a meeting he had been attending at Hounslow, was stopped by footpads; but he happened to have an umbrella lying across his saddle, and this, in the gloom, the fellows mistook for a blunderbuss, and the clergyman being a sharp-witted man, and well mounted, instantly observed their hesitation, and cried out that they were dead men if they approached him, whereupon they turned and fled. I had urged Mrs. Kent to make an earlier start, but she, loth to say good-bye to her sister, replied, "What, Eastwick, are you afraid?" "Why, yes," I answered, "so far that I neither wish to risk the loss of life or money without necessity." At which she rallied me. It was quite dark when we left. Changing horses at Hounslow at seven o'clock, I heard the man say to the post-boy before he started, "Mind, be civil." This was a very common thing, to prevent post-boys making any resistance if attacked, for fear of getting the horses shot. I knew the meaning of the expression, and considered it indicated more than the usual risk. When about half-way over the heath, we saw a person walking towards us, and Mrs. Kent, in dreadful alarm, implored me to tell her what to do, and where to hide her jewels and money. I was myself anxious, and told her this was the folly of stopping so late, and that we must do the best we could. However, it was a false alarm, the fright being occasioned by a woman tramper; and as we travelled at a good speed, by ten o'clock we were at her mother-in-law's—Mrs. Kent. Here we found everything most sumptuous and hospitable, and stayed two days. Old Mrs. Kent was an extraordinary strong woman, and after hearing about our fright on the road, told us that a few days previous to our arrival, a stout, impudent beggar had called at her house. Finding the back door open, he walked into the kitchen,

and to the great fear and surprise of the maid-
servants demanded money. Mrs. Kent having
accidentally observed the man in the garden, went
to the kitchen, and overheard him say he would
not leave without he had something. The stout-
hearted old lady immediately entered, took hold of
his collar, and said, " You won't leave my house,
won't you ? " and handled him so roughly, that he
walked out and down the garden path, she with
her hand on his neck all the time, and on opening
the gate she pushed him with such force that he
fell in the middle of the road, where it was very
dirty. He went to the tap of an inn close by, and
stated what had taken place, observing he was glad
all women were not so strong and resolute, or his
occupation would be gone.

After spending a couple of days at Frimley, we
continued our journey, and arrived at Portsmouth
without any further adventure.

Here we had to wait some time for a change of
wind. The day before Sir John Moore's troops had
returned from Spain, and the officers were hurrying
up to London. As it was understood we should
be detained at least ten days before sailing, Captain
Harington and myself thought we would take a run
up to town, and started in a post-chaise for that
purpose. But at Petersfield, where we stopped to
change horses, there were no fresh ones to be got,
the house being filled with officers back from Spain,
waiting for conveyance to London. It was go or
return with us, for we had no time to wait. So

Captain Harington and I went to the stables, where we seized hold of a pair of horses, which the post-boy swore we should not have. But by dint of argument and a little bribery, we slyly got them harnessed, and away we galloped. After remaining two days in town, we returned to Portsmouth, and immediately afterwards sailed in company with three other East Indiamen.

The ship we were in was the *Neptune*, Captain Donaldson. She was one of the largest in the East India Company's fleet. One of our fellow-passengers was Colonel Backhouse, the same whom I had met at Monte Video. He was very much taken with Mrs. Kent, and made her an offer of marriage on the passage out, but she refused, being certain of marrying a gentleman in Bombay, which was in truth the reason why she was going out.

The day after we sailed a storm dispersed the whole of us, and one ship, the *Addington*, struck on the Bognor rocks, and with great difficulty got back to Portsmouth. We ourselves were in great difficulty near the Channel Islands. Captain Donaldson, in the extremity of danger, having ordered the second mate to go up aloft, and assist taking in the foretopsail, the man refused, and was instantly broke. I volunteered to fill his place, and was gladly accepted. Having arrived safely back at the Mother Bank, the second mate's place was filled by Mr. Alsagar, late M.P. for Surrey. After refitting, the wind having shifted to fair, we made a second start with the same four vessels in company. The weather was now beautiful, and two days out from England Captain Donaldson gave a dance to the passengers of all the ships, which was followed the next evening by another given by Captain Tweedale, of the *Addington*. Notwithstanding that both went off very well, I did not consider it prudent at such a season of the year to do these things at sea. We had a fine voyage to Table Bay, and after rounding the Cape, the *Scalesby Castle*, Captain Lock, the *True Briton*, Captain Bonham, and ourselves shaped our course for Bombay, whilst the *Addington* was obliged to stay behind to repair a bad leak that had broken out afresh.

Approaching Madagascar, Captain Donaldson invited Captain Bonham and Captain Lock to dinner, and the conversation chancing to turn on the disagreeable weather sometimes met with during the south-west monsoon on going into Bombay, and not getting a pilot, I offered my services to pilot them in, which were gladly accepted. The next day we had severe squalls and lightning. About four o'clock, Mrs. Kent, Captain Donaldson and myself were sitting in the stern gallery, when a heavy clap of thunder, so loud it sounded as though a hundred great guns were going off, broke just over our heads, and was followed by an extraordinary brilliant flash of lightning, and so close to us that we saw a considerable number of electrical balls darting into the water. Mr. Shee, the chief officer, who was on watch, came running aft, looking very pale, and said he was sorry to mention the ship had been struck in the foremast, and that the lightning had knocked down four men, and was afterwards attracted by one of the guns into the water. This accident employed all hands for sixteen hours to repair the damages, getting up new foretop-mast, foretop-gallant-mast and yards, for the old ones had been rendered completely useless by the burning force of the electric fluid.

We had no further adventure, except that we came in for the south-west monsoon, with very thick, dirty weather, and a tremendous sea running. When within a day's sail of Bombay, Captain Bonham, the commodore, made the signal: "Will Eastwick stand by his promise?"—which being answered in the affirmative, another was immediately run up: "*Neptune* go ahead, and lead the way." Next day, having made the land, I took the fleet into the harbour, nor did we get a pilot till we were ready to drop anchor.

Having safely made over Mrs. Kent to the care of her sister, Mrs. Gordon, I only stayed a few days in Bombay, and then took passage, intending to go to Calcutta, where I hoped that the vessel, the command of which I had been offered by Mr. McTaggart, might be still available, or at any rate some other of the many that he owned. But on touching at Madras I was asked to take the command of a very fine ship and cargo belonging to the house of Harington and Company. Had I remained in Bombay only a fortnight longer, I should have received a letter written by Mr. McTaggart, to inform me that the ship he had mentioned was built and awaited my acceptance. My stopping therefore, at Madras, instead of proceeding direct to Calcutta, was quite a misfortune; for when Mr. McTaggart found I was engaged with the house of Harington, he sold his new vessel and cargo to Captain Nicolls, who made a prosperous voyage with her to London, where he sold her and closed the concern with a profit of sixteen thousand pounds.

The vessel to which I was appointed at Madras was the *Ganges*—a most beautiful craft. Captain Allen had a half-share in her, but for private reasons Messrs. Harington and Company desired me to take his place. After considerable exertion I got her ready to sail by the 1st of September.

It was just about this time that Sir George Barlow, the Governor of Madras, had quelled the mutiny that had arisen in the army of that Presidency. Owing to the stoppage of certain allowances, a great deal of discontent had been created, and it ended in open rebellion. The Madras European regiment had actually put its own commanding officer under arrest, and chosen another to lead them. It was considered to be a time of great danger, till the Governor, with the assistance of the king's regiments, put down the insurrection. He was now very anxious to send his despatches home, so that he might receive the credit of the affair, and he offered us five thousand *pagodas* to take them. But the elder Mr. Harington, who was a high Government man, thought it better to await the arrival of Lord Minto, the Governor-General, who was expected every day, and take his despatches, considering that they would be more satisfactory to the Court of Directors. This preference annoyed Sir George Barlow very much, it being exactly the thing he wished to avoid. I urged the advisability of sailing at once, but without effect, and we were consequently kept waiting till the 16th of September, when Lord Minto arrived. But in the meantime I got a stroke of the sun, and became so dangerously ill that my life was at one time despaired of. As an only chance of saving it I was put on board my ship, where, by the blessing of Providence, and through the great skill of a passenger, Dr. Dove, I recovered, and was able to resume the duties of my command just before we reached the Cape.

We made a wonderful quick passage to soundings, being only eighty-six days out from Madras, and on our way overtook and passed the *William*, that had sailed ten days before us, and in which Sir George Barlow had sent his despatches. But when almost in sight of England, the wind changed round to the eastward, and we were nearly a month in getting to Portsmouth. Passing the Bill of Portland we were boarded by a king's cutter, and I took the opportunity of sending a private letter to Lord Minto's lady, and another to the secretary at the India House, keeping the despatches to take up myself.

The *William* reached Portsmouth just before we did, but having been nearly overhauled and on the point of capture by a French privateer, she had thrown the despatches she was carrying overboard.

I landed at Portsmouth at eleven o'clock at night, and without an instant's delay proceeded in chaise and four to London ; and reaching the India House, where I was expected, delivered my despatches to Mr. Ramsay, the secretary, who was pleased to remark that during the many years he had been there, none had ever been so anxiously awaited, nor, when read, given such unqualified satisfaction.

It was not unnatural that I should expect some recognition, but the Court of Directors said they never rewarded such things but at the recommendation of the Governments abroad, and referred the matter to Sir George Barlow, who being highly incensed against us for not sailing at the time he wished, used his influence, and also persuaded Lord Minto not to allow us anything. At the East India House they took advantage of this, and refused any special grant for our service ; and the end was that, what with letters to India and letters back, we never got anything at all.

This was not the only loss I suffered, for our detention at Madras, under the advice of Mr. Harington the elder, cost us at least thirty thousand pounds in the disposal of our cargo of cotton. If we had

sailed at the time we were ready, and not waited
for the arrival of the Governor-General, and
made the same quick passage home (which there
is no reason to doubt we should have done), the
westerly winds that had been prevailing for three
months in the Channel would have carried us immediately in, and brought our cotton to market
a month earlier than actually happened.   This
would have enabled us to forestall a large fleet of
American cotton ships, loaded at Charlestown,
and ready to sail as soon as the embargo on the
article was taken off, and whose arrival just before
us so overstocked the market that it reduced
the price of cotton from two shillings to eight-
pence per pound, at which latter ruinous rate we
were obliged to sacrifice our cargo.   It was, in
fact, a repetition of my speculation in Jesuit's
bark during my previous voyage, and I doubt
whether ever any man has been so truly unfortunate
as in two succeeding voyages to bring to market
articles that had fallen in price just previous to
his arrival.   I was never more thoroughly disappointed in my life.   It seemed as though the very
Fates were in league against me, and that I had
but to enter upon any reasonable venture to make
it utterly fail.

The house of Harington did not like to engage
in shipping, it not being their regular business,
and they had consequently sent home orders to
their agents, Messrs. Porcher and Company, to sell
the *Ganges*, which was a really beautiful vessel

about five years old. Our private arrangement bound both them and me, that in case either wished to get rid of the share, it should be offered at the original price of £6,000 to the one disposed to keep. The ill-luck which had attended the ship on this voyage, created a prejudice in my mind. Sailors are often superstitious mortals, and I very foolishly determined to have nothing more to do with a vessel that had so grievously disappointed me. Therefore, when £8,000 a share was offered I agreed to sell, and the *Ganges* was consequently bought by Mr. Flemming. She ran for many years afterwards in the same service, clearing in the next two years alone £30,000, and making the fortunes of several commanders. This caused me to regret that I should have allowed myself to be influenced by a stupid feeling of superstition, and so lost an opportunity that would doubtless have yielded me as much benefit as it did others.

On my return home I found my wife had removed to a new house nearly opposite to the one in which I had left her, and wherein she had not been comfortable. I stayed at home till the end of the year, enjoying the delights and tranquillity of domestic life. My son William had grown a fine strapping child of two, and immediately attached himself to me, so. that we became inseparable companions all day long. As for my daughter, she was now a handsome girl of thirteen of whom any father might feel proud, and there seemed nothing too much for her to do for me. Truly I have been blessed in my children, who have been to me a joy and comfort in all stages of their existence. I could wish to live those happy days again, when, despite the material troubles of life, I had my son and daughter to brighten the house, and my wife to make it a dear and passing pleasant home. Days like these are the green calm islands in the rough voyage of a sailor's life, met with at long intervals of time, and their delights enjoyed in a greater degree than is possible to men who never leave the land. How often in my career have I sailed away to sea, leaving behind me everything that I loved most in the world! How many partings have I felt the keen pain of! How many anxieties have I suffered during periods of long absence! The retrospect of them would be indeed bitter, were memory not cheered by the recollection of the happy meetings that followed, and the sweet spells ashore.

What wonder, then, that I lingered at home as long as I dared, and deferred my departure on a roving life until I felt that my duty recalled me to my profession again? The last few years had consisted of misfortune following misfortune. Everything had gone against me; nothing had succeeded. I had not only been living on my capital, but losing it. I now determined to put what was left to the touch, and endeavour by another effort to retrieve the disasters of the two voyages just finished.

CHAPTER XIII.

THERE was an acquaintance of mine, a Mr. Hutton, who had formerly been a purser in the East India service, and made a considerable sum of money, and was now owner of a ship called the *Elizabeth*, which was loading in London for

Calcutta. Happening to meet him in the city one day we entered into conversation, and it ended in his inducing me to take a one-sixteenth share in the vessel, and also to invest £3,000 in the venture; and I further agreed to accompany him out on the voyage to India.

It being necessary to insure my interest in the *Elizabeth*, I was persuaded by a Mr. Allport, who was clerk to my agents, Messrs. Porcher and Company, to do so through him, and without acquainting the firm, whereby he declared I should protect myself at a lower rate. I unwisely agreed to this, and nothing could have turned out more unsatisfactory, for in the end it caused me delay, anxiety, and loss, and proved the truth of the old proverb that says, "Penny wise, pound foolish."

We sailed in November with thirty cabin passengers and 300 lascars (of whom we carried 256 as passengers), and a large mixed cargo, making a freight altogether of £13,000. The weather was very unfavourable, and we with difficulty made Portsmouth, where we had to call, and having anchored off Spithead, lay there for some days, windbound, owing to a heavy gale continuing from the west.

Here one of our passengers, a Captain Jackson, had arranged to join us. He had not long been married to a beautiful and accomplished young wife, who, having never before parted from her family, and especially from a favourite sister, became dangerously ill through grief, which brought on a premature confinement. Captain Jackson now wished to give up his passage, although it had cost him four hundred guineas, and remain for another ship. Knowing that he was a poor man I did not like to see him sustain such a loss, and therefore persuaded him to act on the doctor's opinion, which was in favour of the lady proceeding, provided she could be got comfortably on board. It only remained for her embarkation to be suitably arranged, and for this purpose I called personally on Admiral Curtis, who commanded at Portsmouth, and represented the case to him, and he very kindly tendered the loan of his yacht, in which we reached the *Elizabeth* just as she was passing through the Needles. I mention this circumstance because I had afterwards a dreadful reason to regret my successful interference to change Captain Jackson's plans.

Almost immediately after we got into the Channel bad weather again set in, and we were obliged to beat against adverse winds and in a very heavy sea. The ship strained so much, and made such bad weather, that when we were between Scilly and the Land's End she sprung a leak, and began to make water very rapidly. And just about this time the wind shifted to due south, and blew a hard gale, which prevented us from weathering either point. A consultation being called, the captain and officers, on my suggestion, determined to run through; and this was accomplished in safety, despite the thickness of the atmosphere, which quite hid the land from view and made the navigation most difficult. The leak continuing to gain on us, we were obliged to bear up for Cork, and reached the harbour of that place early in December.

Here we stayed some time refitting, and awaiting a favourable wind to sail again. We also shipped twenty more Lascars, a European carpenter, gunner, steward, and baker, and three gentlemen as passengers. The latter were Company's marine officers, one of them being a friend of mine named Calder, who had recently come home from India as chief mate of the *Warren Hastings*, a fine vessel of 1,200 tons burden.

At last the wind shifted round, and under convoy of the *Brisk*, sloop of war, from whom we received our sailing instructions, we started again. For a week we experienced fair weather, and had reached considerably to the west of Scilly, to latitude 49 North and longitude 8 West, when we encountered another gale, and before long the *Elizabeth* again sprung a leak.

To keep her from sinking we were obliged to bear up before the wind, and thus found ourselves once more steering a homeward course. So hard did it blow that, although under double-reefed topsails only, we ran eastward at the rate of ten knots an hour, the ship plunging in a furious sea, and the pumps constantly at work. Owing to the danger of heaving to, we dared not enter Falmouth, which we passed about midnight, though we had four and a half feet of water in the hold, and nearly three feet between decks. The cold was intense, and the lascars so benumbed and affected with fright, that they could only be prevented from running-below by Europeans standing over the hatchways with drawn swords.

Captain Hutton now desired to make Portsmouth, and at 6 p.m. the following evening we hauled close to the wind, head inshore, and with not more than a knot weigh on, and about eleven o'clock sighted the Bill of Portland right ahead. But just at this time it unfortunately happened that the pumps got out of order, and the leak gained so fearfully on us that we were obliged to bear up till morning to get them repaired, and in so doing overshot Portsmouth.

After this it blew a regular hurricane from W.S.W., and we lost our fore and main sails, which were blown to pieces. The lascars had by this time become perfectly useless, and the officers were themselves obliged to go aloft and cut away the pieces of the sails, which were flapping with the report of guns. The night was as dark as pitch, and the ship was tossed about completely at the mercy of the waves, many of which were breaking over her. For two days and nights the passengers had all been assembled in the cuddy, which was half full of water, and where boxes and chests and bedding and miscellaneous articles were being washed about in a manner that added greatly to the noise and general confusion. It was very distressing to see the fear depicted on the faces of these poor people, and observe the different phases in which it was exemplified. Some were praying and lamenting, others moody and silent, and others again wildly excited and delirious in their talk.

When at last daylight came, we bent on another foresail and reefed it; but, owing to the violence of the gale and coldness of the weather, we were unable to get up a fresh mainsail, our strength in Europeans being nothing near sufficient to work the ship properly, and the few lascars we managed to drive aloft refusing to stir out of the tops, and ready from cold, fright, and weakness to surrender life and tumble into the sea when urged out on to the yards. We therefore set the main and mizen staysails, and the weather abating a little towards midday, began to cherish a hope that we might get safe into the Downs.

We succeeded in getting through the Straits, and were approaching the South Foreland, when the main staysail blew to pieces, by which the little weigh the ship had on was so much diminished that the strong tide obliged us to anchor about three miles distant from the shore.

We held for a few hours, but during the night the wind increased, and shifted to north-west, and we began to drift, and by the morning found ourselves across the Channel and close between Calais and Gravelines, in a situation which prevented us from clearing the coast to the westward, or the sands to the eastward, and with the gale dead on shore. In this extremity we got out a new Europe sheet cable and stout anchor, that was part of our cargo, and this was now let go, and to our intense relief it brought the ship up; but only till the evening, when with the change of tide she began to drift again.

And now our position became exceedingly critical. It was soon apparent that nothing but a cessation of the tempest would enable us to escape the destruction that threatened, and which could no longer be disguised or hidden from our passengers. All through the storm I had endeavoured to cheer and encourage them whenever I could spare a few moments from the deck—which was seldom enough, since the navigation of the ship had been made over to me. The series of misfortunes that had followed the *Elizabeth* since we first set sail from Portsmouth created a general feeling of superstitious despondency, not perhaps to be wondered at. Two months ago we had passed Dover Straits on our outward voyage, and here we were again at the end of that period, in the same place, and in much sorrier condition. Landsmen are at the best of times all adrift at sea, but in gales and foul weather their ignorance of nautical matters often magnifies the peril in their eyes, and causes them to exaggerate danger. I have always endeavoured to affect a cheerful bearing before my passengers, even when I have myself felt anxious, finding that a good laugh is the best physic for such folk. They repose such an implicit trust in the captain of a ship, and are so guided by his demeanour, that much depends upon how he conducts himself. Whilst we had plenty of sea room I made it my care to frequently visit the cuddy for a few moments at a time, and cheer all there with the assurance that such blows were common at sea, and that the gale would soon abate, or we be safe in some harbour. But now, with a lee shore under us, and the ship drifting on to it, I did not feel justified in assuming the same confident bearing, although most anxious to avoid creating a sudden panic. I was very deeply concerned about Captain Jackson and his young wife, and being desirous to prepare him for any emergency, I called him into the captain's cabin, and privately pointed out to him on the chart a sand bank, on which I thought it probable we should strike within an hour. But I particularly begged him not to mention this to any one, but only to go to Mrs. Jackson, and keep her from being too much alarmed when the shock occurred.

Poor Captain Jackson was himself under such strong apprehensions of alarm on account of that amiable woman, that he seemed unable to grasp my warning, and immediately mentioned what I had confided to him to the third mate, and also to the three officers who were on board as passengers. These at once determined to get the larboard quarter boat ready, and leave the ship privately directly she struck. Being told of this, I at once went and remonstrated with them ; but in such hours of danger words are useless, and just as I was speaking the catastrophe I had anticipated occurred, and the *Elizabeth* took ground with great violence.

All was now confusion and alarm. The lascars, who had been huddled below like so many sheep, rushed up on the deck, which soon became crowded, and filled the dark night with their loud foreign cries, as they ran hither and thither in companies, frantic with fright and uncertainty as to what was best to be done. The Europeans, seeing that they were like to be overwhelmed by these natives, gathered together on the poop, and, forming a line, seized cutlasses, belaying-pins, or any weapon they could lay hands on, and kept the lascars from encroaching. Meanwhile minute guns were fired, whose loud reports added to the fright of the poor women clustering on deck, and who appealed with cries and tears to every man they came in contact with to save them.

And now the party who had proposed to leave in the boat began to launch it, and Mrs. Jackson and the three officers got into her whilst she hung in the davits. But the lowering was effected so hastily, that when about half-way down a great sea caught it and dashed it to pieces against the side of the ship.

Hearing a shouting and commotion I hurried to the spot, and the first thing I saw was poor Mrs. Jackson clinging on by the after-tackle. It was a terrible sight to see a woman so fragile and beautiful thus situated. Her thin white hands clenched the rough ropes with the grasp of despair, whilst her face was turned upwards, and her golden hair becoming uncoiled streamed out into the gale. I at once endeavoured to render what assistance I could to her husband, who was trying to reach down and catch hold of her, but almost immediately another great wave came, and with a pitiable shriek the poor lady fell back into the foaming sea, and was carried away by the resurge into the darkness beyond and never seen again.

Captain Jackson now became frantic, and I was forced to draw him on to the poop with all my strength, as he was preparing to plunge after his wife. I implored him to control his feelings, but he wrestled violently with me and cursed me for keeping him back. Seeing his condition I called four men to my aid, and between us we lifted him up and carried him below to my cabin, where I locked him in until he should again become master of his actions.

Mr. Calder, one of the three officers who had been washed out of the boat with Mrs. Jackson, managed to catch hold of a small coir rope that hung over the stern of the ship, and the third mate (a great friend of his) seeing this, seized it and tried to haul him on board. But when he had all but succeeded a sea washed him from his grasp. A second and a third attempt—for Calder still clung desperately to the rope—were equally as unfortunate, and at last the poor fellow became exhausted, and losing his hold perished miserably.

I learnt this incident from Laird himself, who came down into the cuddy just as I was returning from confining Captain Jackson in my cabin. Noticing that he was much agitated and also that his hand was bleeding profusely, I asked him how he had hurt it. He seemed surprised at the question, and holding it up close to the lantern, found that he had nearly lost three fingers, which had been sawn to the bone by the friction of the coir rope running through his hand. It was marvellous that he should have remained unconscious of so severe a hurt, but it showed his deep anxiety for the preservation of his friend Calder.

All this time we were bumping on the sandbank, with the sea around us boiling like a caldron, so that I expected the *Elizabeth* to go to pieces every moment. But the tide falling we presently remained fast, with a heavy list to starboard, and so continued until morning. With the following tide the ship floated again, and began to drift rapidly towards another bank. And now, as a last hope of saving her, we endeavoured to make sail again, with the object of running between the two shoals into deep water, but before we could get sufficient weigh on she struck with such violence as to beat in her bottom, and the water immediately poured in so fast that it was now certain she was past all hope. The wind began, also, to increase again, and the seas to break so furiously over us, that it seemed merely a matter of minutes before the end must come.

At this juncture Captain Hutton came and implored me to try and get ashore in the cutter and obtain assistance, our minute guns and signals of distress having met with no response. The task seemed an impossible one, for the sea was like a whirlpool, and between us and the land there lay a long narrow bank, over which the surf was breaking with such a fury that no boat could hope to cross it. Since the fatality that attended the launching of the quarter-boat, every one seemed to realize that it was impossible to escape by this method, and no further attempt had been made to prepare any other. But the lives of many human beings depending on it, I thought it my duty to respond to the call, and consented to make the attempt. I therefore went down to my cabin to get my watch, which I had left there, and as I came out Captain Jackson followed me.

Having reached the deck I called for volunteers. At first there was no response, until Captain Jackson stood by my side, when several others came forward, and at the last moment a lascar jumping into the boat, he was at once followed by ten or twelve of his brethren, until I stopped the inrush by hitting into the thick of them with an oar, or they would certainly have swamped us on the spot.

How the cutter drifted clear of the ship I do not know. For some minutes we seemed to be leaping into the air, and falling away again on the broken waves close to the vessel's side, shipping great quantities of water, and unable to obtain any purchase with the oars to push off. Every moment I expected to see the boat either capsize or be dashed into pieces and sink, but by some great mercy of Providence we gradually drifted aft until we found ourselves clear of the *Elizabeth's* hull. Then our oars went out and we pulled for dear life.

The cutter proved more seaworthy than any one would have given her credit for, and with half the hands bailing and half rowing, we kept her afloat and headed for the shore. When within a mile of land we came upon the sand-bank I have mentioned. It ran parallel with the shore, and over it the breakers dashed in one continuous turmoil, so that it seemed to us as though there was not a moment's rest or stay.

I dared not alter our course, as this would have brought us broadside on, when we would have instantly capsized. All we could do was to lay on our oars, and watch an opportunity of running through if such occurred. Standing up in the stern-sheets with the tiller-ropes in my hands, I kept the cutter's head up, whilst a man in the bows signalled to me as each wave came on. At last there was a slight temporary cessation, which every one recognized as by a common instinct, for immediately a great shout went up of, " *Pull! Pull!* " and straining to our utmost endeavour, we rowed direct for the bank.

As we reached it the surf began to make again,

and the first wave coiling at least ten feet above our heads, allowed us no hope of saving ourselves. I bent down and prepared for death. It seemed hovering over me. But at this supreme moment, as if from the depths of despair, the great breaker in its curling fall pitched clean beyond the boat, and only buried us in a large body of water, whilst the momentum it gave us hurled us forward and stranded us on the narrow bank as it dispersed. The next surf following broke short behind us, and threw the cutter forward again with such a shock that it sent a great part of the water we had shipped out of her, and so actually helped us across the grim barrier and into smoother water on the other side, and through this we were able to pull to shore with the two oars that were left to us.

The place where we landed was close to Dunkirk. There were hundreds of people on the beach ready to receive us, many of them women, with little pots of hot tea in their aprons ready to revive us, and their kind eyes full of tears at witnessing our distressing situation. Not a soul of us had expected to reach the shore when we put off from the *Elizabeth*, and many times during the passage we had braced ourselves to meet death. And now, by the Divine goodness of God, we were safe on land, and tended by hospitable hands, that snatched us from the waves and assisted us into a place of safety.

Directly I could speak I pointed out the position of the ship, and by means of signs and gesticula-

tions, and the few words of the French language
with which I was acquainted, entreated that help
should instantly be sent to her. In reply I was
informed that several efforts had already been
made, from the time our first minute guns were
heard, but that all had failed, it being totally impossible for any craft to face the gale blowing in
from the sea. This was indeed true, and when I
reflected on the terrible danger of the journey we
had just made, with the wind abaft us, I was
fain to confess that no boat could make way in the
teeth of such a storm. I had therefore to content
myself with the promise that, were the gale in
any way to abate, another attempt to reach the
ship and succour the crew should at once be made.

And now an officer with a company of soldiers
came marching down to where we stood, and caused
us to be mustered, informing us we must go to
prison at once, such being the destination awarded
us by the law of the land and the fortunes of war.
It seemed harsh and undeserved treatment to thus
use people who had but just been saved from the
jaws of death, and I thought I observed signs of
disapprobation amongst the populace. But there
was no help for it, and we had to fall in and were
conducted to jail between two files of gendarmes.

Shortly after we left the beach, another boat containing two officers and six seamen succeeded in
getting ashore from the *Elizabeth*, and they joined
us in prison within an hour. They informed us
that a little while before they put off from the ship

the captain's barge was hoisted out for the ladies, and the two officers were in it, preparing for its equipment, when it broke away, without any oars, and getting broadside on to the sea capsized. A gig that hung over the stern was then lowered to recover the barge, but the crew of it, instead of doing so, pulled straight to the shore after picking up the two officers, who were too exhausted to remonstrate or do anything. And before they had got half-way to land the *Elizabeth* went to pieces, and all the people on board perished.

When she struck on the sands, which occurred on the 27th of December, 1810, her crew and passengers numbered 380 souls, including several ladies. Of these only twenty-two persons were saved, though one other poor gentleman, Lieutenant Tench, of the 3rd Ceylon Rifles, managed to reach the shore alone, but only to meet with a more barbarous fate a few hours afterwards.

And now I was a captive in a French prison, and without any hope of liberty before me, for our ship-wreck occurred during the middle of the war in Spain, where we were fighting Buonaparte, and there were at this time no signs of peace. My feelings as I marched along with my comrades to the town prison were those of a captive condemned to transportation. I thought of my wife and family, and tortured myself with a thousand anxieties as to their fate. Life but a few hours before had seemed very precious; now it appeared almost worthless. In the reaction of mind and body following the great exertion and excitement I had just passed through, a feeling of deep despondency overcame me, which I found it difficult to contend against.

However, I had to rouse myself and act for my fellows in misfortune. Having reached the prison, we were placed in some small, dark, filthy cells, such as were allotted to common felons, three or four of us being crowded into each, with no distinction between black and white. I at once sent for the gaoler, and asked him if he could not accommodate the Europeans of our party better. Whereupon he offered to give us up his own quarters if we would make over to him the whole of the Government allowance we were entitled to receive. This, in default of any other arrangement being then possible, I consented to, and we were removed to three comfortable rooms that he and his family usually occupied.

The next morning, having finished breakfast, we were discussing our situation, when the gaoler entered and said that a gentleman desired to see me. Following him to a private room, I found a large burly man standing there. I bowed to him, and asked him his pleasure.

" Sir," he replied, " my name is Hodges, and I am a countryman of your own, and have come to offer you any assistance that is in my power."

I expressed my appreciation of his kindness, but desired him to explain how, being an Englishman, he retained his freedom.

"The nature of my profession protects me," he replied. "In short, I am a smuggler, and have many friends and clients in this port, with whom I do a large trade. I am bound on business to England to-morrow, and if you, or any of your party, desire to have news of your safety carried to your friends, I shall be very happy to convey the same."

I thanked him very heartily, and immediately informed my fellow-prisoners of his offer, of which they very gratefully availed themselves. Mr. Hodges having followed me into the room, we gave him a list of the names and addresses of all the people we desired him to communicate with, and these he wrote down in his pocket-book, and bidding us good-bye, departed.

Shortly after this, a deputation of townspeople, representing a committee that had been formed on our behalf, called upon us. They informed us, that most of the inhabitants of the town having witnessed our dreadful shipwreck, had expressed a desire to raise a public subscription to assist us, and accordingly arrangements had been made with an innkeeper in the place to supply us with whatever we required for our table, whilst another person would attend to furnish us with any clothes we might want. Furthermore a sum of ready money was placed at our disposal, to obtain any other necessaries we desired. Nothing could exceed the liberality and charity of these good people, whose timely aid and generous sympathy

left us powerless to express our thanks sufficiently.

In addition to this, General O'Mara, who commanded at Dunkirk, directed one of the three
Town Majors to call every morning and see that
we did not want for anything. One of these, on
the fourth day from our landing, asked us if there
had not been a gentleman on board "*who was very
tall and an extraordinary dressing man,*" and
giving such a description of his appearance that
we recognized it at once as referring to Lieutenant
Tench.   He then informed us that the poor gentleman had actually reached the shore by swimming,
but in a most exhausted state, and had been discovered by one of the *Garda Costa*, to whom he
had offered two guineas to assist him to some
habitation. A soldier coming up whilst he was
speaking, and wishing to share the reward, he and
the coast-guard began to quarrel, and it ended in
the former murdering poor Tench in cold blood,
and rifling his pockets, in which were found nearly
three hundred guineas in gold. I remembered
that Lieutenant Tench had taken charge of this
very sum during the storm, for a Mrs. Major Mid-
winter, who was a passenger on board. The
horror of the deed so haunted the coast-guard,
that he presently came into Dunkirk and confessed the act, whilst the murderer fled to the
woods. He was, however, soon captured, and both
men were brought and confined in the same prison
with us. On the first examination the coast-guard

denied all that he had confessed, saying he had spoken out of malice, as he had a private quarrel with the soldier; but my recognition of the murdered man from the description which the coast-guard himself had given, and my knowledge of the money found upon his person, proved that the confession was true. Search parties were then sent out to try and find Lieutenant Tench's corpse, and it was eventually discovered much wounded and hacked about. The inhabitants—particularly the women—were outrageous against these two vile men, who never quitted the prison for the court without being hooted at and pelted on the way; and they both eventually expiated their crime by death.

Nothing could exceed the kindness of every one in the place to us. I daily received invitations to dine out, which by the courtesy of General O'Mara, who granted me parole, I was able to accept. A short while afterwards the deputation paid us a second visit, when they signified their intention of petitioning for our release, and a day or two later brought a letter ready written, and addressed to the Emperor Buonaparte, for my signature, which I appended on behalf of my fellow-prisoners. It was forwarded to the Minister of Marine, but many days elapsed without an answer. Whereupon the commandant of the town, who had great interest, his sister being married to the Minister of War, and his brother being *aide de camp* to Buonaparte, drew up a petition which he sent to his brother, desiring him to present it personally to his

Majesty. This was done, and no sooner had the Emperor read it, than he sent for the Minister of Marine, demanding the letter which I had signed. This being presented to him he read it, and immediately with his own hand wrote on the back of it an order for our release, and directed that we should be sent back to England at the expense of the French Government.

This joyful news was soon transmitted to Dunkirk, and the Deputy Commissary of Marine of that place, dressed in full uniform, waited upon us in prison to announce the Emperor's order. Our surprise and joy was unbounded, the reprieve being one quite unheard of in those days. General O'Mara immediately gave us permission to quit the prison, and we received numerous invitations from the townspeople to stay with them so long as we remained in the place. On the following evening I was invited to the theatre to receive the congratulations of several families who had interested themselves on our behalf. It was surprising what an effect our shipwreck had created, the many terrible circumstances connected with it having occurred under public observation, and excited a universal sympathy that found an outlet in all these acts of kindness.

Hearing of our good fortune, the deputation waited upon us again to say that "under our present circumstances they left it to us, as gentlemen, to determine whether we chose to leave Dunkirk under obligations for the expenses we had incurred." Having thanked them for their frankness, we assured them that nothing was farther from our thoughts than to remain indebted to them after we were free, and we forthwith settled to repay them the sum they had expended directly we reached London.

I then asked if there was anything we could do to prove our appreciation of their treatment of us, and in reply they gave me a list of about 150 of their townspeople who were prisoners in England, and the places of their confinement, asking my good offices to procure their release if possible. This I gladly agreed to. I was especially interested in the fate of the son of an old gentleman, who had formerly been a banker, but who was now confined for debt in the same prison as we had been; and also of a fisherman, the husband of a woman who waited upon us at our meals; and for both of whom I promised the exertion of my best endeavour.

I must not omit to relate, as a small tribute to his worth, the noble integrity of the smuggler, Mr. Hodges. He had taken my address, and called upon my agents, Messrs. Porcher and Company, to acquaint them of my safety, directly he reached London. He further offered, as he was leaving again on business for France, to deliver to me any letter they might entrust to his care. Mr. Porcher was so pleased with this man, that he desired to give him a cheque for ten pounds. But this the honest smuggler sturdily refused, protesting that he had come to London on his own business, and not on mine, and that he would accept no reward for such an act of common humanity to a fellow-countryman in distress, as he had been able to render me. He called the next morning for the letter, which he gave to me at Dunkirk three days afterwards. Drawing me on one side to deliver it, he said he had brought me two pounds of coffee and four pounds of sugar for my acceptance, and he capped this act of kindness by offering to supply me with any money I might want.

This, at such a season, and to a person situated as I was, appeared a favour of no ordinary kind. I said I would accept twenty guineas, and further desired him to take charge of a valuable gold time-piece and deliver it to my wife, which he readily consented to do. I then proceeded to write out an order on my agents for thirty pounds, for the money he was lending me, and the balance for the trouble and care of taking my timepiece, which had cost me a hundred guineas, so that I was most anxious to send it to a place of safety. On reading the bill to him, he said I had made it too much, as he had bought the guineas for twenty-three shillings each, which made my debt to him only twenty-three pounds, and that he would not accept of any recompense for the care of the watch. "In that case," I observed, "I will take it back, for the obligation is too much." "You can do as you like," he answered; "I can only say I shall be very sorry if you do." Perceiving he was hurt, I at once said, " Take it, and God bless you for a friend in need."   I then wrote out a new order for the lesser sum, and gave it him, and also three letters,* all of which, together with my watch, he safely delivered to my agents.

To return to where I broke off in my narrative.

* One of these letters is before the compiler now, the ink grey and faded, the paper yellow and stained, and the rude wafer still adhering to its back, that sealed it eighty years ago.   Here are its contents :—

" DUNKIRK PRISON, *January* 16, 1811.

' MY DEAR LUCY,

"I have left nothing undone to make up as much as possible the blot I am at present to my family and the world.   After, my dear girl, suffering in danger and horror of mind attending our wreck, to be led a prisoner and captive, and confined in a jail with felons full of vermine.   This, Lucy, would be nothing, did not keen reflection come over my mind for the fate of my family.   Thank God, with strict economy, you will be able to live comfortably on the interest, and spare your poor husband a mite.   Fifty guineas a year shall be the outside.   What is against us is the total loss of cloathes, and being obliged to buy at an enormous price.   I have already laid out £15, which will do but little.   I have no business with much cloathes, they must be put over one's shoulders during the march, for we are considered as Prisoners of War, and expect to be marched up-country to Arras immediately.   We have been very kindly treated by some of the inhabitants, particularly by the house of Richard Faber and Company, to whom all remittances are to be made.   A Mr. Hodges, who is going to England, has proved a kind friend.   He takes over my gold timepiece to be delivered to Messrs. Porcher and Company.   I have desired it to be sent to you.   For God's sake take care of it, as it is of considerable value through the correctness of its going.   I have written to Messrs. Porcher and Company and Mr. Morris to assist you.   I hope all the papers are taken care of.   The letters of Captain Hutton for £400 insurance are of the utmost importance.   I hope Mr. Allport and some friends will assist you.   God Almighty bless you is the prayer of your unfortunate husband.   Write to me by bearer, for God's sake, by this gentleman to whose kindness I am much indebted.   Love to Eliza and Willie.   Your affectionate husband,
" R. W. EASTWICK.

" P.S.—For God's sake write instantly by this good friend."

Arrangements were made for our leaving Dunkirk, and on the morning of the 30th of January we embarked on a large French pilot boat, with a post-captain of the French navy to accompany us, and flying the Cartel flag. We had a fair wind, and made the passage across the Straits in six hours. Our sensations as we neared the shore of our own country I will not attempt to describe. We, who had expected a long captivity in French prisons, found ourselves free, and the white Kentish cliffs were a glad sight to eyes that had given up all hope of seeing them for years and years. Our release from captivity seemed almost as wonderful as our escape from the shipwreck.

Having entered Dover harbour, we landed, and were at once surrounded by persons from the different hotels, clamouring recommendations of their several houses. We went to Wright's, and having obtained permission for the French captain to dine with us, I ordered a hasty dinner, so as to leave in an hour, which was all the time he could spare, It was a very plain meal, and we drank but little, yet the charge was exorbitant—four pounds fifteen shillings for a party of seven, I think. I did not say anything, but handed the waiter a five-pound note, telling him to keep the remainder for his trouble. Whereupon the impertinent fellow said he considered it very little. My anger was now aroused, and I desired him to return the note, but as he did not do so I rang for the landlord, and when he appeared mentioned what had occurred, and declared if the man was not discharged, I would publish the treatment I had received in every London newspaper on my arrival. Mr. Wright assured me he felt so indignant at the waiter's conduct, that he had already made up his mind to discharge him, even had I not urged it. He made a thousand apologies, and begged me not to injure the reputation of his house by publishing the matter, and he offered to reduce the bill to any amount I considered fair. This, I told him, was not my object; but I recommended him in future to pay more personal attention to the care of his customers, if he would not have comparisons drawn (to his disadvantage) between the treatment at his tavern and that in a French prison.

Saying good-bye to the French officer, Captain Jackson and myself started at six o'clock in the mail coach, and by seven the next morning I was at my home, it being rather more than twenty-four hours since I had left Dunkirk. It is needless to say with what transports of joy my wife received me. She signalized the occasion by presenting me with my second daughter, Anna, five days later.

As for poor Captain Jackson, who had hastened back to comfort an affectionate mother, whom he had left in good health, he found that the shock of hearing of the shipwreck and his subsequent imprisonment had been too much for her, and that she had sunk under it, and was buried two days before his return. So that in one short month the unfortunate young man lost a young and beautiful wife, whose amiability of character attracted all who were brought into contact with her, and a kind and devoted mother to whom he was deeply attached. He was shortly afterwards obliged to set out again for India to rejoin his regiment, and I heard of his death a few months later, a victim to a violent fever.

The day after I arrived I waited on the Marquis of Wellesley, who was Secretary of State for Foreign Affairs; he was engaged, but I stated the circumstances attending the release of the survivors of the *Elizabeth* to his secretary, Mr. Harrison, and expressed a hope that his lordship would view the kindness of the inhabitants of Dunkirk in the way they desired. The next day his lordship sent for me, and informed me that as a matter of policy alone it would be wise to do as I requested, but that the matter did not depend upon him, and he could only promise me his interest, and referred me to the Transport Board, to which I immediately proceeded. The commissioners received me, and heard my story, and Captain Bowen very kindly agreed to all I asked, requesting me to give him the names and also the particulars of the French prisoners whose release was desired. This I immediately did from the list which was in my possession, and he promised me he would at once institute inquiries about them.

About nine days after this, on taking up a newspaper, I read with much gratification that their freedom had been granted to as many French prisoners as there were English captives sent home from Dunkirk. And not long after I received a most handsome letter from the committee of that town, returning me their grateful thanks for what I had done, but begging as a favour that their letter should not be noticed in the public journals, as the known partiality of the inhabitants of Dunkirk for the English might displease the Emperor. There was also an enclosure from the old gentleman the banker, who prayed God to bless me for having restored to him and his family a beloved son, whose freedom had enabled the father to arrange his affairs and procure release from prison; and also a message of thanks from the good woman who had waited on us in prison, and who was made happy by the return of her husband the fisherman.

Before I quit the subject I must once again mention Mr. Hodges the smuggler. Finding that he had not cashed the order I had given him on my agents, Messrs. Porcher and Company, I desired them, on his coming, to give him a cheque for £40, to repay my loan, and reward him for the safe delivery of my watch. He called on them shortly afterwards, but still adhered to his determination not to accept more than £23, the actual amount of my bill, and when urged to reconsider the matter, he observed that he was sorry that a reward should have been pressed upon him for the second time. My agents, as a last resource, said it was not in their power to deviate from my instructions, and begged he would enable them to carry the same out. But he replied he would rather leave town without getting anything at all than do as they wished, as he could not reconcile it to his conscience to accept payment for what he had done. Such was the noble and disinterested conduct of a smuggler!

We saw him once again, for he called at my house to congratulate me on my freedom, and it was a great pleasure to show him, by the warmth of our welcome and some trifling hospitality, how great an obligation we felt towards him. And I am glad to add that about two years afterwards I had the gratification, through the interest of a friend, of preventing his son (who had been taken in some smuggling transaction) from being sent on board a man-of-war, and securing his free pardon by representing the conduct of his father to us captives at Dunkirk.

NOTES TO CHAPTER XIII.

The wreck of the *Elizabeth* created a good deal of public interest at the time it occurred, as the following extracts from the journals of the day will show:—

MORNING CHRONICLE, *January* 1, 1811.

" We are extremely concerned to state that the *Elizabeth*, Captain Hutton, a country ship of about 600 tons, which sailed from Cork on the 17th of last month, was totally lost off Dunkirk on the 27th ult. She was outward bound for the East Indies, and only 22 of the crew were saved, namely Captains Eastwick and Jackson, Messrs. Barker (second officer), Laird (third officer), Eddis and Heywood (of the 24th N.I.), and sixteen lascars."

THE TIMES, January 1, 1811.

" To the numerous losses of India ships, we have to add that of the *Elizabeth*, the melancholy particulars of which are communicated in the following extract of a letter from Deal.

" ' DEAL, Dec. 30, 1810.

" ' GENTLEMEN,

" ' A person who left Dunkirk this morning brings us the following most melancholy information. That on Thursday evening last the *Elizabeth*, country ship, which was anchored off the South Foreland, drifted from thence into Calais Roads, where she knocked off her rudder, and cut away the mainmast. No assistance coming after her repeated signals, the captain put off to obtain it. But when about halfway between the wreck and Dunkirk, his vessel drove on the outer edge of Dunkirk Break, Dunkirk steeple bearing S. by W., and instantly went to pieces ; when all on board perished except 22 (mentioned hereafter), who landed at Dunkirk, and were instantly conducted to prison, where our informant saw Captain Eastwick and others yesterday, and procured this information, with directions to acquaint us therewith. No letters were suffered by the commandant to be brought away, although some were written to be sent us : he promises, however, that in a few days they shall come.

" ' The following is a list of persons who perished in the *Elizabeth :* The captain and three officers, six male passengers, five ladies, including the captain's wife, two European men, eight black women servants, and 347 lascars.' "

The " person who left Dunkirk " was evidently the smuggler Mr. Hodges, and if he was bound on business, it is interesting to speculate how he brought himself into personal communication with the *Times*' Own Correspondent so immediately after his arrival in England.

MORNING HERALD, January 3 and 4, 1811.

" A letter from Dunkirk received yesterday says that it was in the power of the Governor there to have saved the whole of the crew of the East Indiaman, which ran ashore there ; but he positively refused, saying it was an English frigate."

" The following is an extract from the *Moniteur* :—

" ' Message of His Imperial and Royal Majesty the Emperor Napoleon Buonaparte to the Senate.

" ' PALACE OF THE TUILERIES, December 10, 1810.

" ' I was in the hopes of being able to establish a cartel for the exchange of prisoners of war between France and England, and to avail myself in consequence of the residence of two commissioners at Paris and London to bring about an approximation between the two countries. I have been disappointed in my expectation. I could find nothing in the mode in which the English Government negotiated but craft and deceit.

" ' NAPOLEON.' "

Perfide Albion! This extract shows the feeling at the time in regard to the exchange or release of prisoners of war.

THE TIMES, *January* 17, 1811.

" The following is extracted from the *Moniteur* :—

" ' DUNKIRK, *December* 29, 1810.
" ' To His Excellency the Minister of Marine.

" ' SIR,

" ' I have the honour to inform your Excellency of a very disastrous event which took place yesterday in the roads of this place. The ship *Elizabeth*, of three masts and 650 tons burden, Captain Hubert W. Eastwick, bound for India from London, having proceeded to join the fleet at Plymouth, and having, in consequence of bad weather, put into Cork in Ireland, from which after nine days she set out on her destination to Madras and Bengal, with a cargo of iron, copper, lead, glassware, hats, cloathes, and other goods, having a crew of 100 men on board, including the captain, and also 80 white passengers, and 250 lascars, destined for Bengal by the East India Company, overpowered by the violence of the gales which had continued since her departure from Cork, ran aground yesterday evening during the night amid the sandheads of the roadstead about three leagues N.E. of the harbour.* Soon after she struck against the Breebank, and was observed at daylight making signals of distress, and firing minute guns (she was armed with ten 16-pounders). Mr. De-la-Costi immediately took measures to send assistance to the vessel, but all attempts proved fruitless, the wind blowing furiously from N.N.E., and the sea being in a frightful state of agitation. Hopes were entertained that at ebb-tide something might be done, but these hopes were vain. It was absolutely impossible to send out any sort of boats, notwithstanding all the efforts that were made. The galliot *La Victoire*, with Captain Gaspard Malo, master of a merchantman, on board, who gave on this occasion a proof of his devotion and humanity, as well as several other sailors and pilots belonging to this port, was towed outside the pier, but the captain seeing

---

* For dogged pertinacity in avoiding full stops, this sentence is not without merit !

his galliot overwhelmed by the waves, and not being able to make any resistance, was compelled to abandon the attempt, after having encountered the most perilous dangers. In the meantime the vessel lost her mizzenmast and mainmast, and soon afterwards disappeared, leaving only the foremast to be seen, which was covered with people. Three boats directed their course towards the coast, but two only succeeded in reaching Fort Risban, from which 22 persons were landed by the assistance of the garrison of that fort, and the people employed about the Custom House, who came down to the shore. The third boat was swallowed up by the waves. The sea was instantly covered with wrecks of all description, which came, one after another, on shore along the coast, with numbers of dead bodies. The persons saved are the captain, the first lieutenant, the second lieutenant, an officer of the army of Bengal, two passengers, and 16 lascars. All the rest perished. The night has been still more dreadful than the day, and this morning the winds continue to blow with much violence from N.N.W. and N.N.E., with rain, snow, and hail. Our first care has been to give these unfortunate people who escaped the assistance they stood in need of.

" ' I have the honour to be

" ' C. Fourcroy.

" ' *Commissary of Marine.*' "

The paragraph that appeared in the *Morning Herald* of the 3rd of January, imputing cold-blooded inhumanity on the part of the Governor of Dunkirk, not unnaturally gave great offence to the French, and the *Morning Chronicle* of the 28th of January copies a letter which was published in the *Moniteur* of the 19th of that month " *to refute the calumnies* " of the English journals. This was the letter or petition signed by Captain Eastwick, and runs as follows :—

" Dunkirk, *January* 8, 1811.

" To His Excellency the Minister of Marine and Colonies.

" Monseigneur,

"The merchant vessel the *Elizabeth*, of which I had the command, was of 650 tons burden, and sailed from London the 25th October, 1810. Though not belonging to the East India Company, she was bound for Madras and Bengal.

"I anchored at Cork in Ireland, from which place we sailed on 19th December. After having sustained much damage from a gale of wind, we got aground amidst the sandbanks in the Road of Dunkirk, and our vessel went to pieces in view of that city on the 28th December last. There were on board 380 persons, of whom 30 were passengers, 250 lascars (Indian sailors), and 100 seamen. Out of this number there were but 22 saved, including myself. We were made prisoners of war.

"Although having suffered shipwreck, and having been saved from its perils by our own unaided exertions (it not being possible for the praiseworthy efforts of the marine to afford us any assistance from the shore), we are satisfied to consider ourselves prisoners of war. But our unhappy situation, and the circumstances which led to it, induce a hope that your Excellency will permit of our being exchanged for an equal number of French prisoners at the disposal of the British Government.

"Deeply impressed with gratitude towards the brave inhabitants of Dunkirk, and the members of its naval administration, who most generously supplied us with every comfort after our sufferings, we particularly request that in case of compliance we may be exchanged for seamen of that place, if there be any such in England. I should consider myself eminently fortunate in being the instrument of their liberation. It is the only way in which I may be able to testify my warm gratitude to the people of Dunkirk, without whose prompt and generous assistance we should have all perished.

"Your Excellency will permit me to submit to your notice such means as appear to me best calculated to forward the exchange. Standing rather high in the estimation of the Admiralty, I have no doubt of success in a proceeding dictated by sentiments of gratitude. I require, in the first place, permission to proceed to England in order to negotiate the exchange. I pledge my word of honour for my return, and offer, moreover, a personal or pecuniary security. Secondly, to bring to Dunkirk, or any other place your Excellency may appoint, 22 French prisoners of war, born at Dunkirk, and of equal rank with such of my crew as have been saved. Thirdly, to conduct these latter to England.

"A detail of the generous assistance afforded me by the people of Dunkirk will, I have no doubt, make a due impression on the Admiralty, and on that I ground my sanguine hope of the success of the undertaking.

"R. W. EASTWICK."

This is the letter which Napoleon Buonaparte read, and on the back of which he wrote the order for the unconditional release of the prisoners. And this, viewed by the light of his recent message to the Senate, before quoted, must be considered as a proof of especial favour. It is somewhat disappointing to find that the *Morning Herald,* so far from withdrawing the remarks which gave offence, came out with the following paragraph on the 5th of February, 1811 :—

"The French are stated to have practised an artifice respecting the letter signed by Captain Eastwick, which was published in the *Moniteur*. They presented a letter to him, which he refused to sign without being permitted to correct it. That permission was given, and having altered it, he signed it. But it was, notwithstanding, published in its original state."

It is probable that the alterations were merely matters of detail, there being some palpable inaccuracies in the letter, the composition of which shows it to have been of French construction. But these had certainly no reference to the conduct of the Governor or inhabitants of Dunkirk, to whose humanity and sympathy ample testimony is born, not only in the body of the letter, but also in this narrative.

There is a final touch, characteristically British, contained in the *Herald* of the 2nd of February :—

"On Saturday last, the day before the release of the British prisoners, a most gallant affair was witnessed in the Roads of Dunkirk. A British brig-of-war, dashing in close to the pier, and under the French batteries, cut out from thence a French transport laden with naval stores, bound from Boulogne to Flushing. The enterprise was executed with so much skill and rapidity, that the prize was gone before the batteries could be brought to bear upon the brig with effect. The same brig hailed the *Cartel* in her passage, to inquire after their friends at Dunkirk, and ' *what the folks of that town thought of the prank that had been played upon them the day before?* ' "

A pretty prank forsooth ! Though the captives still in the hands of " the folks of that town " might have deemed it a trifle ill-timed.

CHAPTER XIV.

I call on Mr. Allport to recover the insurance due on the *Elizabeth*—
He puts me off—I discover his dishonest conduct—Sail for India
in the *Portsea*—We are nearly lost off the Cape—Change into
the *Castlereagh* at Table Bay—Sail for the Isle of France—
Being too heavily laden we are in great danger during a storm—
Fright of Mr. Bell, a passenger on board—His clever operation
on a young recruit—Reach Mauritius—Sail for Calcutta with
Captain Bell—Purchase the *Caledon*—Take her for several short
voyages—Return to Calcutta and sell her to a Portuguese, bu
command her during a voyage to Rio Janeiro—From thence I take
passage home to England in the *Express*—We are sighted by the
Anaconda, an American privateer—An action ensues—We are
captured—Crew and equipment of the *Anaconda*—Her captain,
after plundering us, gives us back our vessel—We arrive at
Fernando—Repair damages and sail for England—Reach Falmouth—Many people visit the *Express* out of curiosity—I send
my baggage in a waggon to London—It is robbed on the way—I
go up by post-chaise—Welcome from my wife—We go to live at
Clock House, Warfield—Death of Mr. English—I attend his
funeral—Conduct of my aunt, Miss Archer—She dies shortly
afterwards—Circumstances connected with the making of her
will which proved very unfortunate for me.

SHORTLY after my arrival in London I called
on Mr. Allport, Messrs. Porcher and Company's clerk, to recover the sum of £3,000,
for which I had insured my interest in the
Elizabeth. Twice or thrice he put me off with
excuses of a trivial nature, that presently raised

my suspicions, and caused me to press for an immediate settlement. Whereupon, with great hesitation, he confessed that he had received the money, but had omitted to make it over to my wife, and was not now in a position to pay me. The truth was, not anticipating my release from the French captivity, he had been base enough to yield to the temptation of acquiring, or at least obtaining the use of, a large sum of money at the expense of one whose misfortunes should have excited his compassion rather than suggested such iniquity. I saw it was no good to press him, and therefore accepted an arrangement by which he undertook to repay me by instalments. It was ten years before he settled the account, and then with one hundred pounds short of the full sum. This experience was a lesson to me, which I took to heart, never afterwards to transact business with any but the firm itself.

Being now a poor man and ruined, my destiny again banished me from a happy home, and in June I left Portsmouth in the *Portsea*, Captain Roberts, with troops on board for the Cape. We were one of several ships under convoy of the *Emerald* frigate, and our vessel sailed so badly that the man-of-war had sometimes to take her in tow.

Near the Cape, one dark night, whilst in this situation, a sudden squall struck us, and the tow-line breaking, we fell away. Being under a great press of sail, the main and mizzen masts immediately went by the board, and having cut them adrift, we were obliged to run before the wind. When morning came we were out of sight of the rest of the fleet. We soon rigged up jury masts, with which we sailed as quickly, or, to be more correct, as slowly as before, and eventually reached port, where we found the *Portsea* had been given up for lost. Fortunately I had a letter ready written for any homeward-bound ship we might chance to meet, and on the very day we entered Table Bay, the *Emerald* was under weigh for England, and this letter sent by her contradicted many others in the same vessel, reporting that we had foundered.

Being anxious to reach India I left the *Portsea*, which was likely to be some time refitting, and embarked by the *Castlereagh* for the Mauritius, which island we had lately captured from the French. This vessel was too deeply laden, for her commander, Captain Cowper, being desirous of saving the high charges for ballast at the Isle of France, did not discharge that which he had on board, but, in addition, filled up with a heavy cargo of salt provisions, to the serious danger of the ship, which, meeting with bad weather, and being unable to ride it, shipped enormous quantities of water, and also sprung a leak, and was with great difficulty kept from sinking.

The storm we encountered raged with great violence for five days, driving us out of our course. During this time the passengers on board lived in the greatest state of alarm, and for the last forty-eight hours were all dressed, and ready to take to the boats at a moment's notice. However, the gale happily abated, and we were able to continue our course again. The night after this a ludicrous incident occurred. There was on board as a passenger a gentleman named Bell, an assistant-surgeon going out to India to take up an appointment in the Company's service. Having fallen asleep, he dreamt that there was a great hole in the ship's side, and, jumping out of his cot, knocked over the water jug. Feeling the cold water about his toes, he ran headlong up on deck, shouting out that the ship was sinking. The carpenter and a number of the officers at once hurried to his cabin, where, to their considerable gratification, they discovered the mistake, and were able to relieve the fears of the other passengers, who had all left their cabins and congregated by the boats.

The next day a sad accident occurred. A fine young recruit got his foot crushed between a cable and the hatches, owing to the rolling of the ship sending the former adrift. Nothing could have been more dreadful, and it was some time before the limb was liberated. It was then found that the bone and flesh and muscle were all crushed into a pulp, and that immediate amputation was necessary.

Whereupon Mr. Bell, the same who had created the scare the night before, undertook to perform the operation. We had not any surgical instruments on board, but a carving-knife was sharpened, and one of the carpenter's fine saws set for the occasion. The recruit, who was quite a lad, with a bright intelligent face, lay on the deck, and three or four assisted to hold him. But there was no necessity for this, for he bore the operation with the greatest fortitude. It was the finest display of skill that I had ever seen, the whole affair scarcely taking a minute before the leg was off a little below the knee. I could not help in my mind contrasting the coolness of the performance with the panic exhibited by the performer a few hours previously. Mr. Bell made a fine cure, and I believe got promoted by the *éclat* it gave him; but I·can never recall the incident without thinking of the poor young recruit, who, to judge by his demeanour under suffering, would have turned out a fine soldier, and but for this sad accident might have carved a career for himself in India.

We reached Mauritius without any further mishap. I only stayed there three days, and then sailed for Calcutta with Captain Fell, who had formerly been an officer of mine. The south-west monsoon prevailing, after crossing the line, we made a romping passage to the Sandheads. Here, not finding a pilot, and being unwilling to beat about outside in the dirty sea that was running, I volunteered to take the ship up the river, and notwithstanding a seven years' absence from these waters, did so satisfactorily, bringing her safely to anchor off Garden Reach.

On my arrival at Calcutta there happened to be a ship called the *Caledon* offered for sale, which I bought, and loaded with a special cargo for the Isle of France, believing, from information obtained by me there, that it would be likely to sell very profitably. No one could conjecture whither I was bound, but unfortunately just before I sailed, another Mauritius ship arrived with news which caused me to fear I should be disappointed in my market. In this difficulty I went to my friend Mr. John Palmer, and explained the case to him ; whereupon he very kindly agreed to purchase half my cargo, and pay me a good freight to land it at Ceylon. This I did, and took the remainder on to the Isle of France, where, after all, I sold it well. I was then chartered by Government to take the settlement from the Island of Rodrigue to Bombay ; and having landed them there, was again chartered to carry back a cargo of timber to the Isle of France ; but on my arrival at the latter place, finding it was not wanted, the Governor agreed to pay me for delivering it at Calcutta, which I did.

Here I sold the *Caledon*, at a good profit, to a Portuguese who had dealings with South America, and who required me to take her to Rio Janeiro, to which I agreed. I reached this place early in 1813, and after observing all the formalities that the Portuguese impose, closed the concern very profitably, and made the ship over to the agent of the Portuguese I had sold her to. I then proceeded to arrange for a passage home to England,

I succeeded in obtaining one in the *Express*, packet, a gun brig commanded by a captain who was appropriately enough named Quick. She carried a crew of twenty-eight persons, was armed with ten 4 and 6-pounder guns, and had the reputation of being a particularly fast sailer, whilst her captain was as smart a seaman as could be desired; both of which advantages were very requisite at a time when, owing to the war with America, the privateers of that country were likely to be encountered.

A few days after we started, and when we were in latitude 6° South, a sail was one evening sighted a long distance to windward. We were bowling along at a great pace, and the wind continuing all night in our favour, we thought no more of it. But when morning came we found, to our surprise, that the strange sail was evidently following, and gradually overhauling us. She had during the night come up close enough for us to see her build, and her low, rakish appearance and immense spread of canvas created suspicion.

As I reached the deck I found Captain Quick scanning her through his telescope. Perceiving my presence, he handed the glass to me, saying,

"What do you make of her?"

"She is American built and rigged," I answered, "and she'll sail and shoot two feet for our one. And it is my belief she is sailing in the same direction as she is presently going to shoot."

"I am of the same opinion," he replied, "but

we will soon settle the question whether she is hostile or not."

He thereupon gave orders to haul up the boarding netting, load the guns, distribute small arms, and prepare for action.

As soon as everything was ready—by which time the stranger had approached to within half a mile and hoisted Spanish colours—Captain Quick had one of the longest guns run aft and sent a shot at her, which fell short. She at once hauled down her Spanish colours and hoisted the American flag, and running up abreast of us, fired a shot in front of us as a demand for our surrender.

But Captain Quick was not the man to give in without a blow, and he replied by piping all hands to quarters for the engagement. We opened fire upon her, which she soon returned with interest, keeping, however, at such a distance as to render our pop-guns harmless, whilst her shot went through and through us.

I volunteered to take charge of one of the guns, and an after one was given over to me, which I worked as hard as I could; but it was a hopeless task endeavouring to do any execution, since the enemy kept completely out of range. Captain Quick was everywhere, encouraging his men, even though it was from the first apparent that all the odds were against us. We could neither fight the superior metal, nor run away from the superior speed. Our adversary seeing this, declined, with American caution, to come to close quarters, but standing on and off, gave us shot after shot, all excellently aimed, and gradually cut us to pieces. Towards the end of this one-sided action, which we kept up for an hour and a half, I was wounded by a splinter that struck me on the forehead, and caused a copious bleeding and a stunning sensation. Captain Quick was much concerned at this, and begged me to go below, but I told him that I felt such an admiration for his conduct (which was beyond all praise, both by reason of his determined pluck and his spirited demeanour), that I would not desert the post he had honoured me with, whilst I was able to stand to it, even though I could no longer assist in or direct the work.

At last we found ourselves in a sinking state. Several of the crew were wounded and two killed, the sails were shot away, the spars knocked into splinters, the foremast gone by the board, and the smart little brig rolled a helpless cripple upon the water. It was evident we could derive nothing from further resistance, and so Captain Quick reluctantly hauled down his colours, and ran them up again Union downwards.

The American perceiving our surrender and signal of distress, sent three boats to board us. When they reached the *Express* the first man that stepped on our deck was a native of Falmouth, and known to some of the crew, who called him by name, and cursed him in sailor fashion, which he did not seem to relish, being no better than a base pirate to fight against his own nation and flag.

The officer in command, after having briefly but handsomely congratulated Captain Quick on his gallant resistance, took charge of the brig, and at once ordered his own and our carpenters to plug the shot holes, through which the water was coming in. All our crew were then taken on board the American. It proved to be the *Anaconda*, of 400 tons burden, and mounting twenty long twelves, with a complement of 140 men.

The large size of this beautiful craft astonished us greatly, for she floated so low in the water that she appeared a much smaller vessel than she really was. There was a tautness and trimness about her such as I have never seen excelled, even in an English man-of-war. The boatswain and forty of her men were English, and the discipline on board was just as strict, and the crew as smart in drill and dress, as on a king's ship. But despite all this she had not in any way distinguished herself, for though she was more than two months out from her port of Boston, ours was the first capture she had made.

We had £20,000 in specie on board the *Express*, and this was soon transferred to the *Anaconda*. After an examination of our vessel, the Captain offered us the brig back again, saying candidly she was so much shattered that his prize-crew did not care to venture in her. We accepted this offer, and gave our parole of honour as required. Our guns were then thrown overboard, and everything of value plundered, before we were allowed to return. At the last moment the privateer captain seemed to have some misgivings, for he said he would stay twenty-four hours in our company to see if we kept afloat, and if nothing happened in that time, hoist his colours and leave us. He also, very civilly, gave us a letter in which he desired all his country ships to let us go free, stating we had fought our vessel until she was almost cut from under us, and being no longer worth plundering, we were deserving of the favour he requested.

Although the *Express* was in such a sorry condition, we nevertheless managed to patch her up, and sailed her to the island of Fernando, where we refitted ship as well as was possible, and starting again for England, eventually reached Falmouth in the month of May. At that port several hundred people visited the brig out of curiosity, for she was a sight to see, being patched and tinkered in a most remarkable manner, and showing all the signs of her recent engagement. Everyone wondered how she managed to cross the Atlantic in such a state, and I remember that there was a description of her arrival given in the journals of the day. *

* " *The Express*, packet, Captain Quick, has arrived at Falmouth from Rio Janeiro in 57 days. On her passage, in latitude 6° 26' *South* and 29° 8' *West* she fell in with the American brig privateer *Anaconda*, of 18 guns and 120 men, and after an action of an hour and a half, during which the packet had all her masts and yards crippled, and all her rigging cut to pieces, she was compelled to strike. The privateer had been 75 days out from Boston, and had not made any other

Having said good-bye to Captain Quick at Falmouth, and with great regret at parting from so excellent a man, I made arrangements to proceed to London by post-chaise. I had saved several ornaments and Indian shawls for my wife, being presents which I had brought with me in the *Caledon* from Calcutta, and which the captain of the privateer had very courteously allowed me to retain, observing jocularly that he never plundered the 'fair sex. These I put into a waggon at Falmouth, as most secure to take them to London. A fellow-passenger, who was going to travel with me in the same post-chaise, took his own baggage with him and got all safe to town, but the waggon in which I had sent my effects was plundered by robbers on the road, and I lost all. The presents for my wife were worth two hundred pounds, and their being stolen was a great disappointment to me, after having safely brought them so far, and through so many perils. It was not so much from their intrinsic worth (although that was considerable), as from the fact that I always made it a point to bring my wife some memento of every voyage. But when I expressed to her my regret at the misfortune, she immediately silenced me, observing it was the intention and not the gifts that she prized most. It was always so with her : she never thought of

capture. The privateer took out £20,000 sterling in gold, and all the stores and spars, canvas, cordage, provisions, &c., and threw the guns overboard, and then gave her up, restoring to the passengers their private effects."—Extract from *The Times*, 24th May, 1813.

herself. Whenever I returned to her safe and sound she was satisfied, and would allow nothing to cloud the happiness of our meeting.

I had been absent two years from home, during which time I had only been actively employed for about thirteen months, yet in that short period I had managed to complete seven clear freights, which resulted in a profit of ten thousand pounds. I now felt myself sufficiently well established, and so I determined to settle down to a life of retirement, and no longer risk my fortune in foreign countries and hazardous voyages. I therefore invested my capital in England, and took a lease of Clock House, situated about six miles from Warfield, in Berkshire, and here, on the 13th March, 1814, my youngest son Edward was born, to whom my friend General (then Colonel) Backhouse stood godfather.

Just previous to this event, on the 4th January, my godfather and step-grandfather, Mr. English, died at Lower Edmonton, and left all his property and fortune to my aunt, Miss Elizabeth Archer, who had kept his house for him ever since I could remember. I had not seen much of Mr. English of late years, although I had from time to time paid him a visit, but he had become a very old man, with failing faculties, and for the last few years had not, I think, remembered who I was. However, I considered it my duty to attend his funeral, and did so, and offered my aunt, who was a most inexperienced woman, every assistance in my power. But she appeared very cold in her manner, being strangely under the influence of my cousin, Mrs. Wright, the only daughter of my mother's second sister, and who resided close to my Aunt Archer at Lower Edmonton. I had been for so many years and for such long periods absent from England, that I found I was regarded almost as an interloper by my kinsfolk, and when I presented myself at the house to attend the funeral I saw it created actual surprise. However, I took no notice of this, but comported myself in a fitting manner, and assumed the position that I felt was rightly mine, as the only male member of the family.

Before I left, my Aunt Elizabeth, observing an opportunity for privacy, called me aside and whispered into my ear, "I feel sorry, Robert, at the reception you have been accorded, but be sure I shall take every care of you and your children." I begged her not to be concerned at anything that had taken place, and as to my having been forgotten in my godfather's will (which had just been read), I could hardly have expected him to remember one whom he had not seen more than a dozen times in thirty years. I then thanked her for her kindly expression of feeling towards me, and said good-bye.

I never saw her again alive, for though I went up from Berkshire three times to pay my duty to her, my cousin, Mrs. Wright, on each occasion prevented my doing so.

My aunt, Miss Archer, survived Mr. English

only three months and a half, and died on the 18th
of March following, just five days after my wife's
confinement. I was informed that on the 16th of
that month she had been seized with violent pains
and immediately made her will, and that the disorder carried her off forty-eight hours afterwards.
There were circumstances about the making of this
will which I did not like, for with the exception of
a thousand pounds bequeathed to me, and five
hundred pounds to my daughter Eliza, all the
property, consisting of freehold and copyhold
estate, and money to the value of at least ten
thousand pounds, was left to my cousin, Mrs.
Sarah Wright. This will was actually drawn out
by Mr. Wright, who was to receive the benefit as
husband of my cousin, and who worded it as if
my aunt had been at variance with me, which not
being the case I am positive could not have been
dictated by her. Mrs. Wright the elder, the
mother of the husband, and an interested party,
was one of the witnesses, and the doctor who
attended my aunt was the other. No notice was
given me of my aunt's illness till the day after
her death, and meanwhile probate had been taken
out at Doctors' Commons.

There was, to say the least of it, an impropriety
in having an interested person to make the will
out, but there was also another curious circumstance, which I was at a loss to account for (and
which accident brought to my notice), namely, the
presents made to the surgeon, who not only

attended my aunt, but was also a witness to her will. This person was very partial to a haunch of mutton, and Mr. Wright's servant was twice observed taking over a very nice one to him as a present. I do not wish to insinuate anything against the surgeon, but knowing the parties who gave it, I cannot account for their liberality. I also discovered afterwards that the same surgeon was in debt to my godfather, but I have never discovered any proof that the money owing to the estate was repaid.

My aunt was taken ill on a Monday and died on the Wednesday following, and on the very same day probate of her will was taken out, although it was not until Saturday that a letter was sent acquainting me of her decease. This I received on Sunday morning, and was at Edmonton the same evening. The indecent haste of the proceedings, which were so very prejudicial to myself as heir-at-law, have always struck me as being most unfortunate for me, who stood in as close a relationship to Miss Archer as did Mrs. Sarah Wright, and had in addition a family to provide for. I was strongly advised to contest the will, and cause an inquiry to be made into the circumstances attending it, but I did not care to make the family affairs public, and decided to take no action in the matter.*

* A portion of the Edmonton property came to Captain Eastwick on Mrs. Wright's death, and was a part of his estate at his own decease.

CHAPTER XV.

I NOW remained in England for two years, enjoying the quiet of home life, which suited my
tastes, and left me nothing to desire. My money
being all safely invested, and under my own immediate direction, I had no apprehensions about it,
and had begun to accustom myself to a shore life,
when I found myself obliged to leave England and
sail for India once more.

This was occasioned by my daughter Eliza, who

was now in her nineteenth year, receiving an invitation from her Uncle Bellasis to go out to him in Bombay, where he had risen to be a colonel in the artillery, having been reinstated in his former profession when he returned from Botany Bay. There had always been a great natural affection between my wife and her sister, Mrs. Bellasis, and the latter having no children of her own, begged that we would entrust her with our daughter. For a young girl to proceed to India in those days was to ensure her establishment in life. Eliza had inherited some of my roving disposition, and evinced the greatest inclination to accept her uncle's invitation, and so, after much consideration, my wife and I sanctioned her request to go out to the East. But as I did not like to entrust her to any other care than my own, I determined to accompany her, and in consequence took a couple of passages on board the *Maitland*, Captain Kingsley, who had formerly been an officer of my own.

We arrived in Calcutta in September, 1816, after a slow and tedious voyage. We were first of all invited to stay at the house of a friend of mine, Mr. Dring, who lived at Garden Reach. Here my daughter gained her first insight into Indian life, and I shall never forget the continual state of curiosity and wonder in which she lived. We happened to arrive during the period of a festival called the "Doorga Poojah," when constant processions of people were to be seen parading the streets, carrying images of men and beasts, surrounded by ridiculous paintings, which they afterwards threw into the river: these examples of the idolatry or the country affected Eliza greatly, and filled her with sensations in which contempt and pity ruled her mind in turns. She could at first hardly be brought to believe that these painted daubs were regarded with reverence, but when it was explained to her that such was the case, she was seized with a profound compassion, and her reflections and sentiments did credit to the religious training she had received from her mother, and which distinguished her through life.

Our visit to Mr. Dring was cut short by a sad circumstance. We met at the house a great friend of his, Mr. Hendric, who after many years' residence in the country, was on the point of returning to England with his wife. They sailed a few days after we landed, but the ship coming to an anchor off Fultah, Mr. and Mrs. Hendric went ashore in a boat. Returning at twelve o'clock at night, the latter, either through taking a chill or from some other cause, became violently ill, and died in a few hours. This so affected her poor husband that he went raving mad, and was landed from the ship, and brought to Mr. Dring's house. His constant spectacle there was so melancholy, that I thought it best to remove my daughter, and as we had several other invitations we took our leave, and went to Mrs. Hayes, who resided at Bankshall, which was the largest house in Calcutta.

This lady entertained a great deal, and my daughter had the opportunity of seeing the most fashionable side of Calcutta life. The mornings were passed in receiving visitors from nine o'clock till one, after which the ladies retired for their siesta till three, when dinner was served. In the evening they drove to the Course, a very fashionable drive where every one met : but though extending for three miles, it was the custom not to traverse more than one, so that the carriages did nothing but pass and repass until it was time to return.

There were many amusements going on during the evening, such as concerts, assemblies, balls, dances, and the play. The theatre was small but pretty, containing only one row of boxes and the pit. All the actors were amateurs, and some of them very clever, but the actresses most inferior. Whilst we were there, a performance of *The Poor Gentleman* was given, by which we were greatly entertained; but when it came to *Macbeth*, we wished we had not gone to see so noble a play misrepresented and spoilt. The concerts were held at the Town Hall, a very handsome building, and one of the chief singers was Mr. Linton, a professor, with whom all the ladies allowed themselves to be in love. He sang the " Death of Abercrombie " with equal taste and feeling. The assemblies were held at Hastie's Rooms, and were on the same plan as the subscription balls in England ; but to all these amusements admittance was extremely expensive. My daughter was invited to several dances, which were kept up with great spirit, and Mrs. Hayes gave a very large ball, with a second supper at four o'clock in the morning, to which most of the people stayed. There were also some dinner-parties that we attended, but these proved formal and stupid, and cards were seldom introduced, so that people could only gape and wonder why it was necessary to spoil a good dinner by such a want of mental entertainment after it.

I took my daughter to see all the sights of the city, obtaining permission to go over Government House, which was a veritable palace. On Sundays we attended either the cathedral or the church, where two services were held, as well as one on Thursday evenings, but the preaching was very indifferent. The building of a Scotch church was nearly finished.

One of the pleasantest days we passed was that which we devoted to visiting Serampore. Having engaged a *budgerow*, or large country boat, we sailed up the river with the tide. The scenery on either side was flat, but very pretty, with many *ghauts* and *pagodas*, whilst the different crafts upon the water diversified the view. We arrived at Serampore at two o'clock, and landed opposite the residence of Dr. Carey, a most distinguished and able missionary, to whom we had a letter of introduction. He received us very kindly, and showed us all over the Mission establishment. My daughter was much struck with the printing offices, where they were engaged in translating and printing the

Scriptures in several different languages, including Chinese.

Later in the afternoon we went to call on Dorabjee Byramjee, my old agent, who was living at Scrampore, which belonged then to the Danes, and where people who were involved, resorted, as here they were free from arrest. Dorabjee had for many years availed himself of this haven of refuge, where, owing to his superior manners, he was treated with great respect, despite his loss of fortune. I found him grown very stout. He was much affected at seeing me, shedding tears and saying he was ashamed to meet one whom he had robbed of so large a sum. I told him that so far as I was concerned I forgave him, which he said was more than he deserved. Perhaps it was : for he was living very comfortably in an excellent house, surrounded by a handsome garden, and seemed to want for nothing. He invited me to come in, and we were glad to rest, but after staying a short while I perceived that Dorabjee's agitation made the visit painful to my daughter, and so we took our leave.

Shortly after this I hired a house for our own residence quite close to Entally, where my daughter was born, and this afforded the opportunity of going over many of the walks that my wife and I had been accustomed to take at the time we lived here. It was pleasurable to me to thus retrace former habits and recall the happy hours of twenty years before. In the retrospect that connected me with this place, my mind embraced many varied experiences, many sorrows, many dangers, many joys, showing me how much I had to be thankful for. My daughter entered into my humour as I recognized old familiar spots, each eloquent with association, and was never tired of listening to me. In short, her companionship made the place so pleasant, that, seeing her perfectly happy, and the weather being cool and bracing, I prolonged my stay here until the middle of December, when I took passage for Bombay in the *Commodore Hayes*, a fine new ship of seven hundred tons, commanded by Captain Pelly.

On board this vessel we were most comfortable, my daughter having a spacious cabin situated in the Round-house, in which she was able to sit during the heat of the day, with the large stern windows open, busy with her work or reading. We experienced a pleasant passage down the Bay, and made Ceylon on the 5th of January, in dull, rainy weather. Here we went ashore at Colombo to the house of Mr. Gibson, who invited us all to dinner. In the afternoon a number of native merchants came to exhibit their stock of precious stones and jewellery, and I purchased a set of moonstones for my wife, these being a new gem lately discovered in the island. We left Ceylon after a stay of three days, and meeting with variable and contrary winds were much delayed, being a week in getting up to Cranganore, a place where, it is said, Nebuchadnezzar landed twenty thousand Jews, captives from

Babylon, who were three years on their journey. hither. For some centuries they throve and became an opulent and prosperous people, but after this were gradually reduced both in numbers and wealth, and had become at this time the poorest people on the coast. This place was taken by Tippoo Sultan before the siege of Seringapatam, but after that it passed under our rule.

After leaving Cranganore, the wind shifted, and we made a quick run up to Bombay; but here, to our dismay, found that Colonel Bellasis had been appointed to the command of the artillery in the Peishwa's dominions, and had left a letter for me saying that when we arrived we were to make our way to a place called Siroor, where he was stationed.

This was a great undertaking, for I had no knowledge of country travelling, never having been ten miles inland in India in my life, except round about Calcutta. However, I made all the arrangements necessary, being much assisted by my good friend Captain Dickenson, with whom we were staying, and on the 1st of February, 1817, we embarked in a large and comfortable boat belonging to the Superintendent of Marine, to cross to a village called Panwell, situated on the mainland on the opposite side of Bombay harbour. From this place we were to commence our land journey of over a hundred miles. It was necessary for us to take everything that was requisite for our personal comfort, as the country we were about to march through was native territory, where no conveniences of any sort existed. I was obliged, therefore, to supply myself with tents and furniture—the latter suitable for folding up and carrying on the heads of coolies, or the backs of beasts of burden. Then there were several boxes of stores and wines, with cooking utensils, plates, crockery, and linen, and in fact everything that is required in a civilized state of life. In addition to this I had to engage a dozen native servants to wait upon us, and I also provided arms of warfare for our defence in case of danger on the journey, it being no uncommon thing for travellers to be attacked.

During our passage across the harbour, my daughter was much shocked by the ghastly spectacle of three men hanging in chains from a gibbet situated on an eminence in one of the islands, quite close to which we passed. They had been recently executed, after conviction, for a most atrocious murder. Happily the natural beauty of the scenery soon turned her thoughts into pleasanter channels. The only place that I have ever seen that could vie with Bombay in exquisite loveliness is the harbour of Sydney in New Holland, but the former possesses that additional elegance of tropical surroundings which is so especially charming to the European eye. As evening drew on we were enchanted with the prospect of the sun setting, in a crimson and purple sky, behind the island of Elephanta, bringing out in vivid relief the fringe of palm and cocoanut trees that covered it, and which gave it such a softened appearance; whilst a little later, after the short eastern twilight had deepened into night, the full moon rose over the distant ghauts, lighting up their jagged outlines with its silver rays, and presenting a marvellous scene like some fantastic view in fairyland. To complete our enjoyment, there was a cool breeze which, after the heat of the day, was most refreshing.

It was late before we reached the village of Panwell, where to our great joy, and to my even greater relief, we met Colonel Bellasis himself. He had received a letter from me informing him of our intended departure, and an excuse being afforded him of coming down to the coast to take up a detachment of sixty-one European gunners, he covered the distance in two days, and arrived a few hours before we did.

There was a small tavern at Panwell kept by a Portuguese, and remarkable for being the only one in the Mahratta empire. Here we found a first-rate dinner prepared for us, and everything so comfortable, that all the troubles we had apprehended from the journey were immediately forgotten, and we congratulated ourselves upon having found so clever a cook and so excellent a house of entertainment, in a place where we had expected nothing but a wild jungle. But the good opinion we conceived of the landlord was soon destined to be destroyed, for he proved himself a scoundrel by supplying the soldiers, after nightfall, with a large quantity of cheap country liquor at the rate of a shilling a bottle, and the consequence was that before morning the entire detachment to the drummer boy was drunk !

We were therefore obliged to defer our start till they recovered, for at present not one of them could stand and much less walk. It was impossible to proceed without them, since Colonel Bellasis had taken upon himself the duty of marching them up, and also because he considered their escort advisable, the road being infested with several bands of Pindarees (a wild and barbarous race of freebooters), who had recently committed many depredations and made several daring attacks on travellers.

Colonel Bellasis at once caused the Portuguese to be arrested, and determined to court-martial and punish him forthwith. Seeing the desperate results, and especially the vomiting, that followed the drinking, I was for making the man imbibe a fixed measure of his own poisonous liquor, conceiving he would then be most appropriately punished. But Colonel Bellasis preferred ordering the administration of a flogging, and the fellow received one calculated to deter him from seeking on any future occasion to make a vile profit out of the debauchery of British troops.

At four o'clock the following afternoon we commenced our journey. Our way lay through an extensive plain, producing vast quantities of rice in the rainy season, but now presenting a barren and dry appearance, except for the mango *topes* and tamarind trees, many groves of which were studded about. My daughter travelled in a *palanquin*, which is a sort of covered-in couch, carried on the shoulders of four men by means of a pole protruding from each end. The bearers are trained to this work, and travel at an amazing fast pace, keeping such perfect step that the motion is almost as smooth as that of a carriage on a good road. Colonel Bellasis and myself rode, my horse being a country one, tall and exceeding vicious and given to constant neighings, whilst my companion bestrode a fine Arab charger, in which he took great pride. We made about twelve miles the first day; by which time the Europeans had got over the effects of their liquor; and hereafter we started every morning at three o'clock, so as to get over each march before the sun gathered strength. In two days we reached the foot of the Ghauts, the name of the range of hills that divide the plains from the Uplands, or Deccan country, and commenced the ascent. Four additional bearers were now necessary for my daughter's *palanquin*, the path being very steep, and in places almost perpendicular, often skirting precipices, down which it made Eliza dizzy to look.. During the ascent we met a large party of *Brinjaries*, who are a wandering tribe of people coming from the interior of Hindostan, and carriers of merchandise by trade. They travel all over Asia, and protection is granted them by every nation, since without their aid no commerce could exist. We were almost suffocated by the dust raised by the thousands of bullocks they were driving, each of which was laden with two bags of grain, or bales of other goods, slung across its back.

We reached the top of the Ghauts, an elevation of 4,000 feet, at 7 a.m., and found the difference of climate very perceptible, for although the heat had been most trying down below, the sun was here rather agreeable than otherwise. Our camp was pitched at a very pretty little village called Candalla, where there is a large tank, around which we strolled in the evening; but the pleasure of the excursion was much spoilt by the starting up of no less than seven snakes in our path, which alarmed my daughter greatly.

From Candalla we marched to Carlee, where we stayed a day in order to visit some celebrated caves, and the next morning started for Wargaum, passing on the way the fort of Lowghur, where the Peishwa confines all his state prisoners. We crossed the *Indouranee* river three times, and just before reaching our camp were met by my wife's nephew, Captain Tom Morris, who was able to give us more recent news of England than we possessed. He accompanied us for the last four marches, enlivening the journey by his witty conversation, his spirits, and his genial manner. On the tenth day after our departure from

Panwell, we reached Siroor, the distance traversed being 122 miles.

Here my daughter received an affectionate welcome from her aunt, Mrs. Bellasis, in whose charge I left her with every confidence for her happiness and comfort. She was shortly afterwards married to Major John Ford, an officer on the Bombay establishment, who was then commanding a brigade of infantry in the Mahratta Peishwa's service—an appointment of great emolument.

I returned by myself to Bombay, and from thence took passage in a country ship bound for Calcutta; but putting in at Cochin on the way, I was introduced to a native shipbuilder who was in want of money to rig and finish a brig he had just launched. Upon the security of this I agreed to lend him ten thousand rupees, and when she was ready to sail I took command of her (naming her the *Eliza* after my daughter), with the intention of sailing her to Calcutta, and then selling her to repay my advance. But Captain Robert Gordon, the resident at Alipee, meeting me in Cochin, offered me a cargo of pepper, which I accepted. Unusual exertion had to be made in order to get it on board before the south-west monsoon set in upon us, which it did three days after we had sailed for the Isle of France, which was our destination.

And now we had nearly sunk in consequence of the neglect of the rascally shipbuilder, for in several parts of the upper works of the ship he had bored holes for bolts in improper places, which instead of making good again with wooden plugs, he had merely pitched over. In the gale this worked out, and so nearly filled the ship with water before we were aware of our danger. Our pumps becoming choked by the sand ballast, we were obliged to hoist them up and bail the water out with buckets, and just as we were doing this, the two masts went by the board, and the ship lay nearly on her side. The chief mate was now so over-powered with fear that his example alarmed the crew, and it was with the utmost difficulty that I induced them to wear the ship round, and this, with cutting away the masts, soon put us in a position of greater confidence.

Having got up jury-masts we made sail again, and being favoured with a fair weather passage reached Port Louis in safety, but with pumps going all the voyage. It was not till we docked here to undergo repairs that I found out the real cause of the leak.

Having taken the *Eliza* to Calcutta, I sold her and repaid my advance. The *Granville*, Captain Alságar (the same who had been second mate on board the *Neptune*), being ready to sail for London, I took my passage in her, and arrived home at Warfield in the month of June, 1818, after an absence of two years and ten months, during which I had made a small addition to my fortune.

I was destined to suffer great affliction, for on reaching home I found my little daughter Anna, whom I had left a straight fine child of six, now crippled and deformed with a spinal complaint, brought on by a fright from a servant, which caused her to fall suddenly and so injure her back. After about two years of great suffering, mitigated in some degree by the devoted attention of her mother, she was released from pain, and removed to a happier world.

I have been blessed with good and clever children, five now living and two dead, but I always regarded my little Anna as the flower of the family. Her sense of propriety was far beyond her years. She prayed to live, and said the day before she died that she was very happy with her parents and her brother. A few hours later she was taken very bad, and in such pain that she told her governess, Miss Wright, she was quite unable to pray, and begged her to pray for her. The next day she suddenly called "Father, father!" as she was wont to do when she wanted my help; but as she uttered the words, the breath departed, and when I reached her side I was too late, and never learnt what she desired to say to me. A sweeter spirit than my little Anna never lived.

A short time before her death, she seemed to have some predestination that her end was coming, for, child though she was, she arranged all her affairs, giving keepsakes to every one she knew, and bidding them think of her when they used them or looked at them. And one day she sent every one out of the room saving her mother, and when the two were by themselves, the poor child, with words of strange earnestness, begged her mother not to let any one but herself lay her out when dead. I cannot guess how such knowledge could have entered into the child's brain, but I have often thought of her request, and believe it was prompted by the shame of her deformity. This wish my good wife religiously fulfilled, though the shock and pain of it proved so severe that she never recovered from it, and the memory of the terrible ordeal was present with her to the last day of her life.

Our little girl was buried in a vault in Warfield church, and to her grave my wife would constantly repair to pray and weep. In order to remove her from a scene associated with so much grief and unhappiness, I determined to change my residence; and after one or two moves, at the instigation of my old friend Mr. Harington, who had a house close by, I finally went to reside at 33, Hans Place, in the parish of Pimlico, London.

CHAPTER XVI.

FOR the next six years I continued to reside in
London, and had almost persuaded myself that
I should never go to sea again, when in March,
1824, I unexpectedly received an invitation to open
out a new trade between Holland and China, the

speculation being planned by my friend Sir Charles Forbes and Mr. Anderson. The proposal was a flattering one to my self-esteem, and gave promise of very profitable results, but my wife's health was at this time so unsatisfactory that I fully made up my mind to refuse it, and nothing would have persuaded me to change my intention but her own earnest solicitations. She desired me to accept the offer for the sake of our youngest son Edward, who had become very delicate and was threatened with the same spinal disease that had caused the death of his sister Anna. It was pointed out by medical men that a long sea voyage might assist him to grow out of this weakness, and I was strongly urged by my wife to accept the opportunity that now offered of giving him this advantage. Therefore, much against my own inclination, I consented to go, believing my wife's assurance that her failing health arose from her being so much troubled in mind by the illness that threatened our son, and if she were only satisfied by seeing measures taken for his recovery, she would soon regain her strength and spirits, which now suffered chiefly by reason of the concern she felt for him. Such a devoted woman was never exceeded in goodness and unselfishness !

I therefore wrote to Sir Charles Forbes, and accepted his offer. The ship selected for the venture was the *Asia*, a fine large vessel, and she was partially loaded in London with a freight for Singapore, but also with twenty chests of fine Turkey opium for China, and we were ready to sail in March. My wife, with her sister Mrs. Gordon and Colonel Gordon, accompanied us as far as Gravesend, in order to bid farewell to Edward and myself. It was a great trial to my wife to have to part with her son, who was but a child of ten years of age, but to the last she bore up as bravely as she had done in all the many trials she had met with in life. And this was the last and greatest she had to suffer. I was myself deceived as to the critical condition of her health, but I have reason to believe that she herself knew it, and that when she bade us both farewell she had the secret conviction that it was for ever! I have often and often since that dark sad day mourned my dull perception, which did not discover in her pale fading face the too certain signs of the approaching end, and have lamented with an aching heart the cruel fate that carried me so far away from her when death was at hand.

The *Asia* first went to Hamburg to complete her cargo, and here I made the acquaintance of Mr. Anderson, who insisted upon my going ashore and being his guest at the hotel he was staying at. I did not like to refuse his hospitality, though it put me to some inconvenience. He was much pleased with all I did in the selection and taking in of the cargo, and the speed with which the work was carried out. Sailing from Hamburg we called in at Portsmouth for final orders, and I ran up to town to receive them. I found my wife no better, but, on the contrary, worse in health than when I left her, which was a great shock to me. I would now have given anything to remain with her, but that was impossible, I being too deeply engaged in the concern to be spared, and unable in rectitude to retire from the venture. God knows how much I regretted it!

Notwithstanding leaving Portsmouth with a contrary wind that lasted the whole way to Madeira, my voyage was one of the quickest ever made, and we arrived at Singapore on the 20th of August, after a wonderful run through the Straits of Sunda and Banea without dropping an anchor once, a thing not done before or since. It was the fastest passage ever made up to that time. My son was so improved in health that he was quite a different boy, the voyage have fulfilled all that the physicians promised for it. At Singapore I sold the cargo and loaded up with Straits produce, which I carried to China, where we arrived in September. Here I immediately set to work to secure China goods, and especially the finest chops of tea available, of the quality suitable for the continental market, which had hitherto been supplied solely by American ships.

I must not forget to mention that during my voyage out I experienced much trouble from a passenger, whom I had carried for a nominal payment out of pity. He was a scamping, worthless fellow called T——, and was making the voyage for health, and this circumstance induced me to give him a passage at one-third of the usual rate. But his indisposition was nothing more or less than drunkenness, which, had he been satisfied with getting drunk decently in his own cabin, would have been a matter between him and his conscience. But he soon debauched my mates, especially the chief one, Mr. McIntosh, plying them constantly with liquor, by which their blood got in such a state as to lead them into the most tyrannical conduct towards the crew, and this resulted in a mutiny that required punishment to subdue. I was obliged to put T—— in confinement, and when I landed him at Canton he threatened proceedings against me. Whereupon I told him I would be glad to meet him in any court of law; in spite of which he failed to carry his threat out. He was punished afterwards, for on his return to England the ship he sailed in was taken by pirates, and he being bound, back to back, with the captain, they were both pitched overboard and drowned.

In November we started on our return to Hamburg, and now I was placed under circumstances that I had never before experienced. For my first and second mates, who had become confirmed drunkards, gravely misconducted themselves, and having smuggled a large quantity of liquor on board and hidden it in various places, were continually under its influence, so that their conduct, which had been bad on the way out, now passed all bounds.

Previous to starting on this voyage we had all been made Burghers to sail under a foreign flag, the formality being considered necessary. This circumstance hindered my freedom of action: for I was not quite sure of my legal position, believing that Burghers on board were necessary to constitute the legality of my command, and with the enormous cargo and its insurance at stake, I feared to do anything that might technically alter the conditions of the policy. I was consequently precluded from acting as I should have done, had I been sailing under the British flag. It is needless to say that the two mates quickly perceived this, for I could only reprimand them for their conduct, and this in a very short while ceased to have any effect at all, but on the contrary, by showing the disadvantage under which I laboured, and the immunity from punishment they enjoyed, led to conduct more outrageous than ever on their part, and as a natural consequence their bad example infected the crew, and kept them in a state of semi-mutiny. During the difficult passage of the Eastern seas, they were so absolutely unworthy of trust that I could place no reliance in them. For three days and nights whilst running through the straits I did not once leave the deck, and all throughout the voyage was harassed beyond endurance. Expostulations were vain, and threats useless. At last matters came to such a pass, that, Burgher or no Burgher, I was obliged, for the safety of the ship, to break the first mate, and did so, and placed him in confinement for forty-eight hours, logging the reasons that had forced me to take this course. This had a salutary effect upon the other, whose conduct somewhat improved.

After a week I reinstated the first mate, on his expressing his deep penitence for his misbehaviour and promising amendment. I observed, moreover, that his store of liquor was finished, and in order that he might not have any chance of replenishing it, I resolved not to touch at any port on the way home, but make my course direct to Plymouth, where I arrived in April, 1825.

Here I first learnt the overwhelming news of my wife's death of a galloping consumption in the July of the previous year, just three months after. I had left her. Colonel Gordon, her brother-in-law, had written me information of this bereavement to St. Helena, but as I had not put in at that island, it was left to me to receive the blow with awful suddenness on my arrival at Portsmouth, through the medium of my agents there.

I immediately took a post-chaise and journeyed to Winchester, at the college of which city my son William was a scholar. He was permitted by Dr. Williams, the head master, to proceed with me to London, and we drove to my house at Hans Place. The silent, melancholy home, with no fond familiar face to welcome my return, as I had on every previous occasion been welcomed, made me feel more bitterly than ever the grievous loss I had sustained. My sons endeavoured to cheer me, but it seemed as if nothing could raise the load of sorrow from my breast, and I wandered wistfully over the deserted house, from empty room to empty room, connecting each, by some well-remembered incident, with her who had passed away. The shock was so great that I felt prostrated at this breaking of. the partnership of a lifetime, and it seemed as if I could never again find any pleasure in life. But I had no time to give way to these feelings, however acute they might be. Duty called me back to my ship, and on the second day I was obliged to return to Portsmouth, the *Asia* being ready to continue her voyage. I left my son Edward, who was now wonderfully grown and filled out and strong, with a relative, whilst I obtained permission from Dr. Williams, at Winchester, for my son William to accompany me; and making our way to Portsmouth, took on board a North Sea pilot for greater security, and set sail for Hamburg.

I was very low and troubled with mental suffering, and altogether unfit for work, but I braced myself to complete the task I had undertaken. As soon as we had got into the Channel, the weather came on very stormy, and I was unable to leave my post on deck until I had taken the *Asia* safely through the Straits of Dover. I now began to feel very unwell, and all apprehension of danger being past, I determined to retire to my cabin and seek rest. Having made all the lights and ascertained our exact position

on the chart, I called the pilot and desired him,
if even against his own inclination, to keep the
lead going, and not run under sixteen fathoms,
and on no account to leave the deck without first
calling me. These instructions he promised to
observe, and I went to my berth.

I afterwards learnt that very shortly after I
retired, this unprincipled man went to the cuddy,
and, finding a comfortable corner, lay down to
sleep. A little after midnight, the chief mate,
who was on watch, roused him, and informed
him that there was a light ahead. To which he
replied that he knew of no light likely to be seen,
and that it must be a fishing boat, and that there
was no occasion to disturb him!

I fear the chief officer could not have been
sober, for instead of calling me, as I had ordered
him to do if anything occurred, he allowed the
ship to sail on, until she struck with such violence
as to throw me out of my cot.

To such apathy and unseamanlike behaviour
was my vessel sacrificed!

I immediately ran up on deck, and got the
ship's head off shore in the hope of forcing her
off the sands. But we were too fast aground,
and the effort was fruitless. I then ordered a
constant firing to be kept up, hoping to obtain
assistance, and about 4 a.m. a Dutch pilot boat
came alongside and hailed us.

As the glass was falling, and there were many
signs of a renewal of the bad weather, I sent my

first clerk, Mr. Grassick, and my son William ashore, bidding them go at once to Lloyd's agent at the Hilder, and obtain help. This gentleman at once despatched a number of boats to take out our cargo and lighten ship. Meanwhile my crew were employed in getting down the masts, and preparing to discharge, and by the time the shore boats arrived we were ready for them. But now unfortunately the wind increased, and the sea rising with it, the *Asia* began bumping very hard. We instantly commenced unloading and despatching cargo as rapidly as we could, though much hindered by the weather. Still I must confess that, the damage being done, both the officers, who had up to this time behaved so ill, now tried their utmost to retrieve matters, and the crew worked with a will, never ceasing their efforts for thirty-four hours.

At the end of this time the chief mate came to me, and said that the men were now so completely worn out by fatigue that some rest was necessary.

This I could not deny, but yet every hour meant hundreds of pounds saved, for the wind and sea were rising, and I saw that we should very soon be forced to discontinue our labours. I therefore, whilst commending him for his exertions, urged him to make yet one more attempt. But to this he sullenly replied that it was impossible.

"Get you gone, then!" I cried, for his manner roused my temper, though somewhat unjustly, I fear. "Your neglect and incompetence brought us to this pass, and now you will not assist to save a portion of that which you have been mainly instrumental in losing.   I desire to see you no more ! ''

Then I called for volunteers from the Dutch boatmen, offering them a guinea a-head each for every hour they worked; and having manned the hatches (my own officers and crew had gone below by this time), I continued by myself for six hours to direct the operations of unloading and discharging cargo from all three places, and in that space of time got out of the hold and safely into the boats goods to the value of at least ten thousand pounds sterling.   This, during a dark night and in half a gale of wind, required no inconsiderable exertion, but in spite of my not having enjoyed a moment's rest during the previous forty-eight hours, I was strangely supported by an uncommon physical strength and endurance, which I attribute to the excitement I experienced.   The one predominant determination in my mind was that it should never be said that I had failed in any effort to counteract the misfortune that had overtaken my command.

With daylight it came on to blow a stiff gale. The shore boats had all departed, and we were left alone.   About nine o'clock the pilot lugger returned for the purpose of taking us off.   But I refused permission to the crew to leave, informing them that the shore boats would presently be returning for the remainder of the cargo, there being a good third of it still on board.

The chief mate then made his way to the lugger, and engaged in conversation with the pilot, and about a quarter of an hour afterwards the latter came on board, and represented to me that he would hold me personally responsible for any loss of life that might ensue if I continued to refuse leave to the men to depart; that in his opinion our position was no longer tenable; and that to his certain knowledge no shore boats would put out to sea again in such weather. With that he formally called upon me to express my views.

It was a difficult dilemma in which to act. Of all the men collected there, I was the only one who held out against leaving the ship. The wind had certainly increased very greatly, but the *Asia* had bumped herself firm, and there seemed to me hopes of her holding out. I therefore tried to temporize, and desired the pilot to stand by for another hour, when I would give him my decision. At this a low murmur of disapprobation came from the crew, and one mutinous fellow cried out it would not take that time to get drowned. "Nor to get hanged," I retorted, " as you would find out if you had your deserts."

Whereupon the officers and crew commenced to leave the vessel, and clambered into the lugger, and the pilot seeing this, declined my proposal, saying if I desired to risk the lives of the men, he would not follow my example, and it was his intention to leave at once. And with that he followed my crew.

When they had all got into the pilot boat they hesitated to cast loose. " Come along, sir," cried one or two of the men, in a tone that showed they were not without feeling, "you can do no good by yourself. Why should you sacrifice your life ? " I made no movement, hoping that, out of shame, they would return to their duty.

Then they had a consultation amongst themselves. It pleases me to think, misguided as they were, that they were too English to desert their captain. And then the chief officer and three men came back to the poop where I was standing, drenched with the spray that was now flying over the vessel, and, taking off their hats, begged me respectfully but very earnestly to accompany them, saying that they would acquit me to their last breath of any dereliction of duty, and praying me not to put my blood upon their heads.

I attempted to reason with them, and especially with the chief officer, and asked him to stay by me and set an example to the men, if only for an hour, and by so doing redeem his character. But he replied that his life was precious to him, and that if he stayed he believed he should lose it; and that as for the men, if they would not come back for me, they certainly would not for him !

I now felt I had done all that was possible. When he said his life was precious to him, I could not but reflect that mine was equally so to two orphan sons who needed my care, and the thought of them at this critical moment influenced my behaviour. I hope I did right. I tried to do so to the best of my light. For awhile I stood there, looking round and earnestly endeavouring to estimate my situation. The sea was beginning to break over the ship, and large quantities of water were pouring down the hatches, which had been left open. I looked to landward, vainly hoping I might catch sight of some of the shore boats returning to our aid. But not one was to be seen. I cast my eyes to the sky. It gave me not the sign I desired. All was black and threatening, and the thud of the warning waves, as they beat upon the ship's side, sounded dismally in my ears.

And so I yielded to the force of untoward circumstances. Relaxing my hold of the stanchion to which I had been clinging, I motioned to the men to precede me, and followed them off the ship.

None but those who have been similarly situated can realize what it is for a captain to leave his command. It is like cutting a vein and letting the life's blood pour out. In a career of over forty years at sea, I had never yet lost any vessel for which I was personally responsible; and now, at the close of that career, I felt myself all undone by this terrible misfortune that had overtaken me. And in this particular case the blow was made the harder, by the fact that the venture was a new and promising one, the command and direction of which (I say it not in pride) had been bestowed on me for merit.

Fate was against me! The ship was derelict. The crew had deserted. The waves and the winds were leagued to overcome me. I had done my best. I was left helpless.

We reached the shore with considerable difficulty, and I found my son William anxiously looking out for me. I had no heart to return his affectionate salutations, but accompanied him in silence to the house of Lloyd's agent, where every attention was paid to all the shipwrecked people. For myself I had no stomach for food, but swallowing a cup of broth, I sat myself down by the window looking out to seawards.

All through the night I remained there watching. Towards morning the wind began to moderate, and about four o'clock I left the house, and sought the pier again. Having roused up the Dutch pilot, I prevailed on him to put to sea, with the object of re-boarding the *Asia*.

Through the thick murky morning we made our way, and at length came in sight of the stranded ship, which I rejoiced to see in the same position as when we left her. I now began to congratulate myself upon her recovery, but as we drew nearer I observed, to my great mortification, signs of her having been boarded, and, running up alongside, I found that some Dutch fishermen had forestalled us, and were in possession of my vessel.

This proved of great advantage to them in the suit of law that was instituted about the salvage. For it was shamefully decided that they were entitled to one-third of the value of the whole cargo. And thus, through the incapacity of my officers and the cowardice of my crew, I sustained a heavy and unmerited loss.

Mr. Anderson, to whose firm at Hamburg the ship was consigned, was most severely disappointed in having lost the credit of so fine a cargo being sold by his house, whereby he had hoped to secure the honour of establishing a new trade. And this disappointment influenced his conduct very foolishly; for instead of having the cargo disposed of at once in Holland at high prices, as might have been done, he obstinately directed that it should all be put into Dutch schuyts, and locked down until the lawsuit was terminated. A large portion of the teas having been damaged by salt water, and an immense number of chests broken and injured, and these all being battened down in a confined state and in improper vessels, a natural taint upon the fine flavour of the teas took place, which prejudiced and detracted more from their value than even the damage arising from the shipwreck and hasty salvage. This, from my own knowledge and long experience, I had in so many words predicted, when I saw the filthy state of the boats taken up to contain it. But Mr. Anderson would not be guided by my advice, and when later on he discovered his mistake, he was base enough, as an excuse for his conduct, to ascribe the inferiority of the teas to a deficiency of quality at the time of their selection in China! To show

CAPTAIN EASTWICK IN OLD AGE.

(After a Photograph.)

how much he was lost to shame, from his distraction at this time, he actually sent me a bill for my hotel expenses at Hamburg before I sailed, when he had invited me to be his guest! I paid it without any comment, but not without despising him for so mean an act.

There was nothing to be gained by disputing as to the cause of the disaster, and I have always held recrimination in contempt. I therefore contented myself with doing all in my power to accelerate the closing of the concern, and recover the insurance money of sixty thousand pounds; and the venture ended, after satisfying the claims of the Dutch boatmen, in all parties interested having their claims paid at the rate of four shillings a dollar instead of six. Had Mr. Anderson adopted a more disinterested conduct, and sent the cargo directly up to Amsterdam to be separated and sold, it would have turned out very differently, and no one had any cause to complain of anything more than a misfortune arising from the dangers of the sea.

The *Asia*, though high and dry upon the bank, was eventually got off, and brought to London, where the whole of my time was occupied for two months in superintending her refitment. Having finished this, I was truly glad to be relieved of a concern that had brought me so much loss, sorrow, and disappointment.

I was now in my fifty-third year. The death of my wife had left my sons without a protector at a time when a parent's care was most requisite. I had laid by a small fortune sufficient for my wants, and I therefore determined to finally retire from my profession, and devote the remaining days of my life to the education of my boys. To this end I carefully invested my capital to yield a moderate, but certain income. My youngest son, Edward, I entered at the Charter House School, whilst William returned to complete his studies at Winchester College. Soon after this, my daughter Eliza returned from India, having been left a widow by the untimely death of her husband, Colonel Ford, and, to my inexpressible satisfaction, came to keep house for me at Hans Place.

And so, with my three dear children around me, and the consciousness of having done my work to the best of my ability in that station of life to which it had pleased God to call me, I settled down after forty years of active and adventurous life at sea.

I wish I could have presented this account of my life in a much different way, for the incidents were abundant; but a blind man is at a disadvantage in such a task. Few people have gone through more sea dangers and escapes, with some severe trials in battle. These, added to losses by agents, capture, and other circumstances, make a great mass of trials. But looking back on them, I feel how great a cause I have to thank the Almighty for His deliverance, and for having placed me above want, and with perfect independence in my old age

CONCLUSION.

WITH the wreck of the *Asia* in 1825, the active career of the old Master Mariner terminated. Yet he lived for forty years more, and children, and grandchildren, and great-grandchildren were born to him, and grew up, and gathered round his knees to hear from his own lips many of the incidents recorded in these pages.

In 1829 Captain Eastwick married again, being led to take· this step by his daughter's return to India, whither his eldest son had already preceded her. "It threw me on the world again," he writes, "a solitary being. I could not return to such a life, my habits being essentially domestic." So he took to himself as a partner, one who had been the dear and intimate friend of his late wife, and who after thirty-seven years of wedded happiness, followed him to the grave within a few months of his own decease.

About three years after his marriage he lost his sight, and the last thirty-three years of his life were passed in total blindness. This sad affliction was calculated to try him more than it would have done most men, for his temperament was energetic, his habits active in the extreme, and his characteristics of independence and self-reliance strongly developed. To such a one the restraint consequent upon his affliction fell with a double force. His sense of vision had always been particularly acute. "The account of the failure of your eyes, my dearest father," writes his eldest son from India in 1832, "has affected me beyond measure. I always thought your eyes were the strongest in the world. How often have you discovered objects which no one else could make out at all!" The old man bore his trial patiently and unmurmuringly, his unselfish nature being more concerned for those dependent on him, than for himself. "I cannot help feeling," he writes, "that the want of sight diminishes the efficiency of a parent's care; but I place my trust in Heaven, and that great Disposer of all events who guards the weak and unprotected."

Once, and only once, he broke down. It was when his eldest son—"the pride and solace of my heart; in whose character are united the finest principles of honour, integrity and right feeling "—returned from India. He was a singularly handsome man, who had made a name in his profession, and for whom his father entertained feelings of the deepest affection. The son had left England a lad of nineteen: he was coming back a man of thirty. Long had his return home been looked forward to: news travelled slowly in those days, and at distant intervals there came tidings of his ill-health which caused anxiety and alarm. But at length his departure from India was announced. And now ensued a period of excited expectation. The shipping intelligence was carefully scrutinized every morning, the direction of the wind was daily noted as the time drew near. The father rehearsed his old experiences, how on such an occasion he had been three weeks delayed at the mouth of the Channel, but on another had sailed up in as many days. The qualities of the vessel in which his son embarked were discussed, and the best information about her obtained from the city. At last the ship's arrival was reported, and her passengers might be expected in town at any hour. And so the moment came: there was a knock at the hall door, the sound of hurried footsteps in the passage, and then the son entered the room.

The blind father rose from his chair with outstretched arms. Then he halted, and the workings of his face revealed the agony of his feelings, as in a moment the full privation of his affliction overwhelmed him. His son approached and took his hands: the father spoke not a word, but he trembled violently, and the tears streamed from his sightless eyes. All he could do was to pass and repass his fingers over the features he could not see, in a despairing attempt to convey their picture to his mind. But it sufficed him not, and with a pathetic silence he sank back in his chair. The meeting affected those that were present in an indescribable manner.

Happily there were two little daughters born of his marriage who were "sent to cheer the many hours of my blindness, and, blessed with health and engaging and buoyant dispositions, are a constant source of delight and enjoyment to me." It was a touching sight to see the companionship that existed between them and him, and the care with which they tended to his wants and led him in his walks abroad, he directing the way, and they guiding his footsteps. To them after dinner, which was always served at the old-fashioned hour of three o'clock, he always devoted his afternoons and evenings, joining in their games, or amusing them with stories of his former life. It was their society that assisted him to overcome the depression that might have arisen from his affliction. In 1838 his eldest daughter, on her return to England, thus wrote to her brother, still in India: "Our father is ever cheerful. There is a great reaction about him. His vigour of mind is unimpaired, and his countenance is ofttimes so lighted up that I forget that he is blind."

Even to the end of his life was his countenance so lighted up, as the writer of these lines can remember, when, as a child, he sat on the old man's knee, and listened with an awed attention to stirring adventures of a bygone century, all so bright and vivid with description that they seemed invested with the realism of a passing event. For they were told with the artistic accessories of graphic speech and appropriate gesture, enlivened with

snatches of old sea-song, flavoured with fine sea
phrase, and garnished with many a quaint maxim
or rounded off with some deductive proverb, so that
they conveyed a perfect word-picture of the scene
and incident described, and carried the listener
away, as by enchantment, over leagues of land and
sea to southern latitudes, till the very walls of the
room faded from view and there seemed to stretch
around vistas of rolling waters, or bright tropical
lands, peopled with strange inhabitants, and quick
with the spirit of adventure and enterprise.

The house he lived in contained a perfect
museum of curiosities. Stuffed fishes, reputed to
be dolphins, weapons from India, ivory ornaments
from China, and relics of many voyages, filled the
cabinets and walls. On the latter hung an oil
picture of an exceedingly assertive but friendly
Chinese Mandarin, who, during one of his voyages,
to fulfil a vow, had allowed the thumb-nail of his
left hand to grow through his left palm—and yet
looked placid and happy. Every room in the
house held some memento of the past : precious
treasures never permitted to be touched.

In keeping with the tales he told was the old
Master Mariner's personal appearance. No one
could look at him without a rare admiration as he
sat talking in his accustomed armchair—an old man
eloquent. His figure was somewhat below the
middle height, but squarely and powerfully built,
deep-chested and broad-shouldered. His handsome
face was clean shaven, and its strongly marked

features discovered his determination of character. A finely poised head, with spare snowy locks, surmounted an open and lofty forehead, beneath which two great dark hollows, lacking the accustomed light, revealed their sad story. But notwithstanding this, his face and figure were so irradiated with animation that it almost seemed to raise the blind man up above his affliction.

It was fitting that his sons should repay his paternal care and solicitude. He had stamped them both with the hall-mark of his own character. The elder, the late Captain William Joseph Eastwick, who died in 1889, after serving with distinction in military and political employments in India, was elected a director of the Honourable East India Company, and eventually became deputy-chairman of that body, and was selected in 1859 for a seat in the East India Council. The younger, the late Edward Backhouse Eastwick, was a profound Oriental scholar, an author of repute, and at one time Member of Parliament for Falmouth. Their reverence for their father was undiminished to the end of their lives, and in many of the letters that passed between them there is found some affectionate reference to him. A brief extract may be permitted from one of these, which although dashed off *currente calamo*, as the calligraphy shows, is perhaps for that very reason the better worth excerption. The elder brother in 1878, when nearing his seventieth birthday, thus writes to the younger :—

"I should have liked to have heard P——'s [illegible] sermon on 'Murmuring!' Our dear old father never murmured under all his tremendous sufferings and deprivations. I often think of his stout old English heart, which never quailed in the face of the greatest trials and difficulties, and his unexampled self-denial for the sake of his family. You and I owe him much for the education he gave us, when hundreds with his small fortune would never have dreamed of lifting us out of the common highway."

They were, indeed, "tremendous sufferings" that the old Master Mariner was called upon to endure, for after his ninety-second year he underwent a surgical operation for the excision of a cancerous growth in the ear, from which he suffered excruciating torture. But neither in affliction nor in physical pain did he complain, but endeavoured, as he has in his own brave words recorded, "to bear up against heavy and great trials with cheerfulness and contentment, sensible of the bountiful goodness of the Almighty in having spared me for so many years, and sustained me through so many dangers." And no more beautiful sentiment ever passed a blind man's lips, than his repeated asseveration, spoken solemnly and in all earnestness, that "his affliction assisted him to appreciate and thank God for the blessings he had once enjoyed."

Thus in quiet retirement he passed the last forty years of his life, from his shipwreck in 1825 to his death in 1865. In the spring of the latter year he underwent the operation referred to, and it afforded temporary relief, and enabled him to pass through the summer, and pay his annual visit to Brighton in August. But early in October, after his return to his home in Thurloe Square, London, symptoms of the malady began to reappear, and the medical men were now of opinion that there was no further hope of amelioration. Still he bore up bravely, comforted and tended by his wife, although it was evident that from this time he began to fade away. Early in December an old hurt in his leg broke out afresh, and erysipelas supervening, he took to his bed, from which before long it became apparent he would never rise again.

The torture he suffered from the eating cancer and the sloughing wound increased with a terrible rapidity, and soon became so unendurable, that at times he earnestly, but reverentially, prayed for release. But there were still three long weeks of agony to be endured. The exhaustion of continued pain quickly sapped away his physical strength, until he could no longer move himself in bed without assistance. There was a pathetic resignation in his appeal to his eldest son, who watched night and day by his bedside; " Do not handle me roughly, Willie darling. I am but a poor old man now." God knows none but very gentle and very loving hands were there, that shrank from giving the pain their slighest touch awakened. Often he whispered, as if in clear contemplation of his condition, "This is the high-road of death. This is death." But there was no tremor of fear in his voice. It was the calm realization of the accomplishment of life.

All through that last dread month, while the undaunted spirit was battling with the grim spectre, his family were assembled daily at the house, and twice or thrice its every member gathered round his bed, and, like a patriarch of old, solemnly and in succession he blessed them one and all. But on each occasion the masterful will and the iron constitution conquered the apparent crisis, and he struggled back out of the very clutch of death. And all this while the cold hand stealing on was powerless to chill the warm heart, or turn his thoughts from those he loved. "I die happy," he murmured as he lay there, "knowing that my children will always respect my memory. I have done my duty to my wife and family. I have never had a thought beyond them. I have worked hard." It was the simple and touching apology of his unselfish life, and true to the last letter.

On Christmas night he was seized with a violent fit of choking, but though greatly exhausted and shaken by it, he rallied. "Willie, my son," he whispered a little while afterwards, "I cannot tell you how grateful I am to you and all my good children for their loving-kindness to me in this Hurricane of Disaster. God has been very gracious in giving me such children. Blessed be His Holy Name. And now cover me up, and let me rest!"

But rest was not yet permitted. The "Hurricane of Disaster" had still a course to run : the harbour was not reached. Three more days passed, long drawn out with suffering, and found him alive. He talked at intervals, and prayed constantly, repeating over and over again his favourite text, "The Lord gave ; and the Lord taketh away. Blessed be the name of the Lord."

On the 28th he appeared a little better, and at midnight of that day turned to his eldest son, and speaking in his natural tone of voice, almost as though he were merely a spectator of his own last struggle, he said, " Well, Willie, your old father at ninety-four years of age dies as hard, I think, as any man you ever heard or read of ! "

It was his last lucid remark. Soon after this his mind began to wander, and from the deep wells of his memory there flashed back to him phantom reflections of the long gone past, crowded with scenes finished and forgotten, and actors dead and decayed. In his delirium he discoursed many things : about his old ships, his numberless voyages, the foreign countries he had seen, the strange and barbarous people he had been brought in contact with. . He recalled his past pursuits, his successes, his failures, his dangers, his sufferings, his adventures, his escapes. He addressed by name friends and comrades who had been drowned or buried for three-quarters of a century, and in his imagination wandered forth with the companions of his boyhood. Hour followed hour, and found him recounting and expounding in his delirium this weird and wonderful summary of a long eventful life.

Last of all, as in a final effort of nature, he rose unaided in his bed, and conscious apparently of the presence of his eldest son, who had been with him in the shipwreck of the *Asia* just forty years before, he cried aloud, " This is a fearful hurricane, Willie my boy.   We cannot weather this ! "

Then, in this supreme moment, his old instincts quickened into life and action.   With his gaunt and shrunken arms feebly gesticulating, and his sightless orbs peering into the unseen tempest, he lifted up his voice and called out in swift succession his orders to his crew, as though he were once again standing on his own quarter-deck.   And so for one short space he sustained the struggle, whilst those that watched him held their breath in awe.

Then he paused and trembled.   The hardy spirit succumbed ; the light of hope faded from his face ; the uplifted hands fell helpless to his side. Slowly his head bowed down and down, until crouching low, as before an irresistible fate, he sank back upon his pillow, repeating for the last time—

" This is a fearful hurricane, Willie my boy ; we shall never weather this ! "

Sunday the 31st of December, the closing day of 1865, was at hand.   It was a tempestuous night, and the rain fell in torrents.   The date was not unfitting for the passing of one so full of years, nor the day for the occasion that was to bring rest and surcease of pain to the overtried sufferer. The dying man had fallen into a state of torpor. At eleven o'clock at night the doctor felt his pulse : it was still fluttering, but the end was at hand. For five long hours the worn-out watchers followed each last solemn phase of ebbing life. The old Master Mariner never stirred or spoke again. But at four o'clock in the morning he heaved three deep-drawn sighs, and so passed through the tempest into the calm beyond.

*   *   *   *   *   *

He sleeps in the old parish churchyard of Lower Edmonton, in the vault where his mother and grandmother are buried, and where fifty years before he had laid to rest his godfather, Mr. English, and his aunt, Miss Elizabeth Archer. Here, too, are interred the remains of his cousin, Mrs. Sarah Wright, and her husband, and but a few feet distant is the grave of that surgeon "against whom he did not wish to insinuate anything."

The church itself has been recently restored and enlarged, and is much altered from what it was on that cold snowy January morning twenty-five years ago when the Master Mariner was laid to rest. It has lost the quaint old-fashioned gallery under which, and not far from the memorial erected to the memory of the poet who sang the epic of John Gilpin, a small marble tablet was fixed in wall, bearing an inscription that is here ʼed—partly because it very succinctly summarizes the contents of the preceding pages; and partly that the reader may judge for himself whether the eulogy it perpetuates may not at least claim the justification of truth and merit.

. 𝔖𝔞𝔠𝔯𝔢𝔡

To the Memory of.
ROBERT WILLIAM EASTWICK, ESQUIRE,
Of 39, Thurloe Square, London,
Whose remains are interred opposite the South door of this church.
He was born on the 25th June, 1772,
And died on the 31st December, 1865,
Aged 93 years, 6 months, and 6 days.
He was Master's Mate on the *Inconstant* Frigate in 1788,
Was 5th officer of the *Barwell*, East Indiaman, in January, 1792,
Was one of the seven who escaped from the wreck of an American ship
in August, 1793, at Cape Negrais, on the coast of Burmah,
Was Captain of the *Endeavour* when taken in Belasore Roads
by the *La Forte* frigate, and was recaptured
by the *La Sybille* in the celebrated action of the 28th of February, 1799,
Went up with Sir John Malcolm's Mission to Persia in 1800,
Was with General Whitelock's Expedition to Buenos Ayres in 1807,
Commanded the *Ganges*, which brought to England Lord Minto's despatches
announcing the Suppression of the Madras Mutiny in 1809,
Was one of the twenty survivors who escaped from the wreck of the *Elizabeth*
at Dunkirk in 1810, when 360 persons perished.
After being imprisoned for some months he was liberated
by the Emperor Napoleon Buonaparte,
Was captured after a severe action, in which he was wounded,
by the American privateer *Anaconda* in 1812,
Commanded the *Asia* when wrecked on the coast of Holland in 1825.
He was a skilful and fearless sailor; an honest, energetic, self-denying man,
And a sincere Christian.
This tablet was erected in token of love
By his Widow and Children.
" The Lord gave, and the Lord taketh away ;
Blessed be the Name of the Lord."

FINIS.